WHEN LEGENDS STALK—

Arsen was bending to slice off a knob of rock when he heard a faint noise that seemed to emanate from somewhere behind and above him, and at the same time a stench registered in his nostrils. It was a terrible stench, reminding him of corpses rotting in the sun.

Whirling about, he spied pure horror crouching on a ledge some five feet above him. Man-shaped in some ways, the thing was squatting on its heels, glaring down at Arsen with slitted eyes. Its arms were overlong and as hairy as all the rest of its thick, massive body, except for its face and slightly projecting, long-fanged muzzle. The creature's upper canine teeth were at least two inches in length.

Working in the heat, Arsen had left his shirt, pistol, and all other weapons back in the carrier. Slowly he began to back away from the beast above him. But he knew he would never reach the carrier's safety before this creature of nightmare attacked. . . .

CASTAWAYS IN TIME #5

ROBERT ADAMS

OF MYTHS AND MONSTERS

A SIGNET BOOK
NEW AMERICAN LIBRARY

In memory of Robert A. Heinlein
1907–1988

NAL BOOKS ARE AVAILABLE AT QUANTITY DISCOUNTS WHEN USED TO PROMOTE PRODUCTS OR SERVICES. FOR INFORMATION PLEASE WRITE TO PREMIUM MARKETING DIVISION, NEW AMERICAN LIBRARY, 1633 BROADWAY, NEW YORK, NEW YORK 10019.

SIGNET TRADEMARK REG. U.S. PAT. OFF. AND FOREIGN COUNTRIES
REGISTERED TRADEMARK—MARCA REGISTRADA
HECHO EN CHICAGO, U.S.A.

SIGNET, SIGNET CLASSIC, MENTOR, ONYX, PLUME, MERIDIAN and NAL BOOKS are published by NAL PENGUIN INC., 1633 Broadway, New York, New York 10019

First Printing, December, 1988

1 2 3 4 5 6 7 8 9

PRINTED IN THE UNITED STATES OF AMERICA

PROLOGUE

In one of the larger cities of an Eastern Seaboard state of the United States of America, in the first year of the last quarter of the twentieth century, a man sat at a desk in a modest office which was located in a building that, though it once had been the mansion of a well-to-do family, was now become one- and two-room offices. The man resembled in his physical appearance, dress, and usual manner only what he was supposed to resemble, a businessman of indeterminate age but probable middle years, a run-of-the-mill, middle-class American who was possessed of sufficient business acumen to afford to dress well, drive a midpriced but new auto, pay his bills on time and in full. A bachelor who had been known to make allusions to one or more former wives, he occasionally wined and dined and otherwise entertained acquaintances of the female persuasion and later, in his comfortable apartment, often shared sex with them. That he never allowed any serious or lasting relationships with them to develop was usually ascribed to his understandable fear of repeating the pain of his late marriage or marriages.

In fact, the man was nothing of the sort. In the strictest sense, he was not even a man—male, but not human, not completely human, at least. Not that there had not once been a truly human man just like this being, but he had died and his husk had been used as the pattern for fashioning the body that this being now inhabited; his brain and selected portions of several others had been skillfully merged to occupy the skull of this "man" by a technology so far beyond the "man's" present contemporaries as to be unbelievable.

Although other beings considered this being to be almost young, still had the being been in existence in one or another form for almost half a millennium, by the standards of authentic men.

He sat at the desk, speaking in a conversational tone although he was alone in the office. The language in which he spoke, however, was one incomprehensible to any save two or three other beings like himself on all the earth. He spoke to a dimly pulsing spot of light that hovered in the air before him, its glow all but invisible in the shafts of sunlight spearing between the slats of the window blinds.

"I am certain that it is more well-meant idiocy on the parts of those cretins who are mining the easternmost reaches of the largest northern-hemisphere continent of the world we call 3-9-23-1. It is but more proof of what has been said by beings before this: Their available technologies have far outstripped their intellect and judgment and, are they not more strictly controlled and guided in the proper ways, they will eventually be the innocent instigators of real difficulties for all of us.

"In an attempt to return certain humans to this world which is my current station of duty, said humans having been plucked into the world of 3-9-23-1 by way of a malfunctioning primitive projector out of the world that we call 3-9-18-20, they managed to instead lose all of them somehow, on exactly which world and in exactly which line of time I have yet to ascertain.

"I came upon all of this by way of purest accident. I was called upon in the line of work that this creature I here am conducts to investigate disappearances of valuable items from the properties of a firm that specializes in the sale and resale of weapons of many varieties. Seated with the senior officer of the parent firm in his office, I was able to sense the afterglow of one of the carriers used by the miners of 3-9-23-1. This alerted me and I was caused to recall that close relatives of this very man had but recently disappeared under most singular circumstances. He had, indeed, asked me to investigate those disappearances, and I had so done, my conclusions having been reported to you higher beings in my report #11.523LSP12RF.

"Had immediate remedial action been taken at that time, doubtless none of the present threatened problems would be occurring; but the circumstances prevented speedy action, I was informed, and so we now are faced with the result. I will be unable to report on the degree of gravity of this result until I can discover just where and when these subjects were projected, of course.

"The artifacts being apparently projected from this world are very oddly assorted, and many of the varieties of foods and weapons have disappeared in quantities much larger than the ten or twelve human projectees could use themselves, so I must assume that they are giving them or selling them to humans indigenous to that time and world, and all of us are unpleasantly aware of the certain outcome of such interference if it is allowed to go on for any length of time. It was interferences akin to this, allowed by the lesser ones who preceded us, that brought about the sorry state of affairs now so bedeviling us.

"But worse than the projections of artifacts of this world to another is what I noticed in a research laboratory of the firm on which I was calling. The carrier afterglow was very strong in one room of that place, and certain traces remained as to lead me to believe that the room and some of its equipment had been used to reproduce technologically sophisticated devices of the miners' culture, world, and time. If such knowledge as was necessary to do what was done there falls into the hands of even so primitive a culture as this one the result could be chaos for us.

"It is for this reason that I send this report and why I most urgently request that my other duties be either assigned to other beings or allowed to be suspended until I can put this dangerous matter to rights. The only viable alternative will be to assign an emergency team of beings to the situation, with all that attends to such assignment and preparations of the beings for it.

My report is now concluded."

Immediately his last syllable was pronounced, the dimly pulsing light winked out of existence.

CHAPTER THE FIRST

His name was Brian, the eighth man of that name to reign as *Ard-Righ* or High King of *Eireann* or Ireland, but Brian VIII was only seen on documents or used orally by a *filid* as he sang the long, rhymed, often rambling genealogical records that had never been written in all the many centuries they had been compiled.

He was called Brian the Burly, and burly he was. Scion of a long line of warriors, fighting monarchs and fighting chiefs, he was obviously their true get. Although not truly a tall man, he nonetheless gave a first impression of size, of massivity; though well formed and graceful, his hands were large, strong, hairy-backed, and heavily scarred. His frame was all big bones and rolling muscles sheathing them, the hips as wide as the shoulders that looked almost too broad and thick for his body. His head rested on a neck nearly as thick as the head itself. His lower extremities, though no less solid and strong than his arms, were clearly those of a horseman, with flat thighs. Now, in his middle years, his waist was beginning to thicken slightly and strands of grey were appearing in his hair and beard, but still he looked as powerful, vital, and incipiently dangerous as ever he had in the past.

And *Ard-Righ* Brian the Burly was indeed dangerous in many a way. In his prime, few men in all of *Eireann* had been his match with the fearsome Danish-style axe he favored, ahorse or afoot; and even now, when he was in his fifties, many a younger man would be inclined to think twice before meeting the monarch in lists or on field of battle. But as deadly an opponent as he certainly was sitting his spotted destrier in armor grasping his fearsome axe, this was not the only danger he represented . . . or even the most significant.

For Brian was not only physically strong, he was possessed of wealth and power, wealth, power, and an ambition that gnawed at him without cease, waking and sleeping. Countless men had died, countless gallons of blood had been shed, in his years-long attempts to assuage the pangs of his ambition, and, ruthless as he was, he stood quite prepared and ready to see half the male population of the entire island done to death if it would achieve his ends.

For years without number, Brian's paramount title, High King, had been mostly a mockery, for the high kings had held no more land than any of the other kings in *Eireann*, had had no hint of true sovereignty over these other kings, in fact, had acted as little better than a referee in wars between kings and kings, kings and would-be kings and the like. Brian's sire and predecessor had envisioned an *Eireann* over which the high kings would hold such sway as the kings of other lands—England, Scotland, France, Norway, Denmark, and Aragon—did over theirs, and he had inculcated his son with an equally driving ambition from his very earliest years.

Of course, Brian did not, would not, could not

admit to the fact that personal ambition drove him, rather did he often cite his desire to bring to an end, once and for all, the small wars between the kings that had, for year after year, century after century, racked and impoverished what could have been a rich, fertile, productive land and people. These citations, however, were only taken at face value by foreigners who did not know him or know him well; his kingly opponents in *Eireann* knew better. And foreigners of any intelligence or intuitiveness who served him or had any depth of dealings with him for any length of time quickly sensed a real difference between that in which Brian believed and that in which he wished others to believe he believed.

Such men as these were three condottieri temporarily resident in widely separated portions of *Eireann*. One was an Italian—Ser Timoteo, *il Duce* di Bolgia—who had, along with his justly famous condotta, been hired by one Cardinal D'Este and sent to the Irish Kingdom of Munster to help to modernize its existing army and hold it against the incursions of the High King for the Church and the House of Fitz Gerald, scions of which had been its kings for centuries—the second was also an Italian, actually, the full brother of the first, Roberto, and he now reigned as an Irish king over the kingdom called Ulaid, in the northeast of the island. *Righ* or King Roberto, who had realized even as the ancient crown of Ulaid was lowered upon his brow that his small, weak, impoverished little holding had had all the chance of a wet snowball on a hot griddle against the power and the wealth of the grasping High King, had sought about and then made the short sea journey to the Hebrides Islands, where—after certain negotiations—he had given over the Kingdom of Ulaid to Sir Aonghus, Regulus of the Isles, then received it back of the powerful old man as a feoff.

In due time, the Regulus had sent formal notification to the *Ard-Righ* and all other nearby rulers that, as in archaic times, Ulaid was once more a feoff of the Western Isles of Scotland, its king his vassal and, therefore, henceforth under his fearsome protection. At receipt of that letter, *Ard-Righ* Brian the Burly had, so said his people who waited upon him, cursed and blasphemed most sulphurously, then set about recalling the bulk of his large army from campaign in the Kingdom of Connachta, his fleet from interdicting the ports of that western kingdom, and otherwise had looked to be making every preparation to mount a full-scale invasion of the Hebrides, Ulaid or both.

The third condottiere, Sir Bass, Duke of Norfolk, Earl of Rutland, *Markgraf von* Velegrad, Baron of Strathtyne, Knight of the Garter (England), Noble Fellow of the Order of the *Roten Adler* (Holy Roman Empire), and holder of other honors too numerous to list, in addition to being Lord Commander of the Horse of Arthur III Tudor, King of England and Wales, presently on loan with his condotta by his own monarch to Arthur's cousin, *Ard-Righ* Brian VIII, took alarm at this turn of affairs, not wishing to see troops that he considered to be pledged to the service of Arthur and England sent off to fight Scots who were just then allies of Arthur. He had dispatched a letter and a trusted, noble officer of his command—*Reichsherzog* Wolfgang, who was at one and the same time uncle of the reigning Emperor of the Holy Roman Empire, sometime uncle-in-law of King Arthur, and overlord of the Mark of Velegrad which Sir Bass held in feoff from him—aboard one of the smaller ships of his private war-fleet to London and his own king.

Shortly, *Ard-Righ* Brian was in receipt of a letter from his "loving and concerned cousin" Arthur. The words were indeed loving, the tone was diplomatic and as warm and smooth as thick samite, but still to the knowing reader was the hard steel beneath apparent . . . and Brian was, if anything, knowing.

Distilled down to its essence, the royal missive had said: "The Kingdom of Scotland is now my confirmed ally and the Lord or Regulus of the Hebrides or the Isles is a Scot. If you are so unwise as to attack him openly, then King James of Scotland will own no option but to attack you, and I, being his ally, cannot but lend my own forces if he so request. Haven't you more than enough sworn enemies in Ireland but that you must seek out more and newer ones overseas? In any case, I must forbid you the use of the troops I loaned you—Duke Bass *et alii*—against Scotland, the Scottish Isles, or any vassal or feoff of King James or Earl Aonghus, the Lord of the Isles."

Brian the Burly sat in a cathedra chair in one of his smaller rooms of audience with Sir Bass Foster, Duke of Norfolk, seated in a lower-backed armchair across an inlaid table from him. A ewer of Rhenish wine and a brace of gilded silver goblets sat on the table, along with a loosely rolled letter writ upon flawless vellum and adorned with colorful, impressive, much-beribboned seals. Sir Bass had but just finished reading the letter, while Brian had sipped wine slowly, watching the condottiere over the golden rim of the goblet.

"Well, Your Grace of Norfolk," said Brian at last, "what do you think of your monarch's, my own cousin's, letter to me, eh?"

Bass felt it best to be cautious here, as cautious as he would have been on a narrow, slippery river ford over deep and deadly water. "King Arthur expresses true regard, deep respect, and sincere regard for Your Highness . . ." he began.

Brian laughed once, harshly. "Cousin Arthur, or whoever really dictated that letter, is by it proven a true master at the coating of bitter gall with honey, no mistaking that. Nonetheless, it is nothing less than a threat, a firm promise that if I do the most honorable thing and attack this foxy, poxy Aonghus Mac Dhomhnuill, this aging byblow outcome of the unnatural coupling of a tusked seal and a perverted, udderless cow, then I will certainly stand to be invaded by the combined forces of both Scotland and England-Wales. Was this what Your Grace expected when he sneaked a letter-bearing ship out of the anchorage of his fleet to bear word to his monarch of my advertised intentions, then?"

"I had hoped," answered Bass, "that, being Your Highness's cousin, King Arthur might be able to reason with Your Highness and . . ."

The blank, cold stare of Brian's eyes departed to be replaced by a twinkle of merriment, then he laughed, true laughter, and said, "Your Grace, it has been unfair to dangle you on hooks for so long today, when really you were a large part of my scheme from its very inception, you know."

Bass Foster knew that the *Ard-Righ* was truly friendly again from his use of the first person rather than the royal third person with which he had begun this meeting. "Your Majesty means that he truly *wanted* me to dispatch letters to King Arthur, then?"

Taking the near-empty goblet down from his lips, Brian replied, "Of course I did, Your Grace, else your little dispatch ship would never have made it down the Liffey to the sea. You've seen my forts, man, my gunners are all masters, Venetians, the best. They have the finest of modern, brazen long guns—demicannon, culverins, and demiculverins—to work with, they know the capabilities and peculiarities of each and every piece of ordnance under their care, and they know the ranges to any point in the river within bare feet and inches. Your rakish little ship with the Roman name could have been blown out of the water in a mere twinkling, Your Grace.

"No, I knew from the onset that, whether provoked or nay, any meaningful attack I mounted against Lord Aonghus would require near every man I own and that that would be the truest folly, all other things considered. However, I still saw the need to make the proper-sounding and -appearing noises and actions, lest I lose the respect of such as the kings of Laigin, Connachta, Breiffne, and the Northern Ui Neills, who might have declared that I lacked the will and courage to fight for my honor and possessions against any save those weaker than me.

"And so, Your Grace, I made all of the expected noises and did all that would lead men to believe that I would pool every available resource and strike hard and true at the Regulus, imminently. Had you not sent out a messenger so promptly, so cooperatively, I would have had to prime one of my own to do it, but he would not, I fear, have been nearly so convincing as was your letter borne by *Reichsherzog* Wolfgang."

Bass shook his head slowly. "But . . . but why, Your Majesty? I do not understand it, any of it."

Brian smiled again and indicated that Bass should refill both goblets from the ewer. With a full goblet once more in his hand, the *Ard-Righ* retained his smile and said, "Of course, Your Grace does not understand, but an Irishman would, eke a Scot—that's because both the Irish and the Scots own a common, ancestral race, the Gaels, from which race the most of our customs, usages, and thought processes descend.

"The Gaels of old, Your Grace, inveterate warriors that they all were, still owned many peculiarities of thought as to what was proper or not proper in fighting and warfare, what was most honorable and least honorable as regarded warlike conduct of a warrior, a chief, or a king. The last of the true Gaels have been but bones and dust for time beyond reckoning, but still they and their ancient codes live on in the hearts and minds of us Irish and right many of the Scots.

"For good or for ill, had I seemingly made no move to revenge myself upon the lands if not the person of the Regulus—who is held to be roughly my equal in military terms—the other kings in *Eireann*, even those who are my clients, would have named me either coward or dishonored, and God alone knows to just what extremities that unholy mess would have led.

"These same old Gaels, however, were quite realistic in many a way, Your Grace. They also felt that for a man to decline combat with an opponent or opponents so far superior to him in strength or armament that he was certain to die—such as, say, a naked man with only a small knife against an armored man with sword and axe—was to be held prudent rather than either cowardly or dishonored to decline combat even if that meant flight.

"Now Your Grace may be dead certain that each and every one of my royal clients and enemies on this island is or will shortly be fully aware of what has transpired—of how I was provoked by Lord Aonghus, of how I began to make preparations to gather all my hosts and go against him in his lands as a brave and honorable *Ard-Righ* would and must do, and most importantly of how the King of England and Wales, my blood cousin but confirmed ally of the royal overlord of Lord Aonghus, threatened to bring me to combat and certain defeat with his vastly larger and stronger host was I to strike at the vassal of his ally.

"So, Your Grace must now see, the *Ard-Righ* thus retains his reputation of bravery, honor, *and* prudence. His army remains in the Kingdom of Connachta, his fleet continues to interdict her ports, sink her fishers, and raid her coasts. I am sure that I shortly will be entertaining a noble Mac Dhomhnuill who will come bearing word from Lord Aonghus that I obviously took offense at what he had sent off as a mere declaration of his God-given duty to defend his vassals, both old and new. He will send me some rich presents, offer me more *galloglaiches* as I need them at reduced prices, and promise that, in future, he will try to restrain *Righ* Roberto's obvious land-hunger.

'I will treat the noble messenger with all of my renowned and lavish hospitality, then send him back to his master with equally rich presents—perhaps even a destrier of the leopard-horse breed—and a letter reaffirming my friendship and respect for him, taking him up on the offer of more *galloglaiches* and suggesting an exchange of hostages between our two realms as a seal of enduring amicability. Then I'll get back to business as usual, of course, here in *Eireann*."

The gate guards of the palace compound seemed more than happy to gape the gates, raise the portcullis, lower the bridge over the wide, green-slimy moat, and see Bass Foster and his two squires go clattering across it and, finally outside the high, thick walls, Bass could see why.

He had arrived, when summoned by three of Brian's Knights of the Silver Moon, with merely his squires, his bannerman, and a dozen or so bodyguards, all of whom still awaited him just where he had left them. But now there were far more men than that awaiting him. Somewhat impatiently awaiting him were three to four hundred men and almost all of his squadron officers, most of them dismounted but all of them fully armed, heavily armed. Certainly for the benefit and intimidation of the guards on walls and gate, many of the waiting men were carefully examining weapon edges and primings of pistols or long guns.

A long, loud cheer rose from out that steel-sheathed throng at sight of their leader riding free and unharmed from out the Tara Palace. And another cheer, mostly a relief of long tension, grew up from the guards behind and above him. Several men tightened girths, mounted, and rode to meet Bass.

On the ride back to their camp halfway between Tara and Lagore, Bass asked the big, gruff, jovial *Reichsherzog* Wolfgang, who rode just behind him, wearing his fluted three-quarter armor, his face red and steaming sweat, "What, pray tell, would you all have done had I not come out, had Brian decided to cast me into one of his cells or take off my head?"

"Attack, *mein freund*," was the German's blunt answer. "Attack *und* either free you or avenge you in much red blood."

"Attack a fortified palace complex without engines, cannon, or even infantry, Wolfie? Be serious—cavalry alone can't do that."

"No?" spoke up another of Bass's officers. "And cavalry brigades cannot prize armed merchant ships, either, my lord, yet as I recall, you proved to King Arthur, England and Wales, indeed, to all the world that a cavalry brigade commanded by Your Grace could do and had done just that, some years back."

"That was an entirely different set of circumstances, and you ought to know it, Sir Ali," snapped back Bass. "After all, you were there."

"Bass, Bass, *mein Freund*," rumbled the *Reichsherzog*, "vat ve planned an accomplishment of renown would not haf been. Defenses of such a poorness as those of that palace to Irischers daunting may be, but not to any other. My good Kalymks stood behind, their fine crossbows unseen, vhile those before them kept on their pistols and swords the eyes of the guards. Other of my Kalmyks were vith ropes ready.

"On command, each of the visible guards a quarrel would haf received to take to his heart, then the Kalmyks vould have the moat swum, loops of ropes over the merlons thrown, then all to the top of the wall would have climbed up, and, after any other guards cut down were, the bridge would have lowered *und* the grille raised up and the gates opened and everyone else to ride in would have to either free or avenge you."

Bass believed it, all of it, for the uncle of the Holy Roman Emperor never lied, and he felt a shuddery feeling, a brief prickle of his nape-hairs. He still sometimes felt himself to be basically unworthy, undeserving of such degrees of loyalty.

"Dammit!" he thought to himself. "This bunch would have done just what Wolfie outlined, too. They would've shot down those guards, climbed the walls, opened the grounds to the rest, then butchered every man, woman, and child in there had I been already executed, or they would have all died in the attempt. And goddammit, I'm not, truly not, the kind of man they all seem to think I am, the kind that a pack of howling, murderous savages like my *galloglaiches* can and do all but worship as a living deity, that is just not me, never was.

"But now, God help me, it is. That's just the way they all see me—their own, personal, bloody-handed god-in-the-flesh, their chosen war-chief, battle leader—me, Bass Foster, who, in another world, deliberately passed up a promising army career, a direct appointment to West Point mine for the asking with graduation to come as a captain, not merely a second lieutenant. Bass Foster, who just passed up a lifetime sinecure like that because he said he was tired of killing—tired of doing it himself, tired of sending other men to do it, tired of ordering still others to their deaths. So how did that man of announced peace wind up as a widely hailed war-leader and very personal participant in this world of gory and seemingly never-ending chaos and death wrought by man on man, then?

"I never even tried to write science fiction on the world of my birth, but knowing me, even if I had, I could never in a million years have dreamed up a scenario so ridiculously farfetched and so utterly implausible as this one I've lived and am now living."

It was not really all that many years past, although it now often seemed a lifetime ago to Bass, but still could he hear very clearly the voice of that state trooper shouting above the noise made by the rotor of the nearby helicopter and the rush of the rain on that dark and stormy night on the banks of the Potomac River.

The uniformed man in the rain slicker and ten-gallon hat had made no secret of the fact that he thought Bass's decision to be one born out of insanity, alcoholism, or both together, but he was just too tired, harried, overworked, and hurried just then by the fast-approaching flood bearing down upon them from upriver to waste any further time in argument.

"A'right, Foster, I ain't got no right to force you to abandon yore property, see, but I done done my job, I done tol' you the way she's stacked. The river's goin' to crest at least ten, fifteen foot above where she's at right now. And the way yore house is situated, it'll be at least two foot of water in yore top level, even if the whole house don't get undermined and come all to pieces, see. And thishere's the lastest round the chopper's goin' to make in thishere direction, too. And don't you figger you can allus change your mind and take to your boat, because it won't last in that river way she is and will be any longer than a wet snowball in hell. So you still sure you ain't comin' with us?"

On receiving again Bass's same, firm negative reply, the trooper had blown up at the steady stream of rainwater cascading off the slightly canted tip of his nose and said, shrugging, "A'right, citizen, it's yore dang funeral . . . if'n we ever finds yore body to bury it, that is."

He also remembered sitting at the picture window in the living room of his trilevel home, watching the rampant, widening, deepening, grey and swirling river tear away first his runabout boat, then his dock, sweeping both swiftly away downstream along with its other booty—animal, vegetable, and mineral.

He recalled thinking then that that trooper had been right, he had indeed been some kind of fool to remain behind here. But too this was the only real property that he had ever been able to call entirely his, and the largest part of his net worth was sunk into it and its appurtenances, and he was dee-double-damned if he would leave his home and possessions to the ravages of wind and water, not to mention the packs of looters who were certain to flock from the slums of Washington, D.C., to descend on the affluent, abandoned homes just as soon as they could make it. Besides, he trusted less the dire pronouncements of "authorities" and "experts" than he did his own, unexplainable dead-certainty that he would, somehow, survive the coming disaster.

Not that that inexplicable certainty had not been more than just a little shaken when he, hearing odd noises from above during a brief lull of the storm and the pelting rain, had climbed up to his low attic to find all three of his cats clinging tightly to crosspieces of the rafters and mewling feline moans of terror. More significantly, all three of them—the huge, rangy black tom, the older queen, and the younger silver Persian which had been Carolyn's last gift to him—were good hunters, merciless killers . . . yet they were peaceably sharing those rafters with several flying squirrels and a brace of soft brown house mice. That had been when he had started both to get truly worried and to call himself a fool, aloud.

He had tried to telephone a neighbor, only to discover that the telephones all were dead, and when the lights had all gone out, he had not even bothered to check the circuit breakers. He had dragged an easy chair closer to the picture window, fetched a bottle of Jameson's Irish whiskey to keep him company, and then just sat, sipping neat whiskey and watching the inexorable rise of the angry grey water and reflecting upon his past life.

Through his mind's eye, he had relived the joys and the sorrows, the wins and the losses, the victories and defeats which had studded and marked his forty-five, almost forty-six years of life. And, as the level of the river rose higher and higher, while that of the bottle sank lower and lower, his thoughts had turned finally to Carolyn.

Dear, lovely, loving Carolyn. She and the deep love they two had shared for so tragically short an interlude had been the greatest win of his lifetime. Therefore, her murder at the hands of some junkie musician and his homosexual lover had been the greatest of his losses. That horrendous loss had completely disrupted his life, had driven him almost over the edge into insanity, and the constant longing for her was even now turning him into an alcoholic. He had grieved again for a while, then he had begun to feel that, somehow, his dead love was truly near to him, and, murmuring softly to her, he had fallen asleep in the chair, there before the window.

The hot, bright sun on his face had awakened him, had blinded him when first he had blinked open his gummy eyelids to expose his bleary eyes.

"Well, what the hell," he had groaned, "I was right, after all, and . . . Ugh, my mouth tastes like used kitty litter. *Fagh*!"

Stumbling into the kitchen, he had flicked the light switch out of force of habit . . . and the tubes had flickered into life.

"Well, good God Almighty," he had remarked, "those damn utility crews are really on the ball, for a change. Okay, so let's see if the phone works, too. Shit, still dead, only one miracle at a time, it looks like."

With a pot of coffee perking merrily on the stove top, he had decided to walk outside and see if he could determine just how much damage his house and property had sustained. But he had taken only two steps out of his front door, looked in wondering, terrified disbelief, then reeled back inside to safety, to sanity. He had slammed the door, locked it, thrown the massive barrel bolt, drawn the drapes with shaking hands, sunk down into the familiar chair, and just sat, stunned.

Drawing upon some hidden well of courage, he had at some length lifted an edge of the drapes enough to peer out and see . . . and see . . .

He didn't think it could be called a castle or chateau, not really, although one wing of the apparently U-shaped stone house incorporated a tower at least sixty feet high and, from what he could see, the entire building and grounds seemed to be encircled by a reasonably high wall of dressed stones, pierced by at least one gate wide enough and high enough for a Sherman tank to easily negotiate. A creepy-crawliness had begun gnawing at Bass as he had gazed across his neat, manicured green lawn to behold, where the river had so recently swirled madly, part of an elaborate formal garden and, beyond both lawn and garden, the many windows of that huge house of archaic design, the windows staring back at him like the black, empty eyesockets of some hideous, grinning skull.

But Bass had not been long in discovering that he was not the only person of his world and time to be somehow transported to what seemed to be the English border country in the late Middle Ages or early Renaissance. In all, there were seven men and three women, and of this initial number, the women had fared worst in this ruder, cruder, less comfortable, and far more dangerous world into which they had been willy-nilly thrust.

The first to die had been a man, however, one of four truckers who had been transported, with their trucks, trailers, and loads intact, from Interstate 95 to a stretch of long, narrow, level lea all in the blinking of an eye and with hardly a bump. When one of the men had climbed down from his rig and approached two armored men on horseback to ask the location and how to get back to the interstate, he had been lanced through the chest for his trouble.

The second death had been that of a middle-aged and alcoholic woman, wife of a chemistry professor of fifty-odd years, who had, himself, eventually gone mad. The third death had been that of a young hippie girl, who had the dangerous habit of swallowing anything that looked to be a drug and discovered too late that the pills of this period were quite often deadly in even small amounts.

Since that death, there had been no more, although one other of the truckers had been severely and permanently injured in a great, raging battle between the English army and that of the Scots invaders. The third woman, who now was Bass's wife and the mother of his son, had become murderously insane and had had to be separated from her child and locked away in a convent of a nursing order.

Knowledge and skills and materials from their own world had allowed the survivors of the group to vastly improve and to immeasurably help certain aspects of the world into which they had been so abruptly and surprisingly deposited.

The professor had contributed much to the cause of the beset and beleaguered English and their king and had been ennobled quite early on, before his unfortunate traits of personal cowardice and a hectoring manner, plus symptoms of his encroaching emotional instability, had cost him all that his talents had earned and sent him riding off into an exile that had resulted in his full descent into madness.

One of the truckers had developed new and better firearms and had carried on some of the projects originated by the madman after his departure. He had been aided in this by another of the truckers as well as by the male "hippie" who had been shocked back to normality by the hideous demise of his girlfriend. The third trucker, subsequent to his crippling combat injury, had begun the selective breeding of farm animals on the country estate of a churchman.

Under the circumstances, deeply hidden traits in Bass had emerged and flowered. He had become a superlative cavalry commander, a warrior of some note, and a matchless leader of men. In the society into which he had been thrust, which was unlike the one he had departed—in which the military leader and combat expert was distrusted, derided, and held in contempt—such traits as he demonstrated were considered to be among the highest attainable attributes of a gentleman, and his feats had been rewarded by a shower of honors which had been conferred upon him by nobles and king alike.

Only well after his arrival in the strange world did he find that he and his companions were not the first to be so deposited. Two men had preceded them, these having arrived nearly two centuries before from the twenty-first century. These two had been scientists, both of whom had been the recipients of longevity treatments, and, although one had died in battle since that long-ago arrival, the other was not only still living but was the Archbishop of York, the second-most-powerful man in all of that version of England.

The two scientists had made their arrival at precisely the same location as had Bass and the rest, and it was assumed that a malfunction of the projecting device—still squatting in the ground level of the old defensive tower there—was what had jerked Foster, the other six men, and the three women into the new and different world.

For different it assuredly was from their own world of a comparable time and place. The date that Bass had been given some time after he had begun service with the royal army had been A.D. 1643, which had in his own world been in the late northern European Renaissance era; but conditions in this world were much closer to being late mediaeval than early Renaissance. Over a period of time, Bass had discovered that no really large, strong nations existed in this world, only small, relatively weak countries, and that this miserable, very feudal mess was to a very large extent a result of the constant meddling in lay affairs of the Church.

The Church of this world exercised and was able to exercise far more real raw power than the Church of his world's history ever had owned. Part of the reason for this was the fact that there were no longer any

Moslems in this world, a military alliance of Christians and Moslems against the Mongols at some time in the thirteenth century having gradually and miraculously become a merger of Islam and Christianity. The other source of inordinate power for the Church was her control of the sales of gunpowder worldwide. She had from the beginning of this lucrative trade tried to keep the formula a secret, referred to refined niter as "priests' powder," and savagely punished any layman or group who so far transgressed as to make their own, unsanctified gunpowder—tormenting them, torturing them, maiming and mutilating them before finally burning them alive, the cavities of their mangled bodies stuffed to nigh bursting with their own, unhallowed gunpowder.

The England into which Bass and the rest had been thrust was not the same as the seventeenth-century England of his own world had been, consisting only of England and Wales, owning no suzerainty over either Ireland or Scotland. Moreover, it had been an England sorely beset—the king excommunicated, the entire kingdom under interdict, and, a crusade having been preached against it by Pope Abdul in Rome, hordes of bloodthirsty, loot-hungry foreign invaders massing against it on every hand.

CHAPTER THE SECOND

Worst of the many problems besetting the English king and his army was that as they were in the bad graces of the Church, they had no way of obtaining gunpowder in any quantities or even the refined niter necessary to fabricate really strong powder.

Having for many years been a research chemist in the field of propellants in his own world, the professor, upon being apprised of the current local problem, had rigged a lab of sorts at Whyffler Hall, where he, Bass, and the others had been projected, and had there quickly produced a succession of formulae, each resulting in even stronger gunpowder than the product of Church powdermills. Making good use of the eighty-odd tons of nitrate fertilizer which had been the load of one of the trucks, the Whyffler Hall operation had produced enough top-quality gunpowder to carry the royal army until it had been able to defeat armies of invaders and capture full resupplies of gunpowder.

In the England of this world, the twenty-first-century man who eventually became the Archbishop of York had, through a succession of events, been able to save the threatened life of the eldest son of King Henry VIII Tudor through dosing the boy with longevity booster capsules, the formulation of which included extremely strong antibiotics. Therefore, the boy had lived to succeed his father as King Arthur II Tudor, while his younger brother, Henry Tudor, had died in Angevin of plague while at war against the French king.

Arthur II had reigned long and had been succeeded by his grandson, Richard IV Tudor, who was soon after his elevation wedded to a niece (which was a polite way of saying illegitimate issue) of the then Roman Pope. Not far into his reign, Richard had died, and, fearing instability, the great nobles had had his younger brother crowned as King Arthur III Tudor. Although, more than seven months after Richard's death, his wife, Angela, had given birth to a son, there was sufficient suspicion of her among the bulk of the English and Welsh lords that most of them held forth that the boy was not come of Tudor loins but was certainly a bastard begat on the adultress by one of her multitudinous lovers. Since by this time her papal "uncle" was deceased, all in England thought that that would be the end of that and good riddance to bad, foreign rubbish.

However, the new Pope Abdul had been an old friend of his predecessor and, like him, a Moor, and he would have not liked to see Angela rejected and ejected from her late husband's kingdom in any case. But also, he had looked forward to ruling England and Wales through her as a virtual satrapy, and so the crusade against the "English Usurper" had been pronounced.

At the moment of the arrivals of Bass and the others, the Regent Angela's forces had held the City of London and its immediate environs, while her opponent, King Arthur, had more or less held all the rest of England and Wales. He and his forces had, however, been severely crippled by their lack of gunpowder; Angela had had all of the gunpowder she ever could need, shipload after shipload of all sorts of supplies coming upriver to her from Italy and other places, but she was woefully short of men to use it in the field, her best troops—led by one of her rumored lovers, a papal knight—having been almost wiped out in a recent battle with Arthur's army. And so she and her supporters stayed mostly behind the strong walls of London and awaited the huge, strong force of Crusaders said to be on the way by sea from the Mediterranean lands, led by a world-famous condottiere hired on by Rome.

When the word had been bruited about that King Arthur had, by hook or by crook, secured quantities of gunpowder, his army had nearly doubled in size and, with them, he had marched out of his camp near York to defeat first a force of French and Flemish Crusaders on the banks of the Tees River, then marched clear across the country to shatter a force of Irish Crusaders near to the walled town of Manchester and hotly pursue them clear to the sea, the last, desperate actions being fought on the very sea sands between royal English and Welsh cavalry units and the bodyguards of Irish petty kings and high nobles that these might be taken off by waiting boats.

At length, the great force assembled of Crusaders and mercenaries from Italy, southern France, Savoy, Spain, North Africa, Dalmatia, Hungary, and dozens of other, smaller principalities had been landed in the south of England and had been met and soundly defeated by King Arthur's army—now benefiting not only from the changes wrought by the professor and by Bass and Buddy Webster, but by Pete Fairley's innovations on cannon and harquebuses.

A born tinkerer, sometime jack-of-all-trades, weapons buff, and shooter of reproduction antique arms in his own world, Pete had come up with a simple, effective way to give seven relatively quick shots to each harquebusier, and he also had developed lighter, more easily maneuverable field-gun carriages no less strong and durable than the old, heavier, clumsier ones. These new weapons arrangements had gone far in the thorough defeat of the Scots army, and they proved no less devastating against the largest contingent of Crusaders, ripping the madly charging heavy cavalry into bloody rags in a deadly cross fire of harquebus balls and grapeshot from the batteries of light field guns massed at the flanks of the English line.

With the utter rout of this last and largest Crusader force, all of the diehard anti-Arthur folk fled to the "safety" of the walls of London-town, it having by then become virtually the only place in which persons of such sentiments could continue to live in safety in all of England and Wales. Hordes of gentry and minor nobility, some with their own warbands, began to appear at the royal camp, ready now to fight for King Arthur against the evil, foreign Regent Angela and her assuredly bastard pretender of a son. Southern priests either fled to London or, suddenly having been brought to a realization that it was by far preferable to be a live Englishman than a dead churchman, began to strenuously preach support for the chosen and crowned king of England and Wales, Arthur III Tudor.

With the influx of priests and bishops who had heretofore been rabid supporters of the Regent, hoard after long-hidden hoard of "priests' powder"—refined niter—was brought to light and turned over to the royal powdermills in and around York, where men trained by Pete Fairley used otherworldly techniques to further refine, then mix and blend it with other ingredients to produce English gunpowder, which was slowly achieving widespread renown as a product far superior to the very best grades of hallowed gunpowder—far more stable and dependably more powerful, so that significantly less was required to equal propellants in use.

With no more invading armies to fight, King Arthur and the bulk of his enlarged, much strengthened army had invested London and gone into permanent camps at various locations around it in preparation for the coming winter, dispersing the cavalry to their homes for the season of snow and cold, mostly as an economy measure. So Bass had spent that winter at Whyffler Hall, with his wife and new son, but with the spring he had ridden out with a force of his Borderer veterans to the preannounced site of the spring cavalry muster, at the location of the battle against the Irish Crusaders, near to Manchester.

While still in the north, he had been offered and had eagerly accepted an aggregation of fierce, hard-riding, hard-fighting Scots border rievers led by a justly infamous noble raider, the Laird of Eliot, overiding the inborn prejudices of the rest of his followers and officers.

He had arrived at the Manchester encampment to find most of the troops he had expected, but also a complete squadron of mercenaries, the Royal Tara *Galloglaiches*—mounted axemen from the northwestern isles of Scotland, officered by Irish knights, all well mounted, well supplied, armed to the teeth and beyond, and of such ferocious reputation, appearance, and behavior that they terrified even the ruffians led by Laird Eliot. Although he had grudgingly accepted these troops, doing so only because it was the expressed wish of King Arthur that he do so, he had never yet regretted taking them on.

He had first been truly glad that he had them on the day when he, by then Lord Commander of the Royal English and Welsh Horse, had brought to battle a tardy, mounted force of Crusaders—Spanish, Catalonian, Aragonese, Leonese, Asturian, Galician, Andalusian, Moorish, and Portuguese, with a light sprinkling of other nationalities—that had landed on the southern coast late in the winter and had been since playing hob in the most southerly counties. He had met them on certain croplands north of Lymeport, and the hard-fought encounter had thus become known as the Battle of Bloody Rye.

Between the *galloglaiches* and Eliot's Scots, the Southern Europeans had been almost exterminated on that day, hundreds having fallen on the main field of battle and hundreds more along the line of retreat. Having been borne along with his bodyguards and a large proportion of his staff officers on the crest of an intemperate, unordered charge of the Scots—frantic, lest the already committed *galloglaiches* kill all the invaders and thus reap all the glory before honest Scots got to swing their own steel in the melee—Bass had taken out his anger, frustration, and fear that the battle might go awry without his guidance on the enemy, fighting aggressively, ferociously, rather than merely defensively as was his usual wont in personal combat. In so doing, he had won the deathless respect of the *galloglaiches* and full many another of his officers and men, a respect tinged with awe by more than a few and, therefore, bordering upon out-and-out worship. The Irish nobleman who had led them having suffered permanent injury in the battle, the *galloglaiches* had unanimously chosen Bass to be their new "chief," declaring themselves ready and willing to follow his banner to the ends of the earth, did he so desire, and so they and their knighted Irish officers had been with him ever since, they being the basis of his condotta.

Subsequent to this great victory and, immediately thereafter, his cavalry brigade's extremely freakish capture of three armed merchant ships sailed up from Bilbao to resupply and revictual the now mostly deceased Crusaders, Bass had been summoned to attend upon King Arthur, and, in the castle at Greenwich, he had reaped his royal reward, being named Duke of Norfolk, Earl of Rutland, Baron of Strathtyne, and Knight of the Garter.

The bulk of the royal army had hunkered down in their camps and entrenchments around besieged London, sending the occasional iron cannonball or carcass over the walls, but mostly just waiting for time, starvation, and disease to bring the city to capitulation, as was the king's wish, since he did not desire to damage the city as a full-scale bombardment and assaults would certainly do. Most of the cavalry had been split into very small units and, scattered hither and yon all over both England and Wales, were riding about cleaning the countrysides of surviving foreign Crusaders, native traitors, and packs of bandits, preparing the lands for peace.

There being no place and no need for a Lord Commander of the Royal Horse in such small-scale cavalry operations as now were the only ones in progress, Bass had taken up residence on his duchy and had had built a permanent camp for his *galloglaiches* near to his ducal seat at Norwich Castle.

When word was brought from friendly sources in the Mediterranean area that a large resupply fleet was being collected for the relief of starving and almost powderless London to Sir Paul Bigod, admiral of King Arthur's small but very feisty royal fleet, Bass and

Pete Fairley between them had seized upon another use for the condotta of *galloglaiches*, then sitting idle near Norwich, submitted their scheme to Sir Paul, and been accepted with enthusiasm.

So some two dozen open galleys, rowed by brawny axemen—who all, in their homelands in the Scottish Western Isles, had grown up handling oars as often as axes—and each of the galleys mounting a platform and a rifled, breechloading, Fairley-made cannon, had taken a significant part in the waterborne ambush which had ended in the sinking or capture of the entire papal fleet for the crown and the prizing of a large, fully armed galleon-of-war for Bass.

With this ship, more ships had been taken on the open sea—outright piracy having long, Bass quickly discovered, been a completely honorable profession or avocation of noblemen. The end result had been that he not only possessed a sizable and powerful fleet, but was become wealthy beyond any thought of or need for avarice.

Then, shortly after the beginning of the new year's war season, King Arthur had ordered Bass and his condotta, along with certain volunteer reinforcements, to cross the Irish Sea and enter into the temporary service of Arthur's cousin, King Brian VIII Ui Neill, who was striving to bring all of the petty, ever-warring kings of Ireland under his sway. Bass had obeyed his monarch's orders.

He had succeeded in his first two missions for the charismatic *Ard-Righ*, bringing back into the itching hands of the acquisitive High King no less than three of the Seven Magical Jewels of Ireland—the tangible symbols of sovereignty of the seven original kingdoms on the island—and even bringing down from the north two of the petty kings to pledge their allegiance to the *Ard-Righ* in person.

But then a new-crowned king of the northeasternmost realm, that one called Ulaid, had decided to find a way to secure himself and his new realm against Brian and had voyaged over to the Hebrides isle of Islay, there to give over Ulaid to the Regulus of the Isles, receiving it back from that fierce, powerful Scottish lord as a feoff, which maneuver meant that now any attack upon Ulaid by the power-mad, land-hungry *Ard-Righ* would perforce signify an attack upon a vassal of and lands belonging to the Regulus, who owned forces and resources on at least a par with Brian.

Then, to add insult to injury, the new vassal king of Ulaid had taken advantage of the curious murder of the petty king of Airgialla to his south and west, this kingdom having been a declared client-state of the *Ard-Righ*, to declare the domain to now be his client, he to rule it as regent for the infant son of its last king.

At the announced enfeoffment of Ulaid by the Regulus and the report that a unit of Bass's condotta had been courteously but very firmly turned back from approaching the capital City of Airgialla by King Roberto of Ulaid and his forces, Brian the Burly had given every indication of contemplation of an immediate, seaborne attack upon Islay and the Regulus.

Only now did Bass realize that the sly, crafty *Ard-Righ* had used him and his well-known loyalties to abet his own schemes, having never entertained for even a moment any real intention of upsetting his plans in and for Ireland to go venturing off oversea in what would at best have been a very risky campaign, since he might well have ended having to fight not only the forces of the Regulus's erstwhile overlord, King James of Scotland, but those of his own cousin, King Arthur of England and Wales, King James's new ally, as well.

Arrived back in his semipermanent camp, finally,

much of the dust and sweat of the day laved off, in comfortable clothing and with a full meal resting warmly in his stomach, Bass sat well into the night drinking and chatting with his officers, these men who had stood outside the palace complex at Tara, prepared to kill or to die for him, that day. He felt more than humble at such clear expressions of friendship and loyalty; he felt frustration, too, in that he did not know when or if or even how he could ever express his thanks and gratitude for such extremes of devotion.

It was not until all goodnights had been uttered, and he had been disrobed by his squires and other servants, had bathed in his personal bathtub, had donned his silken nightclothes, and had lain upon his bed that other thoughts came to him.

For the two twenty-first-century scientists and he and his group of twentieth-century people had not been the only ones snatched into this world from their own. Earlier this very year, in fact, thirteen men and women of his own world—most of them second-generation Armenian-Americans, plus a couple of Greek-Americans, a Lebanese immigrant, and a few of other ethnic backgrounds, the whole making up a Middle Eastern band and belly dancers who had been giving an outdoor performance when snatched away by another malfunction of the Whyffler Hall projector—had arrived during a solemn high mass in Yorkshire, appearing between the congregation and the celebrants with their stringed instruments still twanging, their clarinet still wailing, their fiddle still screeching, their rank of drums still booming, and the colorfully costumed dancers still whirling. Only the fact that the Archbishop of York had been on hand, had immediately realized what must have occurred, and had been able to hurriedly summon his foot guards to protect the confused and thoroughly shocked projectees had prevented the deeply superstitious and horrified attendees of the ceremony from killing all of the supposed "imps of Satan."

The Archbishop had lodged them all in a sizable and well-guarded suite in the huge, rambling hall on his country estate southwest of York. He had left most of them therein, ordering them a reasonable amount of freedom on the grounds of the estate, while he tried to decide the best disposition of them—best for them, best for him, best for England.

In order to help him make a decision, he had taken to having lengthy conversations with the eldest of them, a man of fifty-odd years named Rupen Ademian, uncle to the bandleader and two of the others. In the course of these meetings, the two men had become fast friends, and, long before he had made any firm plans for the others, the Archbishop had taken Rupen into his personal service.

Then, of a day, out of a guarded suite inside a well-guarded hall situated on a large estate far from any village or town, all save only Rupen Ademian and a belly dancer named Jenny Bostwick had mysteriously disappeared, just as if they might have been once more snatched up by the Whyffler Hall projector, although such could not have been the case, since the Archbishop had had that dangerous and unpredictable device removed from its centuries-old place and brought down to him at York, where he himself had taken it completely apart, using the otherworldly parts for various of his and Pete Fairley's projects and experiments.

"I wonder," thought Bass, as he began to drift off into a state of pre-sleep, sunk into the soft warmth of the feather bed, "I wonder just what in the seven hells did happen to those poor folks? None of them had learned much of the language here, yet, and God knows the lingo they speak in this England is a far cry from the American dialect of my time and world. Besides, there was no earthly way that eleven people could've been spirited out of that suite and that hall and across the grounds of that huge estate without somebody seeing them at some point and time.

"Well, wherever, whenever they are, I sincerely wish them luck. I have a feeling they're going to need that and a whole lot more."

Dr. Ilsa Peters found Arsen Ademian stomping up and down the length of the crypt, back into which he and she had moved as soon as a habitation had been built and approved by the overly picky Bedros Yacubian as home for him and his wife, Rose. Arsen was half-shouting obscenities in English, Armenian, and what she assumed was either Japanese or Vietnamese. In a corner, Simon Delahaye squatted quietly, watching Arsen and listening to him while skillfully mending a rent in the sleeve of a fatigue shirt.

"What's the problem now?" the tall, slender, blonde physician asked of no one in particular.

Simon answered her. "The noble Captain Arsen be most wroth at the continued lack of resolve of the old sachem, Squash Woman, and the council that sitteth with her, here. I much fear me that if Captain Arsen rage so for much longer he must assuredly burst his skull and his veins-all, my lady."

Only the touch of her cool hand, however, was required to stop Arsen's tantrum and start him explaining the outrages that had precipitated it. "Aw, goddammit, Ilsa, that fucking slimy old cunt, she and those so-called councillors, old farts, the whole damn bunch of the fuckers, they can't make up their goddam so-called minds on anything; they ain't done it yet, leastways, and I'm beginning to believe they won't ever. All they can ever, and her in particular, think about is gimme, gimme, gimme, bad as a bunch of welfare bums in our own world ever was."

Ilsa sighed. It was an old story and long since become a most unfunny one. "What are the desires of her Shawnee majesty now?"

Arsen shrugged disgustedly. "Oh, the usual shit, honey: more sides of beef and frozen turkeys, more fresh vegetables, more pots and pans and utensils, more salt and sugar, more dried fruits, more of damned near everything the cow-cunted old scab-sucking bitch can think of . . . plus one other thing. She wants a silver sky boat and she says there will be no agreement to go west of the mountains until she has one of her own."

"A carrier?" demanded Ilsa. "Squash Woman wants us to give her one of the carriers as her price for letting us help her get her and her people out of reach of the Spanish slavers, out of harm's way? Arsen, you know that I've bent over backwards in months past trying to make excuses for that old woman and her actions and lack of same, but enough is enough. Her demands have by now become nothing less than extortionate. We can't work with a woman like her, so why don't we all just move over to that place beyond the mountains and leave her and her people to stew in their own juice until either they wise up and decide to follow us on their own or the Spanish come back and make those they don't kill wish they had taken us up on our offer while they still had the chance?"

But Arsen shook his head, slowly. "Naw, honey, I couldn't do nothing like that to these folks. They need us and they know it. Lots of them can't hardly wait to get over to this rich land in the west they've heard about; you've heard them asking about it, some have probably even asked you. It ain't their fault, Squash Woman and the rest of the sachems."

"Why the hell don't they just get rid of her and them, Arsen?" Ilsa snapped. "Choose some leaders that will do more than eat and sleep and talk and make demands of us, that's what they need to do, you know. If they'd do that, I might start having some faith in them."

Arsen sighed. "You just don't know them, honey. They're a people bound by custom. They think that age makes people smarter, so the older they are, the smarter they're bound to be, see. Squash Woman is the oldest person in this place, so that makes her the top dog, see. They'd never even think of taking and putting anybody younger and dumber in her place, honey, and was we to suggest it to them, they'd wonder when we started using shit for brains, is all, they wouldn't get rid of her."

She made a face. "So, we just sit here while she thinks up more demands to make of us and you build your castle or whatever that thing is intended to someday be and we all wait for the damned Spanish to march or sail up here in force and we have to kill a lot more of them with terrible weapons that have never even been dreamed of yet, thank God, in this world, and you keep going off to rob our world—segments of it, anyway—blind just to feed the whims of a senile and greedy old woman, huh?"

Arsen looked just then a bit like a kicked puppy. "Honey, look, I can't really explain it all too clearly, but I feel like God or somebody put me down here, in this place and time, for a purpose. I think that purpose was to save these poor folks, and I mean to keep on trying to do it, no matter what I have to do to do it, no matter what it takes. I wish you could understand, honey, I really do."

It was her turn to sigh. "I do understand, in a way, Arsen. I understand that you are deeply motivated, and I respect you, love you for your obvious altruism. You've managed to live and function normally despite the hellish amounts of frustration that old woman has shoveled on you daily for a lot longer than the horny caveman that I thought you were when we were in the other world could ever have done. But, Arsen, even a stone saint can bear just so much weight before it cracks and crumbles, and I don't want to see you reach that stage. I . . . Oh, damn, with all this. I forgot.

"Arsen, I took the river patrol for Mike, today, so that he could go hunting. The Spanish are still running around their town and fort like somebody had overturned an anthill, but they don't look ready to move out anytime soon. The only ship I could see down there was an oceangoing ship, far too deep-draught to make it this far upriver without coming to grief.

"But on the way back up here, I swung inland—don't ask me why, I don't know why—and I spotted a whole hell of a lot of Indians. They're on that trail back about a mile and a half west of the river. It looks like men, women, *and* children, plus dogs, donkeys, and even a few horses. I'd guesstimate that they're one or two days from here and headed this way. Some of the men wore turbans, so I'd guess that they're Creeks."

Arsen beamed the first full smile that she had seen light up his face in some time. "Well, that took less time than I could've dreamed it would.

"Simon, go find Soaring Eagle and a couple of the faster-running braves, tell them what they're looking for and about where to expect to find it, and send them out to guide those folks here, pronto."

After shrugging into the mended shirt, Simon tugged

at his forelock, picked up the ornate Spanish broadsword without which he had never gone anywhere since the night he had prized it off a dead man, and ascended the stone steps to the outside, fitting swordcase to belt as he went.

"*Simon*," Arsen shouted after the man, "give the runners a rifle, a pistol, and the accessories for them to give to the sachem as a gift from me. Tell them to tell him that I'll give a rifle to each of his braves and teach them how to use it if he and they join with us in our anti-Spanish confederation here."

He grinned at Ilsa, saying, "God bless you, honey, I'm starting to get good vibes, really great vibes, again. Everything still might work out, you know, Squash Woman or no Squash Woman, damn her stinking old ass."

Bedros Yacubian, holding doctorates in both pathology and paleontology, had not been one of the group of dancers and band members accidentally projected into this world, though his wife had been. Arsen had gone back—after mastering the uses of the carrier that he had found in the crypt when they had landed with said crypt in the wilderness when some something had snatched them from out the comfortable suite in the country hall of the Archbishop of York, months back—to their old world and used one of the projectors that the carrier had explained to him how to fabricate to bring the erudite man to this world at the instigations of Greek John and Ilsa.

The safe, pleasant-looking, game-filled, and fertile land that Arsen had found beyond the western mountains was abrim with beasts the like of many of which he had never before either seen or heard described—shaggy elephantine creatures, long-horned buffalo, huge elk, leonine cats bigger by far than any lion or tiger of his own world and time, a shaggy canine as big as a Great Dane. Greek John, who in addition to being a member of the ill-fated band had been a practicing dentist in the other world, with one of his hobbies being the study of paleontology, had been taken over to see the singular beasts, and after the trip he had urged Arsen to bring in Bedros. Ilsa had wanted the man brought in in order to assuage Rose's hunger to be again with her recently married husband.

But in the flesh, Bedros had proved to be arrogant, supercilious, patronizing, insulting, and the sort of person who found fault with everyone and everything he chanced to encounter. Moreover, he was extremely impressed with himself and knew himself to be far above doing any work not directly connected to his profession. So very difficult had it proved to get any sort of physical labor out of Bedros that Greg Sinclair, one of the band members, had made the remark that if the academic could find someone else to eat for him, urinate for him, and defecate for him, he would certainly give over those functions into that person's keeping. Of course, Greg had couched his words in basic, four-letter terms. At that point, Bedros had committed the cardinal error of slapping Greg's face, whereupon Greg had punched the man out.

Had not Rose been so obviously happy reunited with her husband, Arsen would long since have taken the man back to where he had been brought from. He would have taken them both back, except that Ilsa frequently needed the help of a skilled nurse, and that was Rose. Therefore, he just managed to put up with Bedros and bade everyone else try to so do.

But Bedros was getting harder and harder to stomach. Arsen did not like him and, therefore, did not trust him. Had it been up to Bedros, he would have spent all of his waking hours in that land west of the mountains, trailing and studying the fauna, examining their tracks and droppings, taking stacks of Polaroid photographs and making ream on ream of illegible notes.

However, there were only three carriers, each holding no more than a single human being at the time, and on most days one was aloft patrolling the river and the surroundings, one was being used by the timber detail felling trees, trimming them and projecting the fruits of the labor back to the environs of the fort Arsen and his men were constructing, while the third was being used by Arsen himself to transport him to that land of strange beasts and an ancient granite quarry he had found and was using to provide stone for the fort.

On occasion, after several of the band members and dancers had been forced to endure a particularly petulant, childish-sounding outburst from the academic, Arsen had been asked by more than one of them why he did not just provide the demanding man with a tent, a sleeping bag, a rifle, supplies, and whatever else he claimed to need, then project him over into the new land, going over for a short time now and again to check on him and be certain that one of the superlions hadn't snacked on him.

But although he did it himself, almost every day, to quarry and project granite slabs, Arsen was leery of sending anyone over alone. Not only could more than a few of the seen and known beasts be deadly dangerous to a careless or unthinking human being, there also was a possible, lurking, hidden danger.

Squash Woman had told him and Ilsa, shortly after he had first discovered the western land, that the ancestors of her people had come east from that land long ago, had lived there for time without counting. They had been protected from the huge beasts by an enigmatic race of bearded white-skinned men she had called the Old Ones—men who could, she averred, talk to almost all the animals and make them friendly toward mankind and his endeavors.

She had gone on to say that these Old Ones had hunted down, slain, and tried to exterminate a species of creature she had described as shaped very much like a man but much bigger, much toothier, and covered in hair. Her descriptions had put Arsen much in mind of descriptions he had read of Sasquatches. Squash Woman had said that, there in the west, these creatures had lived in caves, in burrows in the earth, and behind waterfalls, never coming out in full sunlight, but only after nightfall or on dark, overcast days.

The old Indian woman had said that these creatures were all inveterate maneaters. So long as the Old Ones' hunting had kept the things in check, there had been very few losses to their bestial appetites, but after the Old Ones had departed, had put out upon the northern river in the strange boats they had built, never to be seen again by Squash Woman's forebears, the creatures had begun to breed up, become more numerous and ferocious. At last, rather than continue to live in constant fear of assaults by the hard-to-kill predators, the Indians had left that otherwise blessed land and come east across the mountains to their present homes.

This was the thing that troubled Arsen, that made him reluctant to put even the insufferable Bedros Yacubian down in the place alone and with no means of quickly leaving should he be attacked. Arsen had never seen one of the things, nor had anyone else who had visited, not even any really odd tracks, but as these were said to be nocturnal hunters and as all of his and the others' trips had been diurnal, lack of a sighting really proved nothing, and he still had a gut feeling that such horrors might truly exist in the land of odd beasts.

CHAPTER THE THIRD

Impressed by a returning Creek runner's expressed awe of the approaching sachem who had led his people all the way from what Arsen figured would have been northern Florida or southern Georgia in his own world and a not inconsiderable journey to be undertaken on foot in anybody's world, especially through an uncharted wilderness, Arsen and Mike Sikeena got into carriers and flew out to meet the oncoming people.

Arsen took along the Class Five projector, his personal weapons and equipment, and a flashy Spanish dirk as gift for the sachem, while Mike bore the sachem a GI canteen with cup and cover, an unbreakable hand mirror, and a pair of steel tweezers.

The returned runner, a young buck called Swift Wolf, had said in part, "Ar-sen Silver Hat, he who leads is even older than the old Shawnee woman who rules here. He is called Snake-burnt-at-both-ends and he is very famous. He has fought the Spanish in the south many times and celebrated three great victories over them, and so they fear him, but still they shower gifts upon him because they seek to hire on his fierce young warriors to help them fight other whites and help them catch slaves among other tribes. He it was who sent Soaring Eagle and the rest of us to serve the Spanish, and so it was directly to him that Swimming Elk went when your mighty medicine put him back in the land from which we came, two moons and more ago."

To Arsen, the magic words had been "Older than the old Shawnee woman." That meant that, once arrived, the sachem would assuredly be considered by the Indians to be wiser than Squash Woman and, therefore, would become automatically the head of the council of sachems, and Arsen meant to get cozy with him before Squash Woman and her cronies could get him set into their intransigent mold of total noncooperation and endless demands for foods and gifts.

Mike Sikeena and Greek John having learned—independently one from the other and quite accidentally in both their cases—that the carriers would operate on some functions with the lids fully opened, Arsen and Mike on this day took along as passengers seated in the gaped lids Simon Delahaye—who, it seemed, owned an inborn linguistic ability and had learned to speak both the Creek of his warriors and the Shawnee of his women—and the Creek brave called Two-hand-killer—who was ambidextrous to a marked degree and very devoted to Simon, acting in the capacity of an aide-de-camp.

In the lids with them, Simon insisted that each carry not only his own weapons but a half-dozen of the Confederate States Armaments company's flintlock hunting rifles, explaining this to Arsen by saying, "Captain, you gifted the Micco, true, but . . ."

"The *what*?" demanded Arsen. "You mean the sachem, Simon?"

The brawny Englishman shook his shaggy head. "No,

Captain, sachem be what these Shawnees call their leaders; the Creeks call a person such as this one we go to meet Micco. While a sachem be an adviser, a micco be much more, almost a king, and he hath a council of advisers—the warchief, the peace-chief, the chiefs of the clans, the medicine man, and such others as he may feel need of and name to his council. These fine, light gonnes be for that council, that they may feel kindly towards us."

Arsen shrugged. "Okay, Simon. You sure as hell understand these fuckers better than me, so we'll do it your way." To himself, he thought. "Hell, the more Indians have got guns, the quicker the fucking Spanish are going to get a fucking comeuppance, and it ain't as if we're going to run out of them anytime soon. All I got to do is get in the carrier and make another fucking midnight requisition on Uncle Bagrat's place. Shit, I'd like to give the Indians real guns, modern pieces, but where the fuck would they get ammo for the fuckers? That's the fucking problem. This way, they got all kinds of flint and, if nothing else, they can steal gunpowder and lead and cloth for patches from the fucking Spanish, or better yet ambush and kill a bunch of the fuckers and take what they need off of the bodies. But even as it sits, I'm giving them better guns than the Spanish have got, anyway—some those damn slavers was still using matchlocks, for chrissakes!"

The carriers and those who traveled in them had been described to the southern indigenes by those braves Arsen had projected back down to a place near their homelands and, more recently, by Soaring Eagle and his runners, so the arrival of Arsen, Mike, Simon, and Two-hand-killer was not openly remarked upon by the gathered elders and warriors, though Arsen was willing to bet that every one of them was curious as old hell.

So solemn, formal, and ritualistic was the greeting and welcome in the camp that Arsen kept wishing he had a program and was now very glad that he had thought to bring along Simon Delahaye, for though the silver helmet allowed him to speak into the minds of all of the Indians and, in return, understand what they said to him, it gave him no insight into the customs and rules of behavior that caused them to do and say what they did and said. Simon understood not only the language of his Creek braves but had, through actually living in their first longhouse with them, eating with them, hunting with them, and leading them into combat after having trained all of them in his period's military usages and the proper use and care of the flintlock rifles, learned their minds, their thought processes, many of their customs, and much of their very intricate social structure.

Though clearly shrunken and stooped with age, the Micco proved to be a man about of Arsen's height—which meant, thought Arsen, that he must have been close to giant-size among the Indians and the Spanish, in his prime—but he was no shuffling near-cripple like Squash Woman. Vitality exuded from him, tangibly; his voice was deep and rich, the vision of his black eyes was unclouded, and he gave Arsen the impression of being smart as a whip.

When the Micco's council had been introduced and Simon was engaged in presenting a rifle to each of them, in the formal, Creek way, Arsen and Mike proffered their own gifts to the Micco, Snake-burnt-at-both-ends.

After they had shown the old Indian how to open the canteen, how to remove it and the cup from out the cover, he asked, "Did the steel-breasts make this, too Ar-sen-silver-hat?"

"No, the Spanish didn't make this, Micco, it came

from my own folks," replied Arsen. "Just like the rifles and your pistol."

The aged Indian nodded and said, "But I know that the steel knife, here, with the bright-flashing case, is of the steel-breasts. How did it come to your hands? By trade?"

"No, Micco," answered Arsen, "I took it off the dead body of a Spaniard. I was told he had been a knight."

The old man's lips twitched in what Arsen and the rest would soon come to recognize for a smile of approval, and he said in a serious tone, "Good. Very good, Ar-sen-silver-hat. It never is wise to trade with the steel-breasts, hear you the words of age, of one who has learned bitter lessons and knows whereof he speaks.

"Although I heard long, long ago that there were good men with white skins in the north, men like you who do not go about hung all over with steel, you are the first I ever have met, and so I cannot speak with knowledge of them. But the steel-breasts—and I have met four different tribes of them, in my life—are evil, very cruel, and so deceitful that he who trusts them is a fool.

"The people called Guale, they trusted these steel-breasts, and where are they, today? Once they were strong and numerous, now the few as are left live as almost slaves upon the lands that once were theirs. As the steel-breasts had killed off or driven off all the game from those lands, the pitiful things who were once called Guale must subsist on the refuse of the steel-breasts or beg from them, for they no longer own the courage to steal.

"The people related to my people, those called Appalachee, will one day be like to the Guale of today, I feel. And for long I have feared that, when I go, my own people would be like the Appalachee within the lifetime of a man. But when the young men who had gone away to fight for the steel-breasts came back with news of you and your people and told of how you had given them guns—a something which the steel-breasts never would do—and killed many steel-breasts with their help and freed the people enslaved by the steel-breasts, I knew that you were a man I must meet and know before I go to join my ancestors.

"Now, I would hear your words, Ar-sen-silver-hat."

"Micco," said Arsen, slowly, "there are not many steel-breasts of any tribe here, there never have been as many of them as there are of you Creeks and Shawnees and other tribes, not if you all went after them together, there aren't. But you don't, you never have joined together to kill them all or drive them out of your lands. That's what I'm trying to do, Micco, see enough tribes of your kind join together to make it so fucking hot here for the Spanish that they'll head for easier pickings somewhere else, see.

"Armed with flintlock rifles and a few cannon, plus your usual weapons, and trained right, as few as five hundred of your braves could sweep the Spanish clear back to the sea, probably so badly terrify the fuckers that they'd crowd back onto their fucking ships and haul ass back to Cuba or wherever they came up here from to start out.

"Micco, at the start of all of this, I wasn't thinking any more ahead than just taking care of Squash Woman's little clan of the Shawnee and protecting them from the Spanish slavers. But since I've had time to think about it, I've realized that such a small-scale operation would never work for long. What is needed is not just one tribe or two, but five or six in a confederation devoted to fighting together against all the steel-breasts, see, not just the Spanish. Now, you know the Indians a whole lot better than I do. Which of the nearby tribes do you think would work together best for this confederation, Micco?"

The aged man sat for a long time, his eyes slitted, then he reopened them and began to speak, saying, "Ar-sen-silver-hat, if what you have seen in your dreams would work, it would be a great and brave accomplishment. But so very much stands against it that you must forget it, I fear."

"Why, Micco?" demanded Arsen. "Why won't it work?"

"For one thing," was the aged Indian's reply, "the thing that has crippled us in the south since the first coming of the steel-breasts. Most tribes would rather fight other tribes than join with them to fight steel-breasts.

"Another thing is that tribes and clans will not come to you just to hear your words, brave though those words are; you must fight the steel-breasts and win more than once, then see that the words and proofs of these victories are spread far and wide among the tribes and clans by traders or runners. Only then will men sit in council among the peoples and decide that their warriors should journey to join with you and your warriors, to share with you and them the fruits of victories over the steel-breasts—women, slaves, loot, scalps, ears—and the honor."

Arsen shook his head. "Micco, I'm not thinking of just warriors coming here or wherever long enough to fight and then dispersing, going home, and giving the Spanish a chance to gather reinforcements, establish another beachhead, and go at it all over again. No, I'm in mind of a place where all of the people of the confederation—warrriors, women, children, old people—all can live fairly close together in peace and safety, so that the warriors can always be mustered quickly to go wherever they're needed to turn back the foe."

Snake-burnt-at-both-ends breathed a long sigh. "To see your fine dream in flesh, then, Ar-sen-silver-hat, you must find a place wherein so many of the people can find food, raise it and hunt it, and that place is not these foothills, hereabouts. The soil here is shallow and poor, the game small and chary, mostly."

Arsen nodded and said, "Micco, I have found just such a place as you say I need. If you and three of your council will ride with me and the other silver hat on our boats that fly, we will show you this land and the riches it contains."

When they first rose above the tops of the tallest trees, the shaman, who sat crosslegged behind the Micco, gasped once, then put himself under strict control. But the Micco himself merely sat relaxed, and his only comment was, "Remarkable."

Arsen led the way in his carrier, Mike following, as they flew swiftly north and west. They crossed the eastern foothills, then one range of mountains, flew high over the long, narrow, green-carpeted valley that divided the ranges, then over the second and wider range. The same protective field that would shield the carriers from any projectile—up to and including iron cannon balls, in Arsen's experience—also insulated the passengers from the wind of their swift passage and, to some degree, from the cold of the higher altitudes.

After one brief glimpse of the treetops so far below, the old shaman sat rigid, his eyes tightly shut. But the fearless Micco leaned his body forwards and to the side, grasping the edge of the carrier lid to steady him, and avidly drinking in every one of these strange, new sights.

Arsen chuckled to himself, thinking, "That wrinkled

old fucker's got guts a fucking mile wide and ten miles long, by God. That slimy old cooze Squash Woman won't stand a half of a fucking chance against him."

As they reached the beginning of the western foothills and began to gradually descend, they passed a very startled red-shin hawk, which screamed at them before diving fast and far and out of their sight among the trees below. At the noise, the shaman opened up his eyes, moaned very softly, then closed them again.

But the Micco bent far over the edge and shouted at the disappearing raptor, "Fear not, Hawk-brother, I do not want your dry, stringy carcass in my stewpot," then sat back up, chuckling.

Arsen set down first in the long-overgrown fields just west and north of the stone ruins clustered among the hills. "Much food was grown here for many years in times long past, Micco," he said, "by those who lived in habitations built upon those stone foundations you can see back there. If the land supported folks once, I can't see any reason why it wouldn't do it again.

"Now, get back on the carrier and I'll show you the game. You said all the game back there on the east side of the mountains was small? Well, just wait until you see the sizes of the game here."

They sailed silently over a herd of long-horned bison that straggled for what Arsen computed to be over four statute miles, with bands of the small, big-headed, shaggy horses grazing among the huge, dark-colored bovines. At one point, well out from the edge of the herd, five of the monstrous, spotted, lionlike cats sat or sprawled in the high, weedy grasses, being seemingly ignored by the bison and the horses alike. Farther on, past the fringes of the bison-horse herd, on the side of one of the low hills that lay between the plain and the river, they saw three of the over-sized, wolflike canines tearing apart the still-twitching carcass of an elk cow, while in the valley just below a black bear of good but not really remarkable size gorged himself in a dense tangle of berry bushes.

As he had expected, Arsen found mammoths at the river. There were some ten or twelve of them that day. Two of them were clearly calves and the others were of assorted sizes. All of the Indians seemed thoroughly impressed at the sight of so much ambulatory meat. Following the river upstream, to the east-northeast for some two miles, they found two of the gigantic, scimitar-toothed cats making a meal of the bloody body of a sloth at least ten feet long, while constantly having to fend off the incursions of a horde of canines about the size and shape of coyotes.

Buzzards lazily circled over this scene as they had over the feast of the super-wolves back on the hillside, but here there was also, much higher up, a very much larger bird gliding on wings that looked to Arsen to be ten or twelve or more feet in spread. He rose straight upward to see it at closer range.

"*Thunderbird*!" both the Micco and the shaman breathed together, reverently. Then the shaman began to chant something.

Arsen knew that the humongous bird was the same kind that both Greek John and Bedros-the-Prick had called a condor, but to him it still looked like nothing so much as a vastly overgrown turkey buzzard. He descended and continued the tour until they had almost reached the foothills again, then he headed back for the ruins.

When they all were sitting or squatting among the foundation stones on that same hilltop where he and Greek John had once sat, Arsen asked, "Well, Micco, do you think this land has the soil and the game to support enough people to give my confederation up to five hundred warriors at a time?"

"Yes, Ar-sen-silver-hat," replied the old man. "But this is a very sacred land, the Land of the Thunderbird. I had heard of it many times over the course of my long, long lifetime, but I didn't know if such tales had even a kernel-grain of truth, for no one at all seemed to know even in what direction it lay and no man living could say that he had ever actually trod its earth. I would not bring my people to live in this land—it would be a sacrilege, a great sacrilege that would not end well for any of us. Thunderbird would see us, know that we trespassed, and send monsters to kill us, eat of our flesh. The tales tell of this very thing happening in the long ago, when foolish people disregarded the warnings of the Guardian, Thunderbird, came, dwelt, planted, hunted, and waxed fat for a while, but then were either killed and eaten or fled from here back to the parts of the land that are not sacred."

Apparently sensing Arsen's keen disappointment at his lack of support, the aged Indian added, "However, Ar-sen-silver-hat, on our way to this holy place, east of the biggest mountains, we passed over a long, narrow valley. I saw deer there, and it looked to be rich land within it. If it is as long as it looked to be and as rich as what I saw for all of its length, then many, many of the people could live there, hunt and forage in the mountains on either side and plant maize and squashes and pumpkins and gourds and beans and tubers of all sorts and live well in all seasons of the year. Why do we not fly back now and see just how long and how rich this valley is, Ar-sen-silver-hat?"

"Yes, I knew that it was the sacred land, the Land of the Guardian, Thunderbird," said Squash Woman sullenly, speaking to Arsen, Ilsa, Mike, John, and the Micco.

"Then why the hell didn't you tell me?" snapped Arsen. "Why didn't you tell us all, early on, not just keep us farting around here and waiting on you and those other frauds like you've done, you old bitch, you?"

"Because," she mumbled, "I knew that if you knew the whole truth, we never would go to that land to live, you would stop bringing the people food and all your other trifling presents. You would all leave and the young warriors would all leave, then we would have to start hunting and foraging and making our backs sore tending gardens again, and we would have to break up into small bands along the river and again live in fear of the slavers without you and the young warriors to protect us. Now that you do know the whole truth, you *are* all going to leave this place. I know, I can feel it in my bones," she added, nodding sadly, tears glittering in her eyes.

"Shit!" snorted John. "All you feel in your bones is arthritis and, probably, gout, the way you've been overstuffing your face on all that Arsen could bring you for months, now."

"She's guessed right, though," Arsen informed them. "We are moving."

Squash Woman climbed out of her pit of anguish and woe, reviving instantly, to pronounce, "The people do not go anywhere unless the council of elders says so, the council will not say so unless, I, the eldest of the elders say so, and I will not say so . . . ever, for to try to dwell in the Land of the Thunderbird is to die horribly there."

"No, no one is moving there, Squash Woman," agreed Arsen. "But the Micco, here, and I have found another land, a long, rich valley between ranges of the western mountains, north and west of this place in which we now live. It is well watered, game abounds, and the Micco says that no one except wandering hunters has lived there for a very long time, if ever."

"No!" She shook her head, stubbornly. "I told you, Ar-sen-silver-hat, I will not let the council agree to move an inch from this place unless you give me a silver boat and a silver hat and certain other things. I am the eldest. The Eldest has spoken!"

Mike Sikeena growled, low in his throat, and fixed a baleful stare, from eyes as black as her own, on Squash Woman, where she squatted. "Eldest asshole," he said, softly and feelingly, "you are a colossal pain in the neck. I'd be careful if I was you, woman, old folks are real easy to kill . . . if a man knows how, and I do. And ain't too many questions ever asked when a old woman just drops down dead, not if it's no marks on the body."

"Eldest One," said the Micco with polite formality, able to speak directly to her despite the language differences due to his wearing of one of the silver helmets. Arsen had given him Bedros Yacubian's, telling the academic that he really didn't need it since he spoke to no Indians if he could help it, and then only to insult or patronize them.

"Eldest One, when were you born? Do you know, exactly?"

"Of course I do!" snapped Squash Woman with far less courtesy, showing the aged Micco precious little respect. "The True Human Beings, my people, remember things well and accurately, always, unlike you poor half-humans who live in other places. I was born on the night before the great, black monster tried to gobble up the sun at midsummer. That was ninety-two winters ago."

Micco shook his head and said just as courteously as

before, "No, old woman, that was not ninety-two winters ago, that was only eighty-three winters ago; I recall it well, for I was a boy in my eleventh summer then. I was out hunting squirrels and checking my rabbit snares and I became much terrified in that short darkness.

"No, venerable though you assuredly are, woman, you are not at all the eldest here—you are at most eighty-three, while I number this one my ninety-fourth summer of life. I am eldest. The Eldest has now truly spoken!"

Squash Woman's black eyes blazed out rage and defiance. "You cannot, can never be Eldest here, old half-man, for you are not of the real people, you are only a half-bestial Creek. If you try to even sit on *my* council, you will be driven out like the dog you are. My braves will arise on my command and slay or enslave all your clan."

Greek John laughed aloud. "With what braves will you do these things, pray tell, you old scuzz-bucket? Among all the little bunches of Shawnees that have straggled in here, I doubt there are thirty braves, and a lot of them are near middle-aged. The Micco, here, has got over a hundred and fifty warriors, all in their prime."

"Ah, but we . . . our braves all have thundersticks, now, John-silver-hat," she crowed. "Both the long ones and the short ones, like mine." She patted the flintlock pistol thrust under her sash.

Arsen dashed her hopes with gleeful relish. "So what, Squash Woman? The Micco's Creek warriors all have flintlocks now, too; and don't make the mistake of thinking that the young Creek braves who have been living here among your people will fight for you. No, they're Creeks, first and foremost, and they'll fight for their Micco."

"We don't need the half-man, half-dog things!" snapped Squash Woman. "We still have things that they don't have—the thunder-logs."

"Not anymore, you don't," said Mike, coldly. "The cannon and the swivel guns are all over at the fort, now."

Squash Woman licked suddenly dry lips with a dark tonguetip. "But Ar-sen-silver-hat and the rest of you silver hats, you will quickly kill or rout the subhuman Creeks just as you did all of the slave raiders. You must—the Great Spirit sent you to protect us and care for us, forever. You will lie in your silver boats and sit in your moving-swimming-smoking huts the color of dark earth and you will kill all of the Creek warriors, that we people may enslave the women and children and slay the old, useless ones and take all of their goods; the Great Spirit sent you to protect us and see to our needs. This is a need, Ar-sen-silver-hat, and I, the Eldest of the only True Human Beings, command that you do it! For it is only fitting and proper that submen be the slaves and chattels of true people. That is the will of the Great Spirit."

"*Sieg Heil*!" said John, dryly, starting to hum under his breath what he could recall of the "Horst Wessel Lied."

"Oh, no, Squash Woman," declared Arsen. "Uh-uh, no fucking way, baby! Yes, we'll fight off the Spanish whenever we have to and as many times over as we have to, but that's because they're a severe threat to *all* Indians, not just to you Shawnees. But, you slimy, lying, greedy old douche-bag cooze, you refuse to let the Micco take over the council or go and pick a fight with the Creeks, then you're on your fucking own. We'll just sit back and watch them go through you and your pitiful few braves like shit through a fucking goose. Then us and the Micco and the Creeks will go on up to that valley and what they leave of you lazy, helpless fucking Shawnees can sit here and moan and wait for the Spanish to come back. You try explaining to those boys about how you're the only real human beings and they're just half-men and see how fucking far it gets you, hear?"

Shaking all over, tears cascading down over her wrinkled face, Squash Woman turned to Ilsa, saying plaintively, her voice cracking now and again, all her former arrogance flown away, "Please, Il-sa Bright-hair, make the silver hats help my people. And even if they will not, sunk deep into their evil spirits as they now are, you can use your own silver boat to help us, can't you?"

Ilsa looked at her coolly and said in frigid tones, "I could . . . but I won't, Squash Woman. Arsen is right in this. You have lied to us for long months, used us very selfishly. You and the other elders have hurt your own people by not urging them to garden and gather and hunt and preserve food for the winter. Such elders as you all have proved yourselves to be are in no way wise, rather are you all real, dangerous liabilities to your people and should not be allowed to longer hold power over them or ever again to gain power."

CHAPTER THE FOURTH

Two weeks after the Micco, Snake-burnt-at-both-ends, his council, and a few well-chosen elders from the Shawnee had taken over from Squash Woman and her coterie of nodding stooges, the aged ruler sent a runner for Arsen, of an early evening twilight.

After Arsen had taken as shallow a pull as he could, in courtesy, manage at the foul, ill-cured tobacco stuffed into the ceremonial pipe, then passed it on, trying very hard to not cough and thus possibly give insult, the Micco got down to business.

"Ar-sen-silver-hat, wide as my hunters range, numerous as are the set traps for smaller beasts, hard as do the fishers and the gatherers and the gardeners work, still is there not enough food in this camp every day and we must accept your bounty right often, a thing which pains my heart."

"Look, Micco," said Arsen, "it's not any longer like it was when that damned old con artist Squash Woman was running things, see. You guys don't ask for much—leastways, you haven't yet—and I'll do whatever I have to to help you make it, no sweat, don't you worry about that. You tell me what you need and when you need it and I'll bust my ass to see you have it, hear?"

"Yes, you are indeed a good man, Ar-sen-silver-hat," the Micco nodded, sagely. "But it is far better that the people do for themselves whenever they can, lest they become as one with the Guales, who would all starve without the steel-breasts.

"Ar-sen-silver-hat, you have silver eggs that can transport great bundles of long, very thick trees many miles and easily, or can bring in to the place you are building heaps of flat stones so heavy that a hundred strong braves all together could not raise one of those heaps even a hand-breadth from off the ground."

"Yes, Micco." Arsen nodded. "Those are called projectors."

"Hmm, a rare word," commented the Micco, then asked, "Then can these projectors also convey safely living men and dead beasts?"

"They can, Micco," replied Arsen. "I used one such to send the young warriors back down to your lands from here, in fact. Why do you ask this?"

"Ar-sen-silver-hat," was the Micco's answer, "Swift Otter, here, tells us that for long after his people crossed the mountains and left the sacred Land of the Guardian, Thunderbird, they yearly sent large, strong hunting parties into that land to camp in the unsacred mountains above it and descend into the sacred precincts to slay the beasts. They then bore the carcasses back up to their mountain camps to dry or smoke the meat and dress the skins or hides to provision the tribe during the winter months and the early spring, before most plants could be eaten.

"But in more recent generations, most of the Shawnee roamed too far from the mountains to make such hunts practical. And even more recently, they have been so shrunken and weakened by the steel-breast raiders and slavers that they would not have been able to send enough hunters to bear back sufficient food to make the whole, long process worth the effort.

"Now, however, we have more than a hundred and half a hundred warrior hunters, most of them with the fine, straight-throwing guns you so generously gave and the rest with the heavier ones taken from the steel-breasts either by us when we still lived in the south or by you when you fought the steel-breast slavers and drove them back down this river, so I would begin sending hunters into the sacred land, again."

"But, Micco," said Arsen, wonderingly, "I thought it was a sin to live in that land? That's what you and your shaman and Squash Woman all said."

Nodding again, The Micco said, "Yes, to *live* within the Land of the Thunderbird *is* forbidden, but the Guardian understands the needs of men, too. He knows that, like all the beasts, man must eat in order to continue living. All of the old tales tell us that although man is forbidden to live there, he is allowed to hunt the beasts there.

"Now, while those ancient Shawnees camped in the mountains above the sacred land and could only bring back the best parts of their kills, we are blessed by the Great Spirit with you and the other silver hats and your wonderful projectors. Our hunters can be sent there, by you—if you will?—and make their kills and then be sent back here with them, all in a day. This would provide all of us with meat, hides, sinew, horn, and many another thing we need now, will need for the coming winter and will need for the spring journey up to the long, narrow valley."

Arsen reflected that he could combine the projections of the hunting parties with his own trips to the granite quarry, and even had he not been quarrying there, almost anything was better than any further raids on that abattoir. The last time, he'd been seen and shot at by a guard, and only the protective field of the carrier had prevented his likely fatal perforation by one or more of the slugs from the big—either .44 or .45 caliber—revolver. And he had only one or two pieces of the gold which he had been leaving behind to cover the worths of things he took from his natal world left, anyway; so, many more trips and he'd have to be outright stealing stuff.

There was not as much game on the north side of the river, where the granite outcropped, as there was on the south, so Arsen put the first hunting party—forty-two Creek braves, nine Shawnees, Simon Delahaye, and Greg Sinclair—down about halfway between the ruins and the edge of the great plain whereon the bison and the horses always grazed. Greg, having been "educated" by the carriers he so often used for patrolling the river course and timbering occasionally, had the Class Seven projector and knew how to properly use it, so as kills were made, he would project them and a few of the hunters back to the village. Arsen, with the Class Five projector, would be sending back smaller heaps of stone than usual that day. They had suspended timbering operations for the length of the hunt.

Even with the metal wand that the carrier instructor had told Arsen how to fashion in the benighted lab of his father's business in his own world, even with the Class Five projector to lift and to stack the stones that the wand cut out and shaped and smoothed with only the twistings of his wrist and the pressings of his fingers, Arsen still got hot in the close, almost enclosed spot, the ancient quarry of those who had built the ruins south of the river, so he customarily worked with as little on above the waist as possible, preferring the occasional insect bite to the smothered feeling of wearing shirt, T-shirt, and pistol-belt. In all the time he had been working here, the largest beasts of any kind he had seen had been one or two nonpoisonous snakes, a large toad, and a few flashing streaks of lizards among the rock rubble, so he had come to feel that lugging along the pistol was probably stupid anyhow.

He had projected maybe a ton and a half of granite slabs by midafternoon and had just made a decision to call it quits after the stack on which he was working was projected off, for the blue sky had clouded over completely, the sun was no longer to be seen through them, and he was bedamned if he intended to work in the rain in a place where clear watermarks showed that it had held deep pools of water, in times past.

He was bending to slice off a knob of rock he had missed on a corner of the topmost stacked slab when he heard a faint noise that seemed to emanate from somewhere behind and above him and, at the same time, the stench registered in his nostrils. It was a terrible stench, reminding him of nothing so much as a jungle battlefield after the corpses had had two days of hot sun to rot them well.

Whirling about, he spied pure horror crouching on a ledge some five or so feet above him. Man-shaped in some ways, the thing was squatting on its heels, glaring down at Arsen with slitted eyes. Its arms were overlong and as hairy as all the rest of its thick, massive body, except for its face and slightly projecting, long-fanged muzzle. The creature's upper canine teeth were at least two inches in length, Arsen figured, and the thick arms and hunched shoulders onto which the big head seemed to fit without any neck denoted terrible strength.

Arsen eased down his wand to hang from the lanyard around his neck and slowly reached down to his right waist . . . only to remember that the pistol was still in its holster on the pistol belt in the open carrier. He thought the thought required to trigger the silver helmet to summon the carrier over to him, he thought it twice before he remembered with chagrin that the helmet, too, was reposing in the carrier along with his shirt, T-shirt, pistol belt, and all.

The stinking, hairy thing just hunkered there, staring slit-eyed at him, now and then gaping its mouth to show its full set of fearsome fangs and big teeth, all a sort of orangy-white and the longest ones sharply pointed—stabbing, tearing, predator fangs. Once it raised its muzzle skyward and uttered a long, loud cooing call.

Most of the thing's hair was a dark agouti color, but a crest of tall, stiff bristles ran from front to back on its scalp. With a shudder of real fear, Arsen remembered the story Squash Woman had told him and Ilsa. About the huge, hairy, maneating creatures that lived in caves and underground burrows in this land and hunted either at night or on dark overcast days (just like this one!) when there was no sunlight to hurt their dark-accustomed eyes. The old Shawnee woman had said that they were very difficult to kill, that they would leap over palisades at night, seize a human victim, and then leap back out again so quilled all over with arrows and darts that they looked much like man-shaped porcupines. It had been due to them and their ceaseless depredations that the Shawnee had left the Land of the Thunderbird, she had said.

"So, hell," he thought, trying to stop his teeth from chattering, "even if I can get back to the pistol, get it out, arm it and all, a .45 slug—shit, a whole fucking magazine full of the fuckers—may not be e-fucking-enough! If I live through this, I'll be fucked if I ever take that pistol off again, not over here in this damn place. And I'm going to take the carrier back to our old world, first fucking chance I get, and steal one of Uncle Boghos's fucking African elephant guns, too."

Moving ever . . . so . . . slowly, feeling his way among the rock rubble with his heels, Arsen backed up, keeping his gaze firmly locked on the hairy, crouching, salivating horror above him. Once he had covered a little distance, once he at least had put the shoulder-high stack of granite slabs between him and it, he felt just a little better. But then, seemingly without effort, the beast leaped atop the stack of granite.

A couple more slow, very careful steps, however, and Arsen felt the edge of the carrier bump against his rump. Still forcing himself to not make any sudden move, he felt behind him, searching either for the helmet which would allow him to trigger the carrier's protective shield, which would protect him too, this close to it, or his pistol. But all his frantic fingers could seem to locate was his shirts and the Class Five projector.

Fingering the device, he pondered, "I wonder if . . . ? Hell, it's at least a hundred men in and around that fort, armed with ever fucking thing from knives and hatchets to cannons and M60 machine guns, too. If they can't kill one these stinking fuckers, nothing can."

Once the pile of granite slabs and its anthropoid passenger was on the way to the other side of the mountains, Arsen quickly dressed, put on the helmet, lay down in the carrier, closed the lid, and set out for the other side of the river. But less than two hundred yards from the quarry, he spotted four more of the manlike things, running full-tilt over the weed-grown, rocky ground in the direction of the quarry, moving almost four-legged and quite fast. Circling the carrier back, he came in low, behind the maneaters, and, using one of the carrier's array of available armaments, exploded the big heads of all four. They were definitely not the kind of sidewalk superintendents he wanted overseeing his work over here.

He was fortunate enough to locate Greg and all the hunters not already projected back with kills standing in a defensive ring, all rifles pointed at a group of spotted lions who were stalking round and round, some seventy yards out from the men and the carcasses of a bison and two horses.

He landed near the bulk of dead bison and demanded, "Greg, why the fuck haven't you projected out of here, huh? At least project the fucking carcasses—that's what those toothy fuckers are really after."

"Oh, hell, no, Arsen," replied Greg enthusiastically. "Them's my bait, see. Without them, them lions would all probably just go away and I couldn't shoot one."

"Greg," said Arsen with obvious exasperation that he made no slightest effort to hide, "you out of your fucking what you call a mind, you know that? Greg, that fucking M14 is in no way a fucking big-game rifle, it wouldn't even stop one of the littler lions in Africa in our world, much less those spotted fuckers out there. They're eleven, twelve, thirteen feet long, Greg, and it's at least five of them. They'd take everything you bunch have got to shoot and still end up cleaning the fucking clocks of ever fucker too slow or dumb to run."

"Well, dammit, Arsen," Greg half-whined, "I want a good trophy to take back home to Fredericksburg with me when we fin'ly go back."

Arsen shook his head and said, "Not today, Greg, there's a fucking good reason, not today. Pick up the projector and beam you and Simon and ever other swinging dick back right now. I'll send the kills back with my Class Five. But wait a minute—go back loaded for bear. I had to send something big and very dangerous was on top of my last load of granite back to the fort with it."

Immediately the circle of braves, Greg, and Simon had winked out of sight, Arsen set the Class Five projector and sent the bison and one of the horses winking after them. He left the other horse for the felines. He had always had a fondness for cats of any kind, and, he figured, these had to eat, too.

Then he climbed back into the carrier and set out toward the southeast, at flank speed.

Arsen skimmed low over the last trees and angled the carrier down into the compound, headed for the stone crypt that he and Ilsa now called home. But a line of limping, bleeding, cursing men was waiting to enter the crypt, and when he had pushed past them, he found Ilsa, Greek John, and Rose Yacubian working in what looked like a front-line dressing station after an assault on the perimeter.

While John stitched up the scalp of a Creek Arsen recognized as one of Soaring Eagle's original group of braves, Ilsa was giving an injection to another Creek brave with a compound fracture of a lower arm, while Rose worked with forceps, small surgical knife, and steady, if bloody, hands to remove innumerable splinters and bits of pine bark from the legs and buttocks of Haigh Panoshian, who was turning the air around them midnight-blue with a torrent of curses, obscenities, blasphemies, and depthless crudities, all interspersed with yelps and yips and other indications of pain.

Ilsa was first to notice him. "Arsen, goddam, I'm glad you're back. I'm going to need your help to properly set and splint this poor bastard's arm, so go over there and wash up and find a pair of sterile gloves."

"What the hell happened?" he demanded, thinking that he just might know, anyway, "Did the Spanish attack or what, honey?"

Easing the already-groggy brave down onto a spread tarp, she shook her tousled blond head and said, "As best I can gather from the garbled bits and pieces I've heard, a hairy ape about the size of a gorilla suddenly showed up among the piles of stone and timber down below the fort. Nobody seems to really know exactly what happened, then or for the next few minutes, but I'd feel safe to say that all hell broke loose. I heard it from in here, and there must've been a hundred or more gunshots, then two or three cannon shots, all the Indians in the fort were shrieking out warcries, Al and Mike and Haigh were screaming unprintable things, then things just suddenly got almost quiet and they started bringing these hurt and wounded men in. Fortunately, John got back just in time from his patrol downriver; Rose and I couldn't have handled it alone, no way in hell."

"Well, shit, honey," yelped Arsen, "how about Rose's overeducated fucker of a husband? Where was he? I thought pathologists were kind of like doctors, too."

A smile flitted briefly across her sweaty, tired-looking face. "I think you're going to like this, my love. The most eminent Dr. Yacubian was in the fort, up in the walls, when this ape started after Haighie, who was down below trimming timbers with a wand to shape them for palisade stakes. It was him shooting at the animal with a pistol that alerted everybody else, they say.

"Mike shot it in the back with a flintlock, and when it didn't even slow down that he could see, he stripped the hide cover off a swivel gun and aimed it and started flicking his bic over the touchhole to fire it. Then the good doctor comes running up yelling at him to not fire a cannon at it because it will damage the body of the specimen too much. He grabbed Mike's arm just as the lighter flared and that big swivel fired, so the ball missed the ape and plowed into a pile of pine logs instead. The good news was that the splinters pretty well peppered the ape, but the bad news was that they got Haighie, too, mostly in his butt and legs.

"Mike was so mad that he picked up a spade, turned around, and bashed Bedros flat in the face with the back of it."

Predictably, Arsen grinned broadly. "He kill the fucker . . . I hope?"

She shook her head again, trying to brush back her hair with the back of one wrist. "No such luck, Arsen, Bedros was one of the first they lugged in here. He's certainly got a concussion, his nose is badly broken, both his eyes are going to be black, his lips are badly mashed and split, he may very well lose some front teeth, or so John says, and he bit his tongue so severely he's not going to be willing or even able to do much talking for some little time. John said the jaws weren't broken, but that the joints may have been jammed and damaged. Now, get washed—the brave is out cold."

Arsen chuckled evilly to himself as he prepared to assist his mate in her bloody chores.

Later the next day, he was able to get a little more complete story from Mike Sikeena, Al, Haigh, Swift Wolf, Running Otter, and the Micco.

"I don't know where the stinking fucker came from, Arsen," said Haigh, from where he lay belly-down on his air mattress. "I was at the biggest tree pile and I heard another load of rock come down and I figure that must of shook him out of wherever the hell he'd been hiding at. Anyhow, I smelled thishere godawful stink and I turned around and he was coming over a pile of slabs straight at me. I pulled out my Browning and jacked one up the fucking spout and just started shooting the fucker. Arsen, I shot high expert in the Corps, and at that range, a fucking boot couldn't of missed. I put thirteen fucking nine-millimeter slugs into that fucking monstrosity, I know good and well I did, and Mike swears he put a rifle ball in the thing's back, too, while I was still shooting him my own self, and didn't none of them put the fucker down. Then I dumped the empty magazine and tried to pull the spare out of the holster and I dropped the fucker between a couple logs, I could see it, so I bent over to pick it up and that was when the fucking ball out of that big old drake swivel hit the other log pile and it felt like two, three million fucking yellow jackets had zeroed in on my ass and legs. That stinking critter squalled like I never heard the like of and turned himself around and started for the hills. Before he got all the way turned around, though, I could see he had a great long old pine splinter stick out from his left eye. He must of figured I was the one hurt him so bad with them splinters is the only reason I can think of why he run from me, because I would of been dead meat for him, all he had to do was come and get me."

Mike said, "I turned around from bashing that peckerheaded motherfucker Bedros, and looked down to see that *djinn* or whatever it was coming right up the hill, looked like he was coming right at me, there on top of the wall, and at a damn good clip, too. Well, I pulled the wedge and the breech out the drake, but I couldn't see any more loads for the fucker, so I picked my rifle back up and started loading it just as fast as I could make my hands move.

"Right about that time, Swift Wolf and a whole bunch of braves come climbing up there. The ones that had brought rifles or pistols, they started shooting down at the goddam ape, but it didn't seem to stop him, though he did slow down some, like he might've all of a sudden decided maybe he wasn't going to be welcome up in the fort, maybe. I handed over my loaded rifle to one of them to prime it and shoot it at him and started in looking for more loads for the damn drake. When I still couldn't find any, I ran around to the corner, grabbed up the long sling-piece, and brought it over and had one the braves lift out the empty drake so's I could put the sling-piece in the drake's mounting hole.

"Some more braves had come up, along with the Micco, and all of them had at least one gun apiece, too. They all started shooting the big fucker, but he just kept coming, but real slow, making noises like you'd have to hear your own self to believe, Arsen—sort of like growling but too sort of like a man with a broke jaw trying to talk, too. It was then, just then, I got to thinking we might be up there pumping some kind of a wild man full of lead."

"No, not a man," said the Micco gravely. "I have heard tales of these things, they occur now and then, in the less-well-known swamps and mountains, they seem to especially frequent caves, sinkholes and such. They are beasts who, long, long ago, did aspire to be men, but the Great Spirit found them wanting and refused them, whereupon they did curse the Great Spirit. Spirit then did take away from them the power of true speech, make them more beastlike and less manlike, and scatter them widely, that they might serve as a lesson and warning to the true men of Spirit's awesome powers. They are said to swim well and swiftly. This one must have come down the river."

It was Arsen's perfect out. Did he want to take it? "No, Micco," he said, haltingly at first, "it didn't come downriver or upriver, either. I projected the damned thing over here from the Land of the Thunderbird . . . but please understand, all of you, especially you, Haighie, I had to do it." Then he told them of what had occurred that day in the granite quarry.

"So, you see," he ended, "it was mostly my own fucking fault that all this shitstorm came down. It was all just on account of I was too damn fucking lazy to keep my pistol belt on. But I'll make it all up to you guys.

"Look, Haighie, I'll project you back to a time before we ever went to play that gig up north, like I did Mikey Vranian. Then none of this shit will ever of happened to you and all you'll remember is you decided to not go up there and play with the band, that night. Okay? You ready to go? I'll go get the Class Seven and . . ."

"Hell no! I won't go!" shouted Haigh, trying to get his knees under him, while Al and Mike Sikeena did their best to keep him prone. "Look, Arsen, I *want* to stay here, with you and the rest."

"Haigh," said Arsen, "neither Rose nor Ilsa is sure they got all those splinters out of you and they've got no way to tell if they did. What the fuck it is is wooden shrapnel, Haigh. Not even thinking about infection, pieces of that wood could work around in your legs and do things I don't even want to think about—damage nerves or rupture arteries and shit like that. And, goddam you, if you die, I'll never be able to look Aunt Marya and Uncle Boghos in the face again. So I think you ought to let me project you back. In fact, I think I ought to send you all back. This place can be fucking goddam dangerous, and I got no right to ask any of you to stay here with me anymore. I'm doing what I feel like *I* gotta do, but I can't ask or expect you guys to get hurt or maybe die for me, here. I've been wrong to keep you all as long as I have. I'm sorry."

"Well, I be fucked if I mean to go back," remarked Greg Sinclair, who had come in when he heard Haigh's shout. "Man, thishere's the mostest fun I've had since I was in the Corps, I tell you. Where the hell else could I go out with a bunch of real Indians and shoot real buffaloes and deer and elks and horses and even get a chance at cats so big they'd make Clyde Beatty shit his drawers? Oh, no, Arsen, I ain't going back neither, not yet, for a while, anyway."

"Good God, man," Arsen burst out, "you have or had a business, a wife, a house. Don't you worry about what happened or is happening to them?"

Greg frowned and asked, "Arsen, did you see that moving picture *Zorba the Greek*?" At Arsen's nod, he went on, "Well, you recall of how Anthony Quinn said something about having a wife and a house and a farm and kids and called it the full catastrophe? Yeah, well, that fucker was fucking right, too, man, fucking-A right."

"Yeah, I have a fucking business, all right, and that fucking meant I had to work my ass off twenty-five hours a fucking day just to pay the fucking salaries and taxes and bills and all, too. I couldn't never do any the fun things I wanted to do—except just to play with the band, ever now and then—'cause it takes money to scuba-dive and sky-dive and hunt big game and race stock cars and all, and my fucking wife nagged me into putting every damn cent of profit I ever made back into the fucking business, and where she eased up, my fucking accountants would bear back down on me even harder. And I was getting a fucking potbelly and watching my muscles I didn't hardly ever use no more turn to flab, with my fucking wife all the time nagging me about smoking and drinking beer and eating meat. Man, I could just fucking feel myself becoming a old man, watching grey hairs pop up on my head and my chest and even my fucking crotch hairs, too, and wondering if I could cut the mustard any more because I lotsa times had trouble getting my wang up and keeping it up long enough to toss a fucking boff with my wife, her all skin and bones and a mouth on her that never let up even when I was shagging her.

"But, man, Arsen, I'm free here, really fucking free, goddammit! No, I can't do scuba diving, here, but I can swim and fish any damn time I feel like it, and I can't sky-dive, but the carriers are a hell of a lot more fun than chutes, I tell you, and more fun than driving stock cars, too. And the hunting, hell, man, even the rich swells at home couldn't never ever do this kind of hunting, and I can do it damn near ever day, too.

"Arsen, I feel really like I'm alive, here. I got me a good, sweet woman that knows how to make a man feel like a man and flat enjoys doing it, too. She ain't nagged me about nothing yet, and she can work as hard as I do when it comes time to work. She cooks good and she likes to eat meat and drink beer, sometimes, and she ain't all the time gabbing about how to get skinnier than skinny.

"So, Arsen, buddy, when you go to making up a list of folks you mean to send back to our old world, you better put me at the bottom of the fucking list. I'm plumb happy here, man. You can take our old world and shove it—I don't never want no more parts of it."

Arsen looked as stunned as he felt. "How about you, Al? You want me to project you back?"

"Well . . ." said Al, hesitantly, "well, maybe sometime, someday, Arsen, but not now. I like it here, too, like Greg in some ways, you know. I feel really kind of like free, you know. Everything just kind of like, you know, agrees with me here. I'm in a whole lot better shape than I've been in a long time, too. I don't know quite how to fucking explain it. You know I thought when we first were slapped down there in England, I'd probably freak out if I couldn't find me a way to make a connection, you know, and turn on to some good grass or some hash. But, hell, man, I don't miss that shit at all, here. I can crawl out of my wigwam in the morning and stand up straight and breathe the cool air and look up at the trees and the fucking blue sky and, like, man, I'm higher than Acapulco Gold or Maui Wowie ever put any fucker. I've got good buddies, a good woman, good chow and plenty of it, a beer or two now and then, no worries about school or anything. No, Arsen, I think I'll ship over, pull another hitch, here in the closest thing to heaven any of us will probably ever fucking see."

"You want to send somebody back so bad, Arsen," suggested Mike, "why the hell don't you send that fucking Bedros back, huh? He's about as much good as tits on a boar hog, most the time, and after the way I clobbered him yesterday, I don't think he's gonna be any good at all to any fucking body for a while to come. Fucker try fucking with me again, I'll fucking kill the cocksucker the next round!"

"No you won't," said Arsen, firmly. "You won't kill him or even hurt him this seriously again, for the same reason I haven't sent him back before this. Scab-sucking prick that he is, Rose still loves him and wants to be near him, and we all love Rose, so that's that. Right?"

He grimaced and added, "But I just may have to send him back if he doesn't wake up soon, just like I may have to send Haigh back, like it or not, if he shows signs of trouble inside his legs. I promised Ilsa and Rose that already."

"How 'bout Rose, then, Arsen?" demanded Haigh. "She'll be alone here without him then too."

"No she won't," replied Arsen. "She doesn't know it yet, but if Bedros goes back, then so does Rose. Too bad—we'll miss her."

Then suddenly, Arsen remembered something of vital importance. "Greg, Mike, did one of you do a carrier patrol today?"

"Shit, no," said Greg. "Today's Ilsa's turn and she gets real mad if somebody else goes in place of her, you know that, Arsen."

"Aw, hell, just forget it, man," said Mike, shrugging. "One fucking day ain't gonna matter. All we ever see is water and trees and animals and all, anyway."

"Greg, Ilsa is zonked out in the crypt—she and John and Rose and I worked our twats off most of the night on the wounded and the hurt. You fuckers must've spent half the powder that was fired, yesterday, potshotting at each other."

"It did get kind of hairy inside the fort there, when that ape, with half his arm shot off by the ball from that sling-piece come right up the palisade and over it and then fell down off the wall walk into the fort and everybody started shooting at it surrounded by them sandstone walls and all. But it never did get up again after it landed at the bottom of the wall. Hell, I don't know how it kept going long as it did with all the lead's been dug out of it," said Mike, adding, "Look, if you want me to take a sweep down the river, I will. Laying down in the carriers sure ain't no kinda work, Arsen."

"No, not just you, Mike, we'll both go. Come on."

Arsen led the way out of the wigwam to the row of three carriers bobbing a few inches above the ground. "I've got bad fucking vibes. I want to see for myself what's causing them."

CHAPTER THE FIFTH

Don Felipe al-Asraf de Guego had, from the very onset, realized fully and deeply appreciated the signal honor conveyed upon him by the exalted Captain Don Guillermo ibn Mahmood de Vargas y Sanchez del Río and had striven to conduct himself in accordance with the rare opportunity to garner glory.

In his airy office within the powerful fort at the port-town of Boca Osa, situated at the mouth of the Río Oso, the commander of both fort and civil populace had waved the young knight to a seat on an arm-stool, had smiled at him warmly while an Indian slave served them both cups of rich, sweet, unwatered wine of Málaga in which one could easily savor the climate of that far-off warm and sunny Moorish city, set the mood of comradely informality through the expedient of telling a humorous and bawdy tale of the unexpected relations of a peasant's daughter and a traveling muleteer, then finally got down to business.

"Young sir, you know of course that opportunity for advancements of all sorts virtually abound like unto weeds in this new-style Spain. If you want proof, just look no farther than me or Don Abdullah; believe me, both of us recall well exactly how it feels to arrive upon the quay in Habana with a famous patronymic, a decent sword, personal honor, ambition, and damned little else save, perhaps, a letter of introduction to some midlevel official, for he and I both came west across the Ocean Sea in just such fashion, knowing that we would sink or swim, live or die, prosper or starve by dint of only our wits, our strong swordarms, and the Will of God.

"We two both came ashore at Habana within the very same week, my boy. Did you know that? Yes, Don Abdullah and I, although we had never met back in Spain, departed the very same port on the very same day, but aboard different ships. Blind Fate threw us two together there, blind Fate and the fact that we both bore letters addressed to the same man, a Monsignor Hassan de Sidi al-Frangi—a most wise, rightly esteemed, and holy man, he was, God rest his soul; he died years ago of the summer fever."

Following the lead of his superior, Don Felipe reverently signed himself, but kept his silence.

Captain Don Guillermo sipped at his wine and went on. "Monsignor Hassan it was who found us cheap but acceptable lodgments, sent us to meet the proper people, saw that we each were provided with one squire of creole antecedents but good breeding, had us to dine with him often and advised us sagaciously, especially with reference to the intricacies of this new world, new culture, and the values of its new social order, wherein our pure European and/or Ifriqan blood was worth far more to wealthy creoles here than ever they would have been in the old lands of the east.

"When he was sure of us both and another young man, one Lorenzo de Galdeza, certain that we all were God-fearing and pious, honorable, sober, not readily given to gambling or debauchery, seeking after glory for our names and gold and to help to convert the pagan to Christ, then he dropped a word to certain personages and we three were chosen to serve as ensigns with the force of Don Ricardo de las Murasverdes, who was just then preparing to lead his first attempt against the indio king of the Mexicos.

"It was during that costly, ill-fated, but glorious campaign that both Abdullah and I received the accolade and poor young Lorenzo fell, covered with glory, in battle. May the good God bless and keep for aye his gallant soul."

Again, Don Felipe aped his superior in signing himself, but still spoke no word, not having been yet bidden to so do.

Don Guillermo rang and waved the indio slave who silently padded in to refill the two cups from the ewer wrapped in wet cloths, waiting until the indio was gone before going on with his tale.

"Ah, we two were indeed glory-hungry, we two, brand-new-made *caballeros*, Don Abdullah and I, in those long-ago days, Don Felipe. Although the expedition had been as much a failure as had all those which had preceded it—and, alas, all those which have followed, over the courses of the years since—so very rich is that land that few of us came back completely empty-handed from it.

"As soon as we had paid a call upon the secretary of the council of the Indies and deposited the fifth of our wealth for the King, then visited Monsignor Hassan and given him a tenth of our own four-fifths that he might apply them to the Lord's work, we two outfitted ourselves as befitted our new ranks, hired on a brace of squires each—mine having died and Abdullah's having lost most of an arm—then began to search out new expeditions.

"It was one expedition or campaign after another, then, some lucrative, some not, but all valuable in terms of experience and reputation. We took part in the raid upon the Oyster Coast, fought the Portuguese, the French, the Irish, and once even the Norse, far to the north where white mountains of ice float upon the seas. We both took part in Don Ricardo de las Murasverdes's second expedition against the indios of Mexico, indeed, that unfortunate *caballero* died in my arms, his very lifeblood pumping out of his terrible deathwound onto my cuirass. Abdullah was wounded sorely while we and some few others fought to hold off the indios until the bulk of our force might be taken off by our ships.

"He still lay abed recovering of his wounds when I sailed off on the Rio Víboro Campaign to drive the accursed French back from the southern coast of the northern mainland—it was those swine, trespassing excommunicants, who built the older part of this very fort, you know, Don Felipe—and when I returned to Habana, he was already wed to the daughter of a well-heeled creole merchant. It was through him and his in-laws, in fact, that I acquired my own richly dowered wife.

"It was with the better part of that dowry that I organized and financed my own first expedition at Mexico. Rather than landing on the War Coast as had the most of the *caballeros*, I put my force ashore in the northeasternmost province and marched on south, at a general parallel to the coast, with my ships pacing me. God was most generous to me in those months, my boy, for the most of the forces of the armies of the indios was far to the northwest, locked in fierce battle with certain rebellious subjects and other indios who had invaded from the north, so with but trifling losses—and the most of them wrought by illness, accident, disease, and the like—I marched clear down to the old War Coast, looting with blessed success for all the way, living well off the country and attracting not a few indios as irregular troops before I met any sort of real, organized resistance.

"All whetted keen for action against the pagans, my force cut into the scratched-up force of the indios like thin wire through cheese, that day. For all that these were not in any way the best army of the indios of Mexico, still has it been recorded as a very notable victory and a partial revenge for the massive losses of poor Don Ricardo's last expedition there.

"Knowing our desires of old, the leaders of the defeated indios proffered me gold and other riches to board my ships and sail away, being aware that they could not raise enough force to again meet me in battle. Now I had sworn to the indios who had joined me that I would march on to conquer their Aztec overlords, did they aid me, but of course oaths sworn to pagans are never more than empty words to a good Christian, and so, rather than chance having to fling my remaining force against the main force of the indios who were even then hurrying down from the northwest, I accepted the metals and the pounds of jewels and enshipped for Habana.

"We sailed back in triumph, with gold, silver, gems, and slaves enough to give even the lowliest pikeman or seaman a fairish amount. My officers and I were feted by the governor-general himself, and His Excellency offered me a commission to raise a force and drive out the last French bastion in the southern coast, this one, here at the Boca Osa. Of course, I grieved much then that my old comrade Abdullah was not there to share with me in my glory and good fortune, but it then was believed that he had been lost at sea along with ship and ship's company while returning from a slaving venture financed by his father-in-law against the pagans of southwestern Ifriqah.

"Again, my boy, God favored me, for the accursed French had been decimated and seriously weakened by a pest of some sort and had had no time to bring in reinforcements ere I and my brave men were upon them with fire and sword and cannon. Since the town had surrendered before a single ball needed to be fired into it, I forbade an actual sack. The commandant of the fort, unable to offer any effective resistance, sent everyone out of the fort under flags of truce, then locked himself in the main magazine and discharged a pistol, one supposes, into an opened keg of gunpowder. That was why the new section of the fort had to be built ere we could occupy it.

"After seeing all of the French on their way back towards the north, I left a garrison in the wrecked fort, prized some twoscore indios for slaves, then sailed back south to Habana to render my report. You can imagine my great joy upon being greeted, shortly after first I set foot upon the quay, by my old friend Don Abdullah, looking a bit gaunt and bearing some interesting new scars, and with a most singular tale to spin."

As he lay in the brush under the trees, sweating, swatting desultorily at endless legions of insects and seeking to get some sleep on the soggy leafmold near to the riverside, Don Felipe could but think back to that day with his *comandante*—sipping cool, sweet wine in the breezy room wherein only a few stray flies and the occasional *cucaracha* were to be seen.

Recognizing his experience and basic intelligence, the conduct of the probing patrol had been left entirely at his discretion. He had recalled that he never had seen one of the silvery flying things in times of darkness, and so that had been when his boats had been upon the river. They had laid up throughout every day under trees and brush, preferably near to one of the countless little narrow false channels that lay here and there along both sides of the Río Oso.

At sunset each day, they would set out and row mightly against the strong current until false dawn or a bit after, then steer to a bank or into one of the inlets and draw the boats up onshore with much groaning, cursing, sweaty effort and aided by a set of hardwood rollers brought along for just that purpose. After hacking down enough fresh vegetation to completely cover the boats from a casual bird's-eye view, he and his party would all seek out a covert in which to lie and, hopefully, sleep during the entire length of the day, to repeat the backbreaking form of river travel throughout the night.

Don Felipe allowed fires only on the rare occasions when they found a cache of dry, seasoned wood that would emit no smoke, so the party had subsisted mostly on pickled pork, rock-hard sea-biscuit, smoked stockfish, strong cheese, and river water, eagerly pulling and avidly devouring wild onions and edible greens whenever they chanced upon them. A real treat, about which some of the oarsmen still reminisced, had been the finding of a large, prickly thicket of bushes covered in sweet berries, ambrosiacal to them all.

Most miserable of all had been the days of rain and drizzle, when they lay chilled and uncomfortable and mostly sleepless throughout all of the day, to arise stiff and aching from out their hiding-places, few of them not hacking, coughing, and spitting, to wash down a few forced mouthfuls of slimy cheese with swallows of gritty water, then set about the uncovering and launching of the boats so that they might begin another endless night of cruelly hard labor at the heavy oars.

Of an early morning, the island that had for so long

been base camp to the river slavers hove into view around a bend, and, following a brief reconnaissance that showed it to be completely untenanted, Don Felipe had seen the boats drawn up on the shelving beach. No need had there been to even attempt to hide them, not on a strand lined with similar boats that had been just left where they lay by those who had attacked and destroyed the base camp, months back.

An exploration of the battered, blackened fort in the pale light of dawn had revealed that, somehow, enough sound huts remained with whole or quickly repairable roofs to shelter the entire party for the day. One of these cabins had been Don Felipe's own, and, delving under a certain flattish rock sunk into the dirt floor, he was able to retrieve a deerskin pouch containing a scant handful of freshwater pearls, a very old silver coin punched with a hole and bearing on it the arms of France, plus two broken pieces of an Indian spearpoint knapped from a bright-red stone that he was sure was jasper.

Not all of the onetime garden of the base had been despoiled by animals, and the men were able therefore to gather enough squashes, tomatoes (some folk in Europe still averred that these so-called "love apples" were deadly-poisonous, but Don Felipe had eaten them and seen them eaten by hundreds of his own people and thousands of indios with no ill effects, so he could only assume that the Europeans' fear of both the *tomate* and the equally innocuous *patata* were but the ignorant terror of anything new and different), *pimientos*, and herbs. Using the plentiful charcoal to be found almost anywhere within the well-charred fort, and an earthenware pot gleaned from the tumbled and blackened ruins of the fort kitchen, a tasty stew of the pork, fish, and fresh vegetables was made up and all ate very well that day.

While he lay, almost asleep with his belly full of warm food, Don Felipe let his memory slide back to that day in the *commandante*'s office, hearing once more the strange adventures of Don Abdullah.

With a sailing master, good seamen, and a crew of veteran slavers, Don Abdullah had set sail from Habana aboard one of his creole father-in-law's ships in company with a sister ship commanded by his brother-in-law, Sancho Gomez—only one-quarter European and looking far more like an indio than any Spaniard or Moor. They had made directly for the mouth of the Río Kongo and up the miles-broad river some leagues to the sprawling earth-and-timber fortress which Sancho Gomez called El Castillo de los Tres Hombres—a slave-brokerage establishment some twenty years in place, founded, built, and run by two Arabian and one Ghanaian former mercenary officers. The three kept a large army of black pagans officered by Arabs, Christian blacks from farther north, some Egyptians, and a few Europeans—all of these last criminals of one foul sort or another, outlawed and under sentence of torture and death in their own lands, for only the most desperate of men would willingly continue to serve in such a debilitating and disease-ridden place in so deadly-dangerous a line of work for any length of time.

In company with Sancho, who had made several trips and had come to know these traders well, Abdullah called upon the partners in their fortress. As they two sauntered ahead of the laden seamen who bore along samples of the goods they had brought to trade for the black slaves, Abdullah noted to himself that never had he seen so many heavy guns mounted on a single fortification as studded the riverside wall of this one. Like some immense ship of the battle line, the wall of baked mud and massive timbers bore three "decks" of batteries, with the heaviest—full cannon and some demicannon—on the lowest level, some thirty feet above the moat level, demicannon and long culverins above that, short culverins, demiculverins, and some long sakers on the highest "deck." The tops of the walls were platforms for both long and short lighter pieces—sakers, minions, falcons, falconets, and even a few robinets—plus at least one swivel gun every ten running feet of walltop—patareros, portingal-bases, bases, drakes, port-pieces, stock-fowlers, sling-pieces, and murderers, as well as a few very-large-caliber calivers that had been swivel-mounted.

The corner-bastions and the half-bastions along the length of the walls were all defensive towers and so could be fought on even if the walltops fell to a foe or became untenable from bombardment or other causes. The entryway was S-shaped, with ironwood gates and portcullises at both ends, roofed over its entire length, with walls and ceiling pocked by murder-holes. Emerging from the dim entry tunnel into the bright glare of the central plaza was to note the gaping mouth of a gigantic old-fashioned bombard on a stationary mounting. Abdullah thought that the ancient thing looked quite of a size for a slender man to crawl into, and he repressed a shudder at thought of just how many hundreds of pounds of langrage with which the thing was surely loaded. From the same strongpoint, two other equally venerable bombards glowered at the landward entryway and a smaller sallyport-gate.

For all the European flavor of the defenses of the place, the architecture of the buildings inside the high walls was far more in keeping with the equatorial climate, having high, steeply pitched roofs of thick thatch, but with "walls" of split reeds interlaced with cords that they might be rolled up easily for ventilation or unrolled to keep out rain. The visitors climbed steps made of huge halved logs to a broad, wide verandah raised to the height of a man above the ground, then passed into the residence itself, by way of a broad corridor in which lounged some thirty or so blue-black, heavily armed soldiers—some dozing, some chatting, a knot of them squatting and taking turns throwing knucklebones, but paying little if any apparent attention to the white and red men passing through.

Sancho was greeted warmly by a tall, very fat purple-black man seated in barbaric splendor on a backed and armed bench of richly inlaid hardwoods, having whole elephant tusks for corner supports and sections of them for arms. The back and seat of the bench were covered in leopard and zebra skins, and a garish Turkish-weave carpet covered the dais and the two steps leading up to its apex.

The black man who sat on this throne shared it with a large demijohn, which he frequently lifted to take a long, gurgling nip, and Abdullah suspected that the contents of that container were the reason why the man was sweating profusely despite the efforts of a quartet of chubby brown striplings employing wide ostrich-plume fans to keep air moving about their master and his outré pets.

Fortunately, Sancho had described these pets in advance, so that Abdullah showed little surprise and did not flinch when the pair of Persian running-leopards sat up from their doglike sprawls at the black man's feet, yawned toothily, stared at the white men, then resumed their sprawls and somnolence. He repressed his shudder when the bright green "shoulder sash" abruptly slithered down off the corpulent man to coil on the other side of the wide seat from the straw-covered demijohn, obviously in obedience to some unheard, unseen order or signal.

Appraising the slave dealer, Abdullah estimated that he must weigh in excess of two and a half hundredweight, possibly as much as three, but he would have been willing to wager that thick, firm muscles underlay all that fat, for weaker men did not choose as personal weapon the Danish axe, which required great strength to properly use, and a specimen of that fearsome weapon was precisely what lay in a decorative rack, near to the black man's hand.

In addition to ritual cicatrices on cheeks and forehead, all of the man's skin that was visible showed a network of old scars, hallmark of the veteran warrior. Each of his thick fingers bore at least one ring—massy things of gold or silver and all set with brilliant stones—and among all of the finger-rings, arm-rings, ear- and nose-bobs, ankle-rings, and necklaces, a dozen or more of them, all heavy gold, Abdullah would not have been at all surprised had he been told that the array was worth the ransom of a *duque grande* or a *principe*.

The man's clothing was a rich mixture of both European and Ifriqan. He wore finely tooled and inlaid jackboots into the tops of which were tucked the legs of a pair of baggy pantaloon-trousers of loose-weave Egyptian cotton. The outsides of the boots also bore holsters for a matched pair of small Turkish wheellock pistols, while the inner sides sheathed four throwing-knives. A loose-fitting, half-sleeved shirt of some cloth that looked a little like linen lawn, dyed an orangy-brown and adorned with Ifriqan motifs, was secured at the bulging waist with a broad sash of a snow-white silk fringed with reddish gold. Thrust under the sash was a Yemeni *jhambiya*, its rhinoceros-horn hilt wound about with both silver and gold wire and its pommel capped with a big aquamarine in a gold setting.

Flanking the dais and ranked behind it were half a hundred more of well-armed blue-black soldiers like those lounging the length of the entryway. Over kilts and loose shirts, all wore knee-long mail hauberks, belted at the hips with thick leather bands sporting huge buckles of brass or polished steel from which depended a sword of some description—everything from native shortswords and brass-hilted boarding-cutlasses to European and Middle Eastern military brands—at least one each of dirk and dagger and one or more pistols, metal flasks of powder and *cour bouilli* boxes for lead balls and spanners. About a third of them held arquebuses or calivers; the remainder grasped the hafts of a miscellany of polearms. A few wore differing types of helmets to cover their shaven, oiled scalps, but most went bareheaded or wore a felt fez. Those two on either hand of and closest to the slave dealer leaned on the foot-long hilts of broad-bladed greatswords, four to four and a half feet of blade length.

The slave dealer's voice was a contrabasso growl, albeit a merry-sounding and eminently friendly growl. "Ah, Sancho Gomez, my lad, it is very good to see you again," he said in barely accented Spanish. "And how is your esteemed sire, Cristóbal?"

Sancho grinned. "Papa waxes fatter with the passing of every day, Captain Otei."

The slave dealer rumbled out a laugh that set most of his adipose body to jiggling. "Ah, yes, a man after my own heart, that is your sire, my lad. Conduct your life and affairs just as he has his and you'll wind up like him, rich as a pope." Pointing a thick thumb on which gleamed a broad band of chiseled gold set with opals, he asked, "And who did you bring to meet me, Sancho? He's no merchant, not him; I'd guess he's a veteran warrior. The way he moves makes me think of a master of the sword. Whose army did you steal him out of? Is he looking for employment, perchance?" The eagerness in the last question was ill concealed. "Poor ibn Azizi is dead of yaws since last you were here, and I am in sore need of a swordmaster, just now, as consequence. I can pay handsomely, you know that."

Sancho chuckled, "No, Captain, this is my new brother-in-law, Don Abdullah de Baza, a true *hidalgo*, from Spain."

Abdullah thought flittingly of rendering the former mercenary a military salute, but as he was not at all certain just what all of the arquebusiers and calivermen might do if he drew free his blade, he settled for making a leg, sweeping his hat-plume across the grass matting that covered the floor.

"An old-fashioned gentleman," growled Otei, "with the inborn courtesy of his breed, a precious breed that seems to grow rarer as years go by. You are more than welcome here, comrade. Your stay in my holdings will be more than merely pleasant, I will see to that."

Then, turning back to Sancho, he said, "I hope you brought some decent rum, Sancho. The Portuguese who were here last had only a despicable brandy that would make a Kalmyk puke—the foul stuff is fit for no better purpose than treating saddlesores, I trow! My watchdogs"—he waved back at the ranks of black soldiers—"seem to dearly love the stuff, but then they have some other odd tastes, too." He chuckled.

At a word from Sancho, two of the seamen rolled a fat keg up to the foot of the dais, expertly started the bung, inserted a spigot of carved wood and cork, then heaved the keg up on one end. Squatting beside it, Sancho himself filled his belt-cup and took a long draught of it before handing it to the slave dealer.

Captain Otei sniffed, smiled, sipped, then threw back his head and drained the cup. Throwing the pewter mug at one of the great swordsmen, he growled a few words in a slightly nasal tongue, and the man left his sword stuck into the floor and hurried to refill the cup for his captain.

Another few, somewhat louder, growled words saw servants hurry in with a pair of beautifully carven and inlaid chairs for Sancho and Abdullah, as many large, footed silver trays of Moorish designs filled with wide assortments of nuts, fruits, and stranger foodstuffs. Another servant presented each of them with a heavy, magnificent goblet of solid silver enclosing a golden bowl and rim. Three additional servants brought in a keg-holder, installed the broached rum keg in place, then filled the goblets and Otei's cup, which was once more empty.

"I like this cup, Sancho," said Otei, bouncing it on his broad pink palm. "I'll give you those two goblets for it, eh?" He rumbled a laugh like the roll of distant thunder. "The Dutchman for whom they were fashioned tried to cheat this flamboyant, ignorant old savage, so he no longer has any need for them; indeed, I'm having a drinking-bowl made of his thick skull, in the Tartar mode."

While Sancho cracked nuts, Otei asked Abdullah, "Where have you fought, sir knight?"

"A few little wars, short-term actions, mostly, while still I was in Spain deciding whether to follow my father into the priesthood or opt for some military career. Then, after arriving in Cuba, I went on an expedition against the indios of Mexico . . ."

Otei rumbled another laugh. "And it failed, of course. When are you Spaniards and Moors going to get it through your stubborn heads that the Aztec Empire is simply too tough a nut to crack? But, say on, sir knight."

Abdullah did, feeling more and more relaxed as he conversed with the knowledgeable and most amiable retired condottiere. Following the suggestions of his host, he tried several of the unfamiliar delicacies heaped in profusion on the silver trays and found that he savored most of them.

At length, Otei asked, "Well, from your experiece, Don Abdullah, what do you think of my outer works here, those of them as you've had an opportunity to see so far, that is?"

Abdullah frowned and shook his head. "All that I can say, Captain Otei, is that I pray the Christ that no one ever orders me to lead an attack against your walls. Your riverside wall alone has four or five times the firepower of any *castillo* this side of Spain; not even the great *castillo* that guards the harbor of Habana boasts so many full cannon, demicannon, and tercero-cannon, I think. Pray tell, how did you manage to acquire so many this far from any cannon foundry, Captain?"

Otei smiled. "Curiosity—I like that in an officer, sir knight, it denotes an open mind; it is the ignorant and hidebound men who are not curious and accepting of new things, new weapons, new strategies and tactics. But such curiosity among most Europeans, especially among their nobility and gentles, is rare, alas; had I been gifted with more such as you amongst my commanders, I had still been far to the north of this barbaric place, leading my fine old condotta in the service of emperors and popes, kings and caliphs, princes and grand dukes and bishops and beys, living the hard and often penurious life of the professional soldier, not rolling here in wealth and luxury and growing fat.

"But, about my cannon, yes. I brought many of them, all of the older pieces, from Ghana, when first I and my original six partners sailed down here to go into this so very lucrative business, twenty-odd years ago. As for the rest, well, in the early years here, I let it become known in the trade that I would give good value from out my stock-on-hand for perfect, well-found guns of larger bores, iron balls, granite or basalt balls, cases of grape, swivel guns, and suchlike. It worked well, as you can easily see, and even now I can still be persuaded to take good guns, gunpowder of all grades, cast or wrought shot, small arms, bullet molds, bar lead, and similar military hardware in exchange for slaves, even small sailing-ships, if they be sound and of relatively shallow draught, and I never seem to have enough sound longboats and whaleboats on which swivels can be safely mounted and, in necessity, fired. The recoil of a swivel of any size and power is like to spring the bow or stern of the native river craft, and no man—black or brown or white—wants to find himself swimming in a river full of crocodiles, you know."

Sancho, having eaten all of the nuts he could find, asked, "How many slaves have you got in the pens, Captain? Of what tribes?"

The fat man frowned and sighed. "Not a one, right now, Sancho. But if you'll anchor, bring your crews ashore so that you all may enjoy my hospitality, and have patience, there will be more soon. A great war took place in the highlands in the interior south of here, and one of my partners, Haroun al-Ain, is even as we speak on his way back here with a huge coffle of captives bought from the victors in that war.

"Also, my other partner, Ahmed al-Gahzahr ibn Zoultahn, went off on a little razzia of his own, some weeks back, up in the north, and these two absences are why there are so few troops hereabouts just now. Not that you or your men will be in any danger, for I still have enough men on hand to fight the fortress, should that become necessary. If you wish, you may stay aboard your ships out there in the river, but you'll be less comfortable there."

When, on their way back to the boats in which they had come ashore, Abdullah mentioned that he intended to take advantage of the slave dealer's generous offer, rather than remain on the cramped ship, Sancho shook his head and said, "Brother-in-law, you do what you wish, but I mean to stay aboard, cramped or not, for a coffin is even more cramped, I'm told. On board a ship, you can up anchor and let the current carry you back to the sea, even if there happens to be no wind for your sails. Nor do I intend to off-load one more stick of goods until I see a profusion of brown, two-legged cattle in Michael Otei's pens, with some hundreds more soldiers to guard them and the fortress. Do not be led astray by all you've seen and heard today, Abdullah—this is not in the least a healthful place in which to dawdle. What do you think happened to all six of Otei's original partners? Not a one of them died peacefully in bed. I'll tell you, come back aboard my ship with me for a little while, and I'll fill you in on what your father-in-law and certain others have told me, from time to time; then, if you still have the guts to want to take up Otei's offer . . . well, you'll be far braver a man than am I."

They waited, swinging at anchor for three weeks, sweltering in the sun by day, drenched and shivering in the nightly downpours, but preferring that discomfort to the stifling hell that lay in the enclosed places of the ships. Their few ameliorating comforts were a plentitude of fresh foods and cool spring water. The seamen and sea-soldiers were allowed to take turns going ashore in lots of a dozen or so at any one time while Abdullah and Sancho dined each day with Captain Michael Otei in his palace.

Finally, Sancho had himself rowed over to Abdullah's vessel and, when they were in a place apart, said,

"Look, Abdullah, there are good times to make the crossing back to Cuba and there are ill. We came over here, to Ifriqah, near to the tag end of the good, to start, and do we delay for much longer, we'll be into the season of storms . . . and, my friend, you can't know the true taste of terror till you've been in the middle of the Ocean Sea in the howling midst of a full living, raging gale. I think we must up anchor on the morrow and beat out to sea."

Abdullah frowned. "You heard the Captain, Sancho—the parties could arrive tomorrow, either or both of them."

"Yes, and they could never come back, too, Abdullah. Even as we speak here, those Arabs and their soldiers could be bubbling in stewpots somewhere in the interior as did not a few of their predecessors. Otei knows that too, you know. Why do you think he is become so jumpy and irritable, of late, eh?

"No, we up anchor tomorrow, Abdullah. There is another dealer with whom we've done business and been dealt with honestly. He's up north, a factor of the King of Bornu. Since we have to head north anyway, we might as well stop off there and see what he has on hand. Call your sailing-master over and I'll give him his course. You should learn navigation, too, as I did. One can never tell when it might be the difference between living and dying, you know."

CHAPTER THE SIXTH

They were four days out when the storm struck, almost without warning. By the time the terrifying episode had ended, the mizzen was gone and the foremast sprung, three seamen, two sea-soldiers, and both the sailing-master and the quartermaster were gone, swept away at one time or another. Worse, the *Rosalita* was nowhere to be seen on any quarter. They were wallowing, near unsailable in the midst of a pitiless salt sea with no single man capable of plotting a course, fixing a position, or navigating.

Abdullah decided that the first order of business must be to see to the balking of the numerous small but persistent leaks below the waterline, then to pump out the water collected in the bilge. These things done, he summoned the sailors and soldiers and addressed them from the quarterdeck.

"I know no navigation. Does any of you? Very well, then, we all must make the best of a bad situation. Ifriqah lies somewhere to the east, possibly not very far, for we were only about a day's good sailing off the coast when that damned storm struck us. Therefore, we will rig some sort of sails and proceed eastwards until we sight that coast, then we will sail on northwards, keeping it always in our sight, even if that means halting with sea-anchors rigged by nights. Eventually, we must find ourselves in this Bight of Benin, then we must seek the mouth of that big river flowing from the north. Even if we do not find another Spanish ship, still we have a plethora of trade goods, so we should be able to raise enough to pay the hire of a foreign navigator. I can just now think of nothing else to do. May God bless and keep us from harm."

They had sailed slowly, very slowly indeed, for another two days when one of the seamen placed himself before Abdullah, tugged at his forelock, and stood in silence until given leave to speak.

"My lord? If my lord will look over the side here, he will note the color of the water. This unworthy one dipped up a bucket of it and it is near to being fresh."

Tired and very worried, Abdullah snapped, "So, what of it, man?"

"My lord, offense is not intended, but . . . but, my lord, the water would not be brownish and near fresh were we not far off from the mouth of a river, a big river, and it please my lord."

Mounting the keen-sighted seaman on the bowsprit and ordering the steersman to take his direction from him only, Abdullah saw that the battered ship was kept in the most off-colored water, and, hours later, he saw the coast—a dim, hazy, dark line on the eastern horizon.

At a little past midday, a headland came into view . . . a familiar headland. They were back at the mouth of the Río Kongo!

Captain Otei could not have been more sympathetic or attempted to be more helpful, remarking over and over how much safer and more predictable was a landbound life, even that of a professional warrior, than one spent mostly aboard a frail craft always at the mercy of the fearsome vagaries of the cruel sea.

He suggested that the ship, still badly and inexplicably leaking, be run close inshore, so that should it go to the bottom, it do so in relatively shallow water wherein the work involved in raising it and effecting possible repairs would be the easier accomplished. He lent numbers of men and lighters to offload the cargo and the carriage-guns, along with all else of real weight, to help keep the storm-damaged vessel at least partially afloat.

The *barcagalán* and the *carpintero* reported to Abdullah with the bad, the very bad news. "My lord, a fully equipped shipyard could of a possibility repair this ship, make her once more seaworthy, but we cannot. She is old, this *Aña Gomez*, and has been in almost daily use for most of her fifty-odd years. Certain weaknesses and soft spots in her hull planking were ordered to be ignored when last she was careened, the *Señores* Gomez wanting yet another profitable voyage out of her before they would pay the costs of her proper overhauling."

"Is it so, then, *hombres*?" said Don Abdullah. If and when he ever did get back to Habana, there would be very strong words if not more in reference to his dear father-in-law's putting him in command of a less than fully sound ship for what was at best a long and dangerous expedition at sea. "She cannot be repaired here, then, you say?"

The *carpintero* shook his greying head. "No, my lord, no use in even trying. There be a crack in the keel that I can put all my hand into, and the wood inside it is not splintery but feels like a hard sponge. Moreover, at least three ribs are sprung from the keel in that vicinity. Masts and yards and sheathing, even, I can fashion from seasoned timber and replace, but, my lord, keels and ribs are the province of a true shipwright and his workmen, not a mere ship's carpenter."

Dispiritedly, Don Abdullah plodded back to the fortress to dine, as usual, with Captain Otei, only to find the bridge over the moat fully raised and secured. There was not a man in sight on the walls, and only his repeated shouting at last brought one of the white officers, who recognized him and ordered the bridge lowered. But no sooner was Abdullah across than he heard it being winched back up, heard the crash of the portcullis behind him, and saw black soldiers drop from someplace in the entry walls to close and bar the massive gates, then trot ahead of him to open those at the other end of the entry.

In the large central plaza of the fortress, turmoil reigned. A large party of black soldiers under command of a near-white had drawn the loads of the three huge bombards in battery in the center of the plaza and were engaged in recharging them with fresh powder. He recalled now, though it had not really registered at the time, having heard the unmistakable sounds coming through the walls of the entry passage of heavy guns being moved about on their trucks and carriages on the various levels of the front wall batteries, which had most likely been where everyone had been while he had been shouting for admittance to the fortress.

Outside the workshop of the Egyptian *Cirujano* and his apprentices, a heap of still-bleeding black bodies was already aswarm with flies and other insects, which prey had attracted several of the small, jewel-bright, insectivorous lizards and at least one big brown toad. A line of other blank-faced, wounded black soldiers waited patiently along the side of the building for their turns under the gore-clotted knives of the alcoholic surgeon, ignoring the terrible shrieks and screams coming out of the place. Abdullah just ignored them too; he had heard the like from battlefield surgeries in other lands and other places, and they all were the same, when surgeons were rushed and overworked and the laudanum was running low. As he passed on toward the sprawling palace, a slender man with a Semitic hook of a nose—Abdullah could not discern the tone of his skin, because of all the blood, both old and new; he looked as if he had been plunged full-length into a lake of the stuff—stepped to a window and heaved the shattered remnants of an arm, sawn off above the elbow, at the pile of fly-food. A white shard of ulna pierced the brown toad through and pinned him screaming to the blood-soaked ground.

All over the verandah and the full length of the corridor, the black soldiers were squatting or sitting on the floor, loading breech-cups for swivel guns and horn or wooden load-tubes for calivers and arquebuses, cleaning weapons, reaming touchholes, and checking the actions of wheellocks.

Captain Otei looked worried and, moreover, was cold sober. "Don Abdullah," he said without preamble, "you must have your ship drawn out into deeper water and anchored at least halfway to the other side of the river. Don't bother with trying to reload your cargo and your guns and shot—I'll buy the lot, though I don't really know just what I'll do with those old, rusty, short culverins from your main battery, I'd be afraid to fire one of them fully charged, so aged are they, but I'll send out men to drag them inside, anyway."

Don Abdullah shook his head sadly. "Captain, alas, the ship cannot be repaired. If it is warped out into the main channel, it will surely sink, blocking that channel. I have come to ask employment and maintenance for me and my men until another Spanish ship comes and we can work our passages back home."

Otei frowned. "Of course, you don't understand the gravity of the situation here, today, sir knight. Haroun al-Ain and what is left of his force—more than a full third of our garrison left here with him—having had to fight and lose a battle, lost all of the slaves they had bought and then conducted a fighting withdrawal back to the river and their boats. Seven out of every ten of his original force was killed or wounded, and, worse, we can be almost certain that those larcenous, murderous swine will be on their way down here to try to take the fortress or at least force us to buy them off, as a similar big tribe did seven years ago. And we may have to do just so if Ahmed al-Gahzahr and his third of the garrison do not soon return. What little time we do have will be allowed us because this particular tribe are not boat-oriented people. They mostly don't swim and so they fear the river and will, therefore, be coming down here by land, which will take them somewhat longer. And that is also why you would be utterly safe from them anchored out in the river."

He sighed once more. "But if affairs with the ship are as bleak as you say . . . well, all right, strip the ship of anything and everything that might be of use and when your crew is done with her, I'll send out men to take her apart. All of your crew are familiar with guns? Of course they are. You have how many left?"

"Thirty-seven seamen and twelve sea-soldiers, Captain," replied Abdullah.

Otei nodded. "All right, sir knight, there're the cores of five gun crews. The men will receive all necessaries plus one-quarter onza in gold per month, sergeants or their equivalents will earn one-half onza, and you, their captain, will be paid five onzas. Agreed?"

Abdullah was staggered. "Captain . . . it is too much! And I am not even overfamiliar with the arts of the cannoneer."

Otei smiled wanly. "Pah, you don't know the full worth of an experienced European officer, much less a knighted one, here on this coast. And forget about cannons, man, I want you to take over the command of a company of my Bornu calivermen. They're good troops, from a warrior race, trained from birth—like you—in the arts of the soldier and disciplined; I commanded a company of men just like them for years in Europe and other places, and some of my men were, indeed, the sires of some of these. I think you'll get along well with them—you're the kind of a man that they will automatically respect."

The *Aña Gomez* was reduced to only the skeleton of a ship, lying bleaching in the tropical sun, a perch for birds and a sunning-rest for turtles, by the time that scouts brought back word that the huge aggregation of natives of the interior were within a day's march of the fortress, their journey having consumed better than three weeks.

Looking at the files of spearmen debouching from the forest edge two hundred yards distant through the brass long-glass from off the ship, Abdullah quickly noted that they were obviously not the same race as most of those in the fortress, being dark brown rather than truly black, not so tall on the average, and with thicker bodies, limbs, and facial features. A few had firearms—calivers, arquebuses, and long dags—but most carried three spears—a long, broad-bladed one and two much shorter ones with smaller heads—a warclub or axe of some kind, and a large shield almost as tall as they were. A few wore steel helmets and ill-fitting bits of armor, but most were nearly mother-naked.

They were none of them anything approaching well

armed, not by European standards; even the indios that Abdullah had faced in the Mexico campaigns had been better armed, far better protected in their bodies, and with at least a bare semblance of discipline in their movements. These, on the other hand, looked like just a large, ill-formed, leaderless mob. But Abdullah could also see just why Otei feared the savages: there looked to be thousands of them!

One of the Captain's bodyguards came up at a dead run and bade Don Abdullah attend at once upon his master at the rear gate. When Abdullah arrived he found Otei wearing an oversized mail hauberk and a visored, dog-faced bascinet, edged with gold leaf, a heraldic crest of silver and gold centered on its brow and a wealth of brightly dyed plumes socketed atop its crown.

One of the bodyguards handed a similar helmet and a padded mail coif to Abdullah, and Otei said, "Put it on, sir knight, you're going to accompany me to a brief meeting with whatever unhung thief is just now paramount chief of these grunting brown bush-pigs.

"Here, help yourself, the more garish you look, the better; it impresses these childish barbarians, always. Why do you think I go as I do?" He held out an opened casket jammed with chains and rings, necklaces and bracelets of gold and of silver, some set with gems. "I mean to tell him that you're my new partner, and you have to look the part, you see. Make sure your pistols are loaded and primed and spanned tight—no one can ever be exactly certain just how these parleys will end up, not when dealing with such volatile, demon-ridden pagans as these. The only thing you can put stacks of golden onzas on is that they're all treacherous as snakes, so keep your eyes peeled out there, sir knight."

Just before they entered the exit passage, Otei and

Abdullah were joined by two other officers, an Egyptian hight Ali al-Baz and another Ghanaian, Patricius Olahda, each of them almost as weighed down with barbaric jewelry as Otei and Abdullah, though much of theirs was of silver, rather than gold.

As they walked out from the dim tunnel into the glare of the sun, Otei spoke rapidly to Abdullah. "No need for you to say a word—you don't know the language, anyway. Patricius does, though. Listen for his whisper—he'll be close behind you translating the bestial grunts of that swine's droppings. See that one there who's crammed his misshaped body into a hauberk? He'll be the boar in charge, I can tell from the devices on his shield. I don't like the shape of this affair already. They are fielding no more than the agreed-upon four—that's not like them, and it means that they have something up their nonexistent sleeves."

When they halted, facing two of the four brown-skinned men, Abdullah stood perfectly still, his right hand hanging by his side and his left resting on the pommel of his sword, facing straight ahead but using his wandering eyes to take in the paramount chief, with whom Otei was conversing.

From just behind him, the younger Ghanaian spoke in a hushed whisper. "That animal on two legs is called Ngona. He asked who you were and the Captain said that you were a great warrior from Spain and one of his new partners. The gracious gentleman said that you should have stayed in your own country then, because he had kept the last man of Spain they had captured alive and in agony for four days before he finally died and they ate him, and he remarked that your liver would probably be no less tasty after you have been properly tenderized with torture."

The brown man in the too-tight hauberk said something, Otei said something, then the brown man said something else and grinned widely, showing teeth that had been filed to sharp points.

The whisper said, "He asked where was the Arab called the Butcher, and the Captain said that he was abed of a fever. Then the pig said that he is very familiar with that kind of fever, that one brought about by a spear in the back."

There was a few minutes more of "conversation," Otei conducting his end of it all with a cool hauteur, while the brown man, his face running with sweat in the unaccustomed and weighty confines of the hauberk, began to shout, gesticulate, and finally alternately shake his seven-foot spear and pound its butt on the ground, white patches of froth gathering at the corners of his unbelievably thick lips.

Finally, two of the other brown men took the chief by his arms and turned him about, and then all began to walk back toward the dense line of brown spearmen who, Abdullah noted with a bit of alarm, had slowly shuffled forward until they had halved the distance at which they had been standing at the start of the conference. Whirling about and setting a stiff pace in the direction of the fortress, Abdullah spoke swiftly in Arabic, a language that he knew all three of them understood. "Immediately that son of a sow is back to his littermates, they are going to attack, on all three sides and in full force. That's what has happened before when they moved up that way during a parley, and they're too dumb to realize I would remember something like that.

"We won't have time to reach the gate, I don't think, before the guns are going to have to fire for full effectiveness. So when I give the signal, all of you drop flat and stay that way until all of the big guns have fired and drawn inside for swabbing and reloading. Then get up and run as fast as you can to the gate".

There was a roar of sound from behind them, men's deep-toned voices chanting something over and over again, and then, through his bootsoles, Abdullah felt the vibration of thousands of big, calloused feet striking the hard earth. A quick glance over his shoulder showed him the entire long, dense line of savages running straight at the wall of the fortress, waving spears and clubs and shields over their heads and shouting.

Bugles pealed from within the fortress, drums rolled. Then all along the length of the wall within sight, gunports gaped open and with a deep rumbling audible even at the distance, the guns of all levels were wheeled up into battery, their barrels extending out from within the walls' casemates.

Otei dropped flat on his huge belly, and the other three quickly followed suit. Seeing as he dropped that the other three men had closed their visors, Abdullah did the same. The feet kept drum-drumming, coming nearer and nearer, and his every instinct ordered Abdullah to get up, either to flee or fight, but not to just lie supine and be speared in the back; nonetheless, he controlled himself and stayed put.

He heard one or two guns fired off, from somewhere far down the wall to the northeast. Then, suddenly, he was in the midst of a living noise so loud that he nearly swooned of its effects and just lay there, feeling drugged or very drunk, hearing nothing, until something began to beat upon the backplate of his cuirass insistently. He raised his head groggily to see the Arab officer standing over him slamming the flat of his drawn sword yet again onto the backplate. With the man's aid, he got up and staggered the distance to the gate. Immediately they passed under the spikes of the half-raised portcullis, it was slammed back down into place and the crew strained to close and rebar the ironwood gates.

The batteries along the walls roared once more while still they were passing through the passage to the inner gate, but although he felt the pressure and vibration, Abdullah heard the cannon fire only dimly.

Hours later, after he had rested in the palace, changed his bloody, befouled clothing, and washed his face—blood having sprung from his ears, nose, and even the corners of his eyes as he had lain on the ground outside the walls—he and Captain Otei returned to the top of the rear wall, then slowly walked the circuit of the walls before descending to tour the casemates and praise the tired gunners, all gunpowder-black now, no matter their original colors.

"They got a bloody and very deadly surprise, Ngona's swine did," remarked Otei, as they surveyed the hundreds of square yards upon which bloody brown bodies and chunks of bodies lay still or twitching or writhing and screaming. "The last time they tried it, seven years back, I had far fewer heavy pieces on this wall and the two flanking ones, all of my heavy guns were in the front wall back then, and that's where they took their heaviest losses on that occasion and that's why they wouldn't attack it today. But the simpletons didn't stop to think that I might've added guns since they were here before."

"How many do you think we killed or wounded, Captain?" asked Abdullah. "It is said that very few ever reached the walls and none of those ever left the foot of them. Will they have enough men left to launch another attack, do you think?"

"Oh, yes, sir knight, they'll attack again, probably tonight, but surely in the morning, for all that at least half of their effectives are lying out there or dying slowly in the bush of their wounds." Otei's voice bore a tinge or more of admiration for his persistent foes. "They are a brave, determined, often suicidally stubborn people. They'd make first-rate soldiers, could they be disciplined and taught the proper use of modern arms. The firearms that some of them bear are used as clubs, you see, not reloaded and fired at those they're captured from. With the exceptions of their javelins and thrown clubs or axes or knives, they have no missile weapons in war, although they use bows and arrows for hunting. They are a backward, superstition-bound race of pagans and I hate having to deal with them at all, but they fight a lot and therefore take many captives. They can't eat them all, usually, so they sell them to me or to others. But sometimes they get bigger ideas and either try to or succeed in taking the captives back to resell to another buyer. When Ngona's older brother first became chief, he marched down here and attacked us, and, because of a number of factors, I ended it all through dint of buying the bugger off. He was killed in the course of their latest war, up country, and Ngona was chosen to replace him. It was he who led the ambush of Haroun and took back the captives, and, I suppose, he just decided to try to do what his brother had done seven years ago all over again. I can only hope that the pig is lying somewhere out there in the open and that he still is alive enough to feel it when the hyenas come for him tonight."

There had been no waiting at all for the vultures and lesser carrion birds. Thick as flies, they had descended onto the feast so thoughtfully spread for them and now could be seen stalking and hopping about, sometimes rising to fly a few yards to another tempting morsel—internal organs, entrails, and gobbets of more solid meat attracting most of the larger birds, the smaller dining upon eyes, tongues, and brains from smashed skulls. Occasionally there was a ghastly screaming from somewhere around the body-littered fields as a cannibal warrior too badly injured to move or defend himself was eaten alive by the avian scavengers.

On the flanks of the lines of attackers, a few wounded individuals, desperate for water, had crawled toward the riverbanks, and some of them had made it. These dead or bleeding bodies had piqued the interest of nearby crocodiles, and soon the river was debouching the scaly, toothy beasts in numbers and in a vast assortment of sizes. Abdullah could never have dreamed that so many of the reptiles had been lurking unseen in that section of river; he had never seen more than a few, here and there, sunning themselves on the riverbanks as the ships sailed past, and none at all around the area of the fortress.

But there they were, clambering out of the water, climbing the banks and moving amazingly fast to the edges of the area of carnage. Before their advances, the vultures and other birds protested loudly but in vain, for their sharp beaks were useless against the thickly armored water-beasts. Long, tooth-studded jaws opened and clamped down on dead men, pieces of dead men, and some not yet dead, to drag them all relentlessly back to the riverbank and down it to disappear with delicacy under the brown water of the Río Kongo. Here and there occurred a furious, tail-lashing tug-of-war between the big beasts over a tasty bit, but there was more than enough for all and even the loser of these was certain to leave with a prize of its own.

They dined early that evening in the fortress, for all in the reduced garrison would have to take turns watching for a possible new attack by the cannibals. Prior to the meal, Abdullah had tried to return the costly golden baubles to Otei, only to be told to keep them and the antique helmet, in case another conference occur, so the Spaniard dropped them into a suede bag, dropped that into his sea chest, and forgot about them.

There had been a handful of deaths or severe injuries that day, all due to unavoidable accidents, though not a single spearman had ever reached a position from which he could have killed or hurt anyone in the garrison.

After the hurried meal, Otei addressed the assembled officers saying, "Gentlemen, that was a beautiful piece of work out there today. I am justly proud of all of you and of your men. I'd guess that we killed or close enough to it above two thousand of the pigs. And I doubt me not that not a few more had painful cause to regret that they laid up in the bush over there within range of our catapults, too. I know that some of you wanted permission to blast carcasses out of the mortars into the bush, but I forbade it, and, presently, you'll learn why.

"There may be another attack tonight and there may not; it's dependent on a host of variables over which we have and can have no control. These are not in the least subtle opponents. If they attack tonight they'll do it in the same full-tilt, suicidal way they did it today—chanting, shouting, screaming, and running right into the range of our weapons. If the moon is visible tonight, most likely they won't attack until moonset; if not, if it's a cloudy night, then expect it at any time.

"I pray, however, that they not attack tonight for this reason: gentlemen, those splendid cannonades today burned up a great deal of gunpowder. My plans had been to treat them to two volleys, but when more and more kept coming out of the bush, we had no choice but to fire two more, than blow apart the diehards with the swivels, and even then some dozens made it to the walls and had to be downed with long guns and pistols.

"I've assigned more men to the powdermill and it will be at it all through the night, but there is a limit to how much can be made, for the stocks of priests' powder are very low. Yes, we do have some hundredweight barrels of raw niter, but in order to make decent gunpowder of the stuff it has to be refined, and that is a long process.

"So I am not saying don't touch off a piece if it is really necessary, just be damned certain that it is before you blow away at a hyena or three with a twenty-two-pounder culverin. If you have to fire or feel you have to at a suspicious something, then please do it with a swivel gun, a small-bored one, or better yet, with a caliver loaded with ball and shot. God be praised, we own still a very good amount of charging and priming powder for the smaller arms.

"But, as I said, let us all pray that they elect to launch their next attack at a time when we will have enough light to clearly see just what we're shooting at."

Michael Otei's prayers were apparently heard and answered, for the cannibals did not offer to attack that night, with the huge equatorial moon riding high above the beleaguered fortress and its heterogeneous garrison of defenders. But from somewhere back in the bush, drums rumbled sullenly through all the hours of darkness, a satanic-sounding accompaniment to the lunatic cackles of hyaenas, the hissings and bellowings of crocodiles, the low coughing of leopards, and the hundred and one other noises made by other feasters on the cleared land outside the walls.

The approaching drums and the chanting voices commenced at dawn, first a distant grumble and murmur, but growing louder and louder as the cannibals neared. They came from the north, where they had probably camped the night through, but they divided somewhere out of sight of the fort to once more emerge on three sides, another and smaller contingent of them issuing from out a swampy area just downstream of the fort to threaten the riverside wall. They were none of them brown that morning, however. Save only for rivulets cut through by sweat, each of them was whitish-grey from pate to horny soles.

"By the well-crisped pecker of Saint Lawrence," blasphemed Otei, who had happened to be standing near Abdullah and his two dozen Bornu calivermen atop the river wall when the attackers appeared, "this will be no day on which we can save powder, sir knight. See the way those buggers have coated themselves with ashes? That means they mean to fight until we kill all of them or until they take the fort and kill us. They've never done this when they attacked me either of the other times. Someone of real importance must've been killed yesterday, then, one of their pagan juju priests, most likely—they wouldn't make themselves moon-white over a mere chief.

"When they rush this section, Abdullah, have your calivers try to drop those men carrying the notched logs. Not one in dozens of them can swim, so there's no way they can cross the moat here without those logs. There're not many of the maneaters on this side, anyway—I think they're only here for the purpose of keeping us, those assigned here, here, so that we can't go to the aid of any of the other three sides."

He turned and addressed the officer in overall command of the cannon batteries on this wall. "Captain Latiq, unless a lot more of them show up after I leave, don't loose off anything big until they're nicely bunched together on the far side of the moat, then fire only enough guns to shred them and put them on the run, eh? Leave the survivors of your guns to the swivels and the calivers—they burn less powder."

Turning back to Abdullah, the fat but efficient Otei clapped a gauntleted hand on the Spaniard's armored shoulder. "Get yourself one of the spare calivers and join the fun, sir knight, but"—he chuckled—"try to not waste any powder."

Then he and his bodyguards were away up the wall at a fast pace.

Forever after, for all of his life, Abdullah recalled that early morning as a butchery, pure and simple. His veterans dropped all the log-carrying men at long ranges, then those who picked up the burdens and those who followed the second lot, and so on, their reloading times giving the near-naked savages just about enough time to lift the long, heavy, ill-balanced, and unwieldy sections of tree trunk and take a few steps with them before they began to be flung down by the heavy leaden balls. Abdullah himself was not a poor shot, and he did his part with the extremely heavy, wall-rested long gun.

Arrived at the far verge of the twenty-foot width of filled moat, the ash-coated spearmen hurled some javelins, clubs, axes, and even stones upward, but mostly just milled around while more closed in behind them and some few brave souls ran back to try to bring up the logs, most of these being dropped long before they could reach the artifacts.

Then the lowest level of casemate ports had swung open, the barrels of full cannon and cannon-royals had been run out and then touched off, all of them at point-blank range and all loaded to almost the muzzle-bands with tightly packed langrage—chopped-up metal scrap, imperfect small-arms balls, shovelsful of gravel and shards of broken glass bottles. The effect on the "targets" was unbelievable, unforgettable; more than one of the veterans atop that section of wall hurriedly thrust his head far out and retched his stomach's contents into the reddening waters of the moat. Abdullah was among them.

Then it became business as usual for the swivel-gunners and the calivermen. They opened fire on the stunned, bemused attackers still standing there amid the incredible carnage wrought by the loads of langrage and continued to drop the survivors as they ran or staggered away, back toward the reed-grown swamp from which they had so recently emerged.

By the third hour after sunrise, it was over and another feast had been lavishly spread for the scavengers, on all four sides of the fortress, this time.

There were a few, too-short hours of rejoicing, but then, down the river in long war-boats, came Otei's other partner with news of fast-approaching doom.

CHAPTER THE SEVENTH

With the arrival of the Arab partner called al-Ain—"the Eye"—and his battered force, the Egyptian surgeon and his apprentices again became very busy, while Otei, the injured al-Gahzahr, and the third partner engaged in a night-long conference from which the Captain and al-Ain emerged looking haggard and very grim. Michael Otei first issued a spate of orders to various subordinates, then sought out Abdullah and closeted with the Spanish knight.

"There is not much time, my boy, so don't waste any of the precious stuff arguing with me," he said, in preface. "Abdullah, you are a brave man, a good officer, you have served me well here, and I can but wish that our relationship had been of longer duration, but such is the will of God. The intelligence that al-Ain brought with him down from the north is, in a word, dreadful; under the existing circumstances, it could probably not be worse, and I feel a powerful sense of impending, utterly inescapable doom bearing inexorably down upon me, my partners, and my men, but I refuse to see anyone it is within my power to save dragged down into death with me. That includes at the top of the list you and your valiant Spaniards.

"Presently, there will be a ship anchored in the river just far enough out to prevent her grounding as she is laden. She is a Dutch caravel of some four hundred tons, with three masts and drawing some eleven feet, laden. She is pierced for twelve guns on each side on the lower deck, seven on the higher decks, plus two stern-chasers.

"Your crew should already be aboard her by now, for she was not moored far away from here. Although the crew that sailed her in here was twice the size of yours, you'll just have to manage, for she is the only ship of any description I have on hand. My men will be rowing all of the lighters down and they will then set to work loading. They'll load all of the ship's gear that came off the *Aña Gomez*, provisions and water, sacks of charcoal and suchlike."

"You and your officers will be sailing away on this ship, then?" asked Abdullah.

Otei smiled sadly and shook his head tiredly. "No, my boy, none of us have anywhere else to go, you see. I am of the opinion that God has ordained we all die here in final retribution for our many and heavy sins. I would not have lived for much longer, in any case."

"You are ill?" demanded Abdullah. "You didn't look it yesterday or the day before, Captain."

"Not ill, not that I know of, my boy, but old, old and just now very, very tired." At Abdullah's disbelieving look, Otei added, "Yes, old, my boy. My fat hides my wrinkles and the fact that my servants shave my face and head each morning disguises the whiteness of my hair and beard. I was sixty-two on my last saint's day.

"But such trivialities aside, for as I earlier said, time is now of the essence. My men will be loading aboard the ship twenty-four fine bronze culverins, their trucks and necessaries for your main batteries, each of them throwing twenty-two pounds. There will be two long culverins of twenty pounds for your chasers, twelve demiculverins for your waist-guns, and a brace of twelve-pounder demicannons for your quarterdeck. There will be a plenitude of shot and waddings, but I won't be able to give you much cannon-grade powder, of course. Take all of the swivels you want, them and small arms of any description and in any quantity—calivers, arquebuses, dags, pistols, polearms, edge-weapons, armor, anything.

"Those Bornu calivermen that you commanded so well these past days are honest mercenaries whom I hired on only some few years back, not homeless exiles and criminals like me and the rest, so you will carry them as passengers as far as the Port of Saints Peter and Paul, at the mouth of the River Niger or to another port if they so choose. When once they are all safely landed, the ship and all within it become yours, Abdullah."

The Spaniard sighed and shrugged, spreading his hands. "I'll do as you order, Captain, but I am not at all sure I can even find the place you indicate, not without a sailing-master."

Otei asked, "Will you settle for a man who, though no seaman, has studied the arts of the navigator? Then look no farther. You of course recall Patricius Olahda—well, he will be sailing with you, also. He is a young man of depthless curiosity, and this led him at one time to secure and absorb books on navigation, instruments, and charts and maps. He is my only full sister's grandson and I have made of him my legal heir, for though I never can return to my homeland, I still hold title to properties there. For some strange reason, I never in my life have been able to quicken any of my many wives, mistresses, or concubines, such has been the Creator's divine Will, so there will be no questioning the right of Patricius to succeed to that which was mine."

With a mighty rattling and clanging of his armor and weapons, the fat man heaved himself to his feet, saying, "Now I must see to so many other things, my boy. I will try to meet with you once more before you sail. Patricius will see that you receive almost anything that you find you will need for the voyage. God keep you, Abdullah."

At the Captain's request, expressed through Patricius Olahda, Abdullah spent some time in a rope chair slung over the side of the fine northern-type caravel marking the outlines of letters for the crew to paint in—*Nuestra Señora de los Penitentes*. The less than honest Dutch former owner/master had, shortly before he had paid the inevitable wages of his sins, felt constrained to sign over his ship to Otei, and the documents conveying said ship to one Don Abdullah de Baza, rendered in Spanish, Arabic, and one of the languages of Ghana, were given to the Spaniard by a one-eyed Arab who came aboard and introduced himself as the third partner of Otei, him they called al-Ain.

Unlike the other Arab partner, the one called al-Gahzahr, this slender, wiry, greying man spoke and comported himself like the gentlemen he clearly had been reared to be. While his work-force and the ship's crew performed the brutally hard task of getting the world-heavy, cast-bronze gun tubes and the equally heavy, clumsy hardwood-and-iron guntrucks up out of the lighters, then down through the main hatch onto the gundeck, mounted the one onto the other, secured them, and then placed them, al-Ain graciously accepted Abdullah's offer and availed himself of refreshment in the largest cabin of the caravel.

When first the man had clambered up out of the leading lighter, Abdullah had known who he was before he introduced himself, and had known just how he had acquired his present *nom de guerre*. At some time in the past, the Arab had lost his left eye and had filled the emptied socket with a huge and magnificent opal set in solid, ruddy gold. Save alone for this outré prosthetic and a very old silver thumb-ring—now so old that the Arabic script snaking around it was become indecipherable—this partner sported no jewelry.

Abdullah thought that, sitting there in his tight doeskin breeches tucked into the low tops of fancifully tooled boots, his sleeved cotton shirt of European cut, plain dagger-belt, and soft cap of velvet, with his long legs gracefully crossed at the knee, al-Ain—disregarding his "eye"—looked far more the part of a distinguished retired knight than he did that of an active slave trader and fierce warrior.

"I felt that I had to meet you, Don Abdullah," remarked al-Ain, simply. "I have known Michael Otei for more than twenty years and never in all that time have I ever known him to even consider giving so much as one of his precious cannon away, not to anyone for any purpose. Now you come along and he is giving you no less than forty of the best pieces in the fortress—Venetian-cast, every one of them, only about ten years old and sound as the day they were unmolded, real bronzen treasure.

"To be frank, though, I'm as glad to see them go, the larger ones, for we've always had too many guns too big for our needs here; I've had shouting match atop shouting match with Michael about it over the years, too; the only place we have need of anything larger than a saker is on the riverside wall and towers, where we might be compelled to match shot-tonnage with ships' guns. Elsewhere, they are all useless, powder-costly fripperies."

Abdullah, having so recently seen the kind of damage wrought by the multitude of large-caliber cannon upon the attacking cannibals, most of it at distances beyond accurate small-arms shot—thus keeping the vastly more numerous and blood-mad pagans far from the walls or any close-range fighting where their numbers would easily have prevailed—was not so sure that the Arab gentleman was right, but he held his peace, smiling politely.

"I cannot understand," he told his guest, "just why you, the Captain, the other officers, and as many troops as possible do not come aboard this ship, man your boats and lighters, and flee this place if you all expect to shortly die here, as seems to be a fact accepted by everyone. The Captain, at least, owns a great wealth of gold, gems, silver, and other valuables, so you all could live well for the rest of your lives, in comfort, in some more civilized place, I would think."

The thin lips of the Arab twisted slightly, and he shook his head. "Alas, Don Abdullah, you know not just how infamous are we three—Michael, al-Gahzahr, and I, at least. We, none of us, would be safe for long in any more civilized area of this world, not unless we were to make voyage to perhaps Hind, Sind, or the Spice Isles, and quite possibly not even then. We all own powerful and wealthy and most vindictive enemies. One of these—or his son, rather—has searched and found us even here and now is leading a large force down upon us from the north. He is called *Shaikh* Hassan al-Ohsiyahr ibn Omar al-Shakoosh; in the dialect of Arabic from which these two sobriquets come, al-Shakoosh means 'the Hammer,' while al-Ohsiyahr means 'the Short One.' Long years ago, when first we all came here and began slaving, an old, dying juju-man pronounced that Michael would be killed by a 'the get of a hammer,' I by 'something short and red,' and the others of our then-five partners by various means, all of which have come to pass in the ways predicted, and, therefore, we have no slightest reason to doubt but that his predictions will prove accurate in our cases, too. Hassan is short of stature and has red hair, I am told; he also is the get of a hammer. Who, my friend, can long elude Kismet? In what land does a man's fate not finally overtake him? No, this has been the only real home that many of us ever have known; we shall fight for it or we'll die for it, as God wills. But, if die we must, we first will see to it that *Shaikh* Hassan and his men know and long remember that they have been in a fight, have fought men of mettle.

"Now, it is time that I go and supervise the disassemblies and removals of the next load of culverins, Don Abdullah, and you should accompany me to mark the swivels that you want for the ship. After that, go down to the armory and choose whatever you want or need, for far better that they go to a friend than provide spoils and loot to an enemy. Place all of your choices in the outer room in piles and they will be brought out to the ship tomorrow."

By the morning of the fourth day, the *Nuestra Señora de los Penitentes* was completely ready for sea. Before any loading had commenced, however, Abdullah's *barcogalán* and the *carpintero* had seen the bilges pumped completely dry and gone over the vessel from stem to stern, masthead to keel, and had reported her sound in all ways saving only for some sections of rigging that could be easily and quickly replaced, numerous embedded bullets and holes from their passages, these mostly in the waist, and a plethora of old bloodstains in the planking and bulkheads throughout the ship.

At Abdullah's carefully phrased question, al-Ain had replied, "The Dutchman, Don Abdullah? Oh, him, yes, he had an eminently unpronounceable name, like so very many of his ilk. The whole of those tongues when spoken sound like unto angry dogs growling, to me. He was no slaver, but rather a merchant-captain who had heard that the slave dealer here paid hard gold specie for gunpowder in all grades, refined niter—that which the Church still chooses to call 'priests' powder'—brimstone, pig-lead, pig-iron, and cast-iron shot of almost all calibers.

"So he sailed up the river of a day with a cargo to sell, he averred. The two casks and one barrel he brought ashore were all fine-quality, from top to bottom, and the price he demanded was reasonable for the value of such goods brought so far. An agreement was reached, a weight of gold changed hands, and lighters brought a number of barrels ashore and our men bore them into the fortress. Had he upped anchor immediately the last barrel was winched down into the last lighter, he most likely now would be laughing over his tipple somewhere telling the funny story of how he bilked a black savage in far southern Ifriqah, but he did not.

"God was watching over us that day, not over him. In handling the barrels within the fortress, a mischance caused one to roll down a flight of stairs and shatter at the bottom, revealing it to be packed with nothing save powdered charcoal, with not a trace of brimstone or niter. The casks of niter proved, upon close examination, to be niter right enough, but raw niter, completely unrefined; only the brimstone casks contained what they were sold to us to be.

"To compound our righteous rage at being so

cheated, we knew that should we be so stupid as to allow this sharper to escape with his ship, his crew, his life, and our gold, the stories certain to be spread all over Christendom by him and his seamen would shortly see a virtual swarm of dishonest merchants descending upon the simple savages, all anxious to relieve us of some of the burden of our wealth.

"And so, under the cover of darkness, we drew up to the sides of the ship in native rivercraft, which can be propelled more silently than can oared boats. Then we all swarmed up the ship and over the rails and began to kill, but trying to take the captain and his officers alive. Dragged back to the fortress, on his knees in the palace, he and they admitted to everything, all the while begging most abjectly and piteously that their lives be spared.

"After taking a hand and an eye from each of two of the officers, we put them aside to be shipped out aboard the next ship that came to call, that they might be witness to the rewards of those who made to cheat us. When once the perfidious Dutchman had signed over his ship to Michael, he and his other two officers were maimed a bit for sport, then locked away and fed until Michael heard of a nearby column of soldier ants, when he had the swine all three staked out directly in the path of the ants, whose habit it is to eat anything—animal or vegetable—that cannot flee them."

The Bornu calivermen came aboard, all more than simply well armed, for, like Abdullah, they had been given by Otei free choice of all that the fortress armory contained. Patricius Olahda came aboard next, along with men bearing his effects to stow them in one of the three cabins aft of the mainmast, then he returned to shore, and when next he climbed up the ladder, he was followed by the Captain and four of the palace servants whom Abdullah recognized, each of them bearing a thickish bundle and a hammock of woven grass, all wearing abundant amounts of jewelry he did not recall having seen them wearing in the palace. Next to climb up from the lighter was one of the alcoholic Egyptian surgeon's apprentices; then a succession of chests were handed up to be stacked by the port rail.

Otei said, "My boy, Master Abu pronounces that this man has learned enough to pass the testing of any country's or city's Guild of Surgeons, and he is not wanted anywhere for any crimes, having simply accompanied his master here, long ago; he would serve you and your men aboard this ship, if you will have him. He is called Ahmad ibn Wahzi and his chests contain a full set of instruments, medicants, and other necessaries."

Abdullah said gravely, "I would be more than pleased to have a skilled surgeon aboard this ship, Captain Otei. Few, save warships, ever have such, and no man knows just what may chance from day unto day. Master Ahmad should find a place below in which to swing his hammock. I will talk with him later."

Otei drew Abdullah's attention to the four servants. "These men are not slaves, lad, they are all free men, all well trained and most accomplished bodyservants, and they will accompany Patricius.

"Samuel," he addressed one of the four servants, "you and the others bear the four cases I already spoke about and pointed out to you behind us. My boy, let us repair to your cabin."

Following Captain Michael Otei's orders, they destroyed or sank each of the channel-marking buoys as they passed them on their way down the river to the sea. Patricius Olahda stayed in his cabin with his maps, charts, instruments, and books until just before they cleared the rivermouth, then he appeared on the quarterdeck and informed Abdullah that he had plotted a course that, God willing, would deliver them to the Port of Saints Peter and Paul hard by the mouth of the River Niger. At that port, hopefully, Abdullah would be able to hire on a master-navigator to take them back to Habana.

"How far?" asked Abdullah.

"Between four hundred and fifty and five hundred Spanish leagues, Don Abdullah," replied Olahda, adding, "Since none of us knows much about this ship and her sailing peculiarities, I cannot begin to guess the length of time that it will take us to get up to the Bight of Benin, of course."

But the ship, once it had been determined exactly how best to dress her sails, proved a good one, very responsive to helm, not a pitcher or a roller like the late and unlamented *Aña Gomez* had all too frequently proved herself to be. After tossing the log at different times over three days, Olahda opined that they should fetch into the Bight of Benin within seven or eight days, did the wind remain constant.

Of course, it did not. Just off an island marked on Olahda's Portuguese chart as São Tomé, the sails fluttered briefly, then fell slack. Abdullah was trying to decide whether to have sea-anchors cast out to prevent the ship being forced aground by currents or whether to draw in the two trailing boats, have them manned, and set oarsmen to the brutally hard labor of towing the ship when a flotilla of small boats was to be seen approaching from the island. When they had neared enough for Abdullah's long glass to see details of their motley, heavily armed crews, he decided he did not at all like the look of them.

He ordered all guns readied and loaded with grape or langrage, then run out of their ports into plain view. He also bade the Bornu mercenaries and his own sea-soldiers arm and stand ready for action. With the assistance of the four servants, he and Olahda arrayed themselves in half-armor and returned to the quarterdeck armed with swords, pistols, and dirks, these being covered by boat-cloaks, the helmets not yet donned.

When the lead boat, a long oar-barge packed with an ugly pack of scruffy-looking men, numerous spirals of smoke from as many slow-matches curling up above them in the still air, came within easy hailing distance, a man in an old, rusty hauberk too short for even his froggy, not overly tall body stood up in the bow and demanded, "What in hell is a Spanish ship doing off the Isle of São Tomé, anyways?"

"Not that it's any of your business," replied Abdullah in a far more grammatical Portuguese than the questioner had used, "but we are on our way to the Port of Saints Peter and Paul and the wind has just seen fit to die."

"What's your cargo?" snapped the froggy man, who was missing the top halves of both ears, had had his nostrils slit in the past, and owned a left cheek knife-scarred from temple to chin. "Better not try lyin' to me, now, 'cause we'll be coming aboard to check it out."

It was at that moment that the gunports all along the port side opened and the bronzen muzzles of the culverins emerged to grin of death and dismemberment at the islanders on the boats.

"No," replied Abdullah, "you'll not be boarding this ship, not a one of you spoilers, pirates, or whatever you are."

The man grinned coldly, showing a far from complete set of broken, yellow-brown teeth and an expanse of fire-red gums. "You better think twicet afore to let off them guns, Cap'n. It's a lot more of us than it is of you and we can be all over you and your stinkin' little ship afore you can reload them guns, too. It ain't as if we really wants much off you, see. You just let me and my boat crew come on board you and we'll tell you whatall we wants and your crew can load them two fine boats you got with what we picks out and then go on your way. Now ain't that better than killing and hurting a lot of us and getting kilt your own self?"

"We will give you scum nothing, save cannon loads and leaden balls," replied Abdullah with icy arrogance. He raised his voice and roared, "Calivermen, on deck!"

The sight of the blue-black, fully armed, half-armored soldiers crowding the waist of the ship, each with his long-barreled firearm gaping more than an inch at the muzzle, caused the spokesman to pale beneath his deep tan and his scarred chin to drop. The sight also caused not a few of the boats to begin frantic efforts to put about and point their bows shoreward.

Finally managing to start speaking again, the scarred man yelped, "What in the hell are you, a Spanish frigate or what? That there's a merchant flag you flying, you know."

With a broad wink at Patricius Olahda, Abdullah threw off the voluminous boat-cloak to reveal his arms and armor, then replied, "This ship, *Nuestra Señora de los Penitentes*, is a special frigate of His Majesty of Spain, sent out to rid the seas of the threat of you and evil men like you. *Gunners, fire!*"

The ship heeled at the recoil of the larboard culverins. At the range, closely as the boats and barges had been spaced, waiting to move in on the merchantman, there was no way that any of the big guns could miss.

Those who had circled around to the starboard side, however, were too widely spaced to make certain targets for the hard-to-traverse main-battery pieces, so swivels and calivers were used against them, while other calivermen and swivels blasted away at those who had survived the broadside and the one barge that lay close under the stern. Abdullah was saving the demiculverins in the waist, low as were his stocks of cannon powder; fortunately, the swivels were strong-walled enough to take the finer-grained caliver powder, of which there existed larger supplies aboard.

Spotting the scarred man swimming grimly toward the ship's side, a big knife gripped between his rotting teeth, Abdullah drew one of his wheellock dags and, waiting until the swimmer was almost to the ship, put a ten-bore ball through his head.

While the calm lasted, the two ship's boats were used to row parties of the Bornu mercenaries around from one still-floating island boat to another, killing stray swimmers and anyone still breathing in the boats, then taking aboard anything worth taking before bashing out the bottoms of the crafts. A few boats, mere specks at the distance, sat off watching, but made no move to come so much as one rod closer to those terrible guns and the shipload of men who had just proved—proved bloodily—their willingness to make use of them.

With the surrounding sea empty of anything save some floating corpses and several high, triangular fins of piscine morticians come to clean up the carnage, Abdullah—loath to be in proximity to the Isle of São Tomé after sunset, if he could help it—was on the verge of ordering the boats to set to work towing the ship, when, with a first, hesitant flutter, the errant breeze once more blew.

Patricius Olahda's amateur effort at course-plotting

proved very good indeed. On the morning of the ninth day after their departure from the point off the mouth of the Rio Kongo, they spotted the telltale discoloration of the sea that denoted the debouchment of a large river to the immediate north, and by midafternoon, Abdullah was dickering with a pilot who had come out in a barge from the Port of Saints Peter and Paul.

The argument went on for a few minutes, the pilot demanding far more than Abdullah thought his services were worth, then one of the calivermen shouted down something at him in his own language, whereupon the pilot grasped the foot of the swaying rope ladder and clambered up as easily and swiftly as an ape.

Once upon the waistdeck, he asked for Abdullah, a bit aggrievedly, "Why did his Spanish lordship not mention earlier in our discourse that he was carrying homewards-returning Bornu gentleman-soldiers rather than cargo and therefore qualifies, insofar as piloting fees are concerned, as a friendly ship-of-war or a pilgrim ship—that is, I will receive only what your lordship feels my skill to be worth."

"And so," Don Guillermo had told Don Felipe on that day in the fort at Boca Osa, "my old friend Don Abdullah finally sailed back into Habana harbor to find that he was considered dead, that a stone had been raised for his missing body, and that his in-laws had already arranged a remarriage for his wife as soon as the set period of mourning was over.

"The first meeting with his in-laws after his return was fiery. His father-in-law, the grasping, half-breed bastard, claimed the new ship, of course. Abdullah railed at him for sending him on so long a voyage aboard a defective ship to begin, then informed him that the ship would be scuttled in the harbor before it would be turned over to the grasping merchant, whereupon Master Cristóbal ordered Don Abdullah out of his house.

"Abdullah went gladly, fearful that if he stayed longer, his temper might slip and he might do serious or even deadly injury to the older man. Certain that the powerful merchant would soon try to physically seize the ship, Abdullah went directly aboard her and saw her sailed some two leagues eastward along the coast to be anchored in a hidden bay near the estancia of a friend from the expeditions in Mexico. He stayed there that night, then borrowed a horse and set out for Habana before the dawn.

"Somewhat of a celebrity after his miraculous return from the dead, he sought and gained audience with His Excellency the Governor, and spoke to him as one Spanish-born hidalgo to another. The result of that pleasant meeting was that when the creole merchant pressed his claim, the decision was that while the ship should indeed go to Master Gomez, anything not built into the fabric of the ship, anything detachable—guns, swivels, sails, spars, running gear, supplies, cargo if any, tools, and even water-butts—was the property of Don Abdullah. The court furthermore stated that the act of claiming the ship would serve as indication that the firm of Gomez, Gomez and Gomez did agree to absolve Don Abdullah de Baza of any guilt or indebtedness pursuant to the loss of the ship *Aña Gomez*, her fittings and supplies, her guns and her cargo at time of loss.

"It is said that persons on the streets far from the palace could clearly hear Master Cristóbal Gomez's shrieks of rage and grief at the announcement of the decision.

"The greedy bastard screamed even more loudly when another court, after hearing evidence, decided that Don Abdullah, since he had been assumed dead a bit prematurely under the law, might keep all of his wife's dowry, whether or not his sometime father-in-law actually obtained the annulment for which he had very recently prayed of the archbishop.

"Of course, my boy, Don Abdullah and I saw that ship stripped of anything and everything that would move, even the stone ballast. As he had promised the governor, half of those fine guns went to the Castle of the Moor, which guards the harbor of Habana, along with all of the powder and shot for them. Everything else, he sold, and I may tell you that those Venetian guns brought a pretty sum from divers shipowners. Each of his crew members received of him a full onza of gold, save the *barcogalán*, the *carpintero*, and the Egyptian surgeon, whom he gave three each.

"To the archbishop himself, into that prelate's own two hands, he delivered a quantity of garish golden jewelry, including a huge, perfect opal set in a strange sphere of solid gold. He asked that the worth of these treasures be applied to perpetual masses for the repose of the souls of one Captain Michael Otei, Captain Don Haroun al-Ain, and Captain Ahmed al-Gahzahr, deceased but most penitent sinners, all.

"He already had a measure of standing with the Church in Habana, since his late father, in Spain, was a bishop. But this offering has elevated him to quite a lofty place in the consideration of all churchmen who matter in Cuba. Therefore, when the ecclesiastical at length heard old Gomez's annulment plea, they referred that plea, itself, to Rome; however, they refused to set aside the finding of the viceregal court that had awarded all of the original dowry to Don Abdullah.

"At this, Master Cristóbal Gomez must have temporarily taken leave of his wits. He railed out first that his larcenous if gently born scapegrace of a son-in-law had bought both courts—lay and church—then began to babble that Don Abdullah surely must be a warlock and that he had apparently bewitched every judge in the province. Can you imagine such a thing, Don Felipe?"

The younger knight had shaken his head in wonderment. "Captain, the man must have been mad. Even to breathe a word of witchcraft in a Church court were enough by itself, but to speculate that the very holy men making up that court had been bewitched . . . ? May I inquire what came of such calumny?"

Don Guillermo smiled grimly. "Certain investigations were shortly thereafter undertaken into the personal backgrounds of the family Gomez, reaching back to Spain as well as to the indio forebears of the *casa*. It is felt, I have been told, that no matter what the creole's state of agitation on that day, some personal knowledge of the black arts must be indicated by such a shocking and baseless accusation lodged against so good and pious a man as our own Don Abdullah de Baza.

"After all of this, Abdullah saw his wife evicted from the estancia that was part of her dot; she now is back in the bosom of her parsimonious family, one hears, awaiting an annulment and a new spouse. Then he bought slaves to farm it and hired on folk to live there and supervise the establishment. After he had bought a small mansion in Habana and hired permanent servants, and bought all needed furniture and slaves for it, he invested the not inconsiderable sum remaining from his adventures in enterprises of *my* creole father-in-law, who is not in the least of the same stripe as the despicable Gomezes.

"Moreover, since he has had his fill of creole merchants, at least on a purely personal level, and since he now is become a man of some measure of wealth and standing in the province, he intends to send back to Spain for a wife, immediately this assignment of mine be ended and another *comandante* be sent to take my place here.

"And so you see, my boy, a man of honor, faith, and discipline can aspire quite high in this new world of ours. No, I am not so wealthy as my old friend, but I am of comfortable means, due to my investments with my father-in-law's ventures over the years. I have—God be praised—three sons to carry on my *casa*, with enough set by to outfit them for war and to properly dower my two daughters. I am held in esteem by His Excellency as a soldier, and I therefore can expect powerful backing in future expeditions, should I feel again inclined to undertake them.

"Persevere, young sir, let your inbred honor and piety guide you in your dealings, and I cannot doubt but that you will rise as far and as fast as have Don Abdullah and I, both of us not yet forty years of age and with our lives and futures as secure as God ever allows."

Now lying up in the prickly brush on the soggy mat of leaves covering the pebbly ground, Don Felipe recalled that day with Don Guillermo in the *comandante*'s office at the fort downriver, remembered the recountal of the thrilling expeditions against the indios—the fabulously wealthy indios of Mexico—and the exploits of Don Abdullah in far away Ifriqah, and he wondered if, ever, on their own adventures, his two superiors had been so thoroughly miserable as he was just then.

On the day before, he and his squires had viewed the nearly completed fort going up just a bit downriver of the Shawnee stockade. They had watched the furious battle against the odd bear or whatever it had been and Don Felipe had adjudged, simply from the numbers of gunmen atop the wooden walls then, that somehow, from somewhere, the objective had been reinforced. And this boded ill for the *comandante*'s plans to attack it.

CHAPTER THE EIGHTH

Mike Sikeena came back around the corner of the charred cabin, saying, "Some fucking body's been here, all right, Arsen, and not just a few of the fuckers, either; leveled out, it's a good three or four inches' worth of fresh turds in that slit-trench latrine back there."

Arsen frowned. "Well, that eliminates an Indian party—they wouldn't of bothered using that latrine, they all just dump where the urge hits them. How in hell have you bastards been missing these fuckers on the river, huh? Those goddam boats are *big*, too, some of them long as the band's station wagon or longer even. What do you do, just set the carrier to run its fucking self and then flake out in it?"

Seeing Mike's expression of hurt resentment, Arsen placed a hand on the Arab-American's shoulder, saying, "No, Mike, not you, Greg maybe, or even John, but I know you always try to do a good job at whatever you do. I'm sorry. I guess I'm just still jumpy from all the fucking shit that went down yesterday and then damn near no sleep at all last night, is all."

"Yeah, I know how that feels, Arsen," said Mike. "I still feel shaky whenever I think back to how that hairy, manlike fucker just kept coming up those rocks with the mosta his fucking arm shot off by that fucking portingal-ball . . . although Simon, he 'lows as how he's seen at least one real man, back in England when he was a horse soldier, do damn near the same thing until he finally got it into his head he was dead and just fell down and never did get up again." He wrinkled his brows and added, "Simon says it's the spirit that keeps a man or a horse going when they're hurt that bad."

Arsen shrugged. "Maybe . . . but I'd say the adrenaline high has the most to do with it. That's why a whitetail buck will keep on running for miles, even after a thirty-ought-six slug has blown his heart into fucking pieces, or why a grizzly bear that's dead on his feet will still come after the hunter . . . and get him, sometimes, too, at least that's what I heard my Uncle Boghos say once, and he's hunted all over the world, too.

"But you and me today, Mike, we've got us our own fucking hunting to do. You head downriver on that side of the thing and I'll do the same thing on the other side. Don't just look on the river itself—those Spanish greasers could of got cagey, they might be figgering that since they've only seen carriers during the day, we can only fly during the day, so they may be traveling at nights and laying up somewheres during the days.

"Now they must of brushed over the most of their footprints around here, but the ones they missed was all made when the ground was real soft, so the fuckers prob'ly was here during that long, drizzly time the end of last week, I figger, so that means they've had two, three days at the most to travel, and, even with the current, they couldn't of got more than about down to where that deep, clear creek joins the river, I don't think, so we won't go down much past there, then we'll turn around and come back up on opposite sides—maybe that way one of us will see something the other one might've missed, see. The one as sees the fuckers or their goddam boats'll let the other one know where he's at and then the both of us will crisscross all around and make sure how many of the fuckers it is and see if we can find out what the hell they're up to up here. When we get back, maybe we oughta take some of the Creek braves off the fort-construction and send them out to get us a few prisoners, huh? We don't want to have a bunch of the fuckers come barrel-assing out of the woods sometime in the middle of the goddam night or something, you know."

Mike shook his head. "Naw, Arsen, way things looks around here, it ain't that many of the fuckers. I don't think they're up here to fight or nothing, they're prob'ly just a long-range patrol, so their fucking officers'll know what *we're* up to, see. The way we tromped them on this here island, I don't figger they're gonna come back in less strength than was here that night, and prob'ly a whole pisspot more, was I them."

Neither man saw anything much on the downriver patrol. Once, both swung abruptly out into midchannel at the sight of a longboat, but closer scrutiny showed it to be empty even of oars and they at length decided that it was just one of the ones left moored to posts at the island that had finally broken loose and been carried away by the current. Nonetheless, Arsen used one of the carrier's weapons to blast out most of the boat's bottom planking.

They went down a few miles beyond the confluence of the river and the tributary, then switched banks and started back upstream, sailing along fairly low along the banks, with the magnifiers set for five yards. Arsen had come back up well past the island before he saw anything other than trees, brush, a few animals of various sorts, and a vast assortment of birds. Then, only a mile or so from the site of the fort and village, he saw something singularly odd.

Swooping in closer and at almost ground level, he saw them: four longboats, their swivels all dismounted and laid in the boats along with the oars, the tillers, and numerous small kegs and other impedimenta, all skillfully camouflaged with fresh-cut brush, small trees, and driftwood. Taking careful bearings, he turned and skimmed off to find Mike.

Don Felipe, done with his second day of quietly observing the fort-building project from a distance, was tramping back toward the cold camp some fifty yards back from the riverbank and the beached boats when the clear noise of someone approaching sent him and his companions prone into the brush flanking the game trail they had been using, single-file. From behind his chosen tree, the knight spotted the runner and stood up, replacing the ready pistol in his belt.

"Damn your lights!" he hissed at his other squire, Rudolfo, who had been left in the camp that day. "You make more noise than a herd of stampeding cattle, you . . ."

Then he saw the stark fear in the eyes of the younger man and snapped, "All right, what's happened, Rudolfo?"

The auburn-haired, somewhat gangly boy gulped and said, "M . . . my lord, two of the glowing silver things, they . . . they're at the camp. They disarmed everyone and asked who was in charge. I didn't . . . I said nothing, my lord, but he . . . one of the oarsmen told them that Don Felipe leads and was . . . is out with a large force that could attack and save us at any time. Then the men in the silver helmets said that I should find you and tell you that if you attack, they will kill everyone." He gulped again and asked, "Does . . . will my lord at . . . attack them?"

The knight laughed harshly. "With what, pray tell, Rudolfo?" He waved at his other squire and the four men who had been with him on surveillance that day. "With the six of you, seven pistols and a few dirks? Besides, balls just bounce off those silver things, indio arrows, too. I'm certain that that oarsman meant us all well with his bluffing lies, but he should have told the truth, even so."

Leading the way, Don Felipe took his course back toward his camp. But just out of sight of it, the knight had his men place their pistols, their powder and balls, and all save one knife each in the convenient hollow of a dead tree, then added both his own pistols, accessories, and his big dirk to the hoard and saw fallen leaves heaped over the lot before proceeding on, then remembered the long-glass and had one of the squires go back and place it too under the leaves with the hidden weapons.

When the seven Spaniards filed into the clearing and approached the carriers, Arsen said, "Mike, take it up and see if you can tell how many are hiding out there and how well armed they are, huh?"

Grinning, he said to the knight, "Well, Don Felipe, we meet again. Damn, but you bastards are stubborn. You got your tail singed first, just a little way upriver from here, then again a few days later out on the river, then the whole lot of you got either killed or driven off that island, and still you're coming back for more. What do I have to do, kill all of you to keep you off this stretch of river?"

Don Felipe drew himself up and cleared his throat.

"It is not in any way your land to hold, trespasser. All of this land was given by the Holy See into the sole domain of the Spanish Crown and the Caliphate of Granada. Any other European or Ifriqan not here for the specific purpose of serving Spain or Granada is automatically excommunicated until the day he leave, confess his sins, and perform adequate penance. This is Spanish land and we will defend it from all foreign interlopers who so transgress as to disturb and corrupt the indigenous pagans."

"Disturb and corrupt, huh?" sneered Arsen. "While all you fuckers have in mind is to kill the ones you don't make slaves out of, huh?"

Don Felipe shook his head. "Not so, excommunicant. All that a pagan need do is profess his Christian faith and he becomes free at that moment."

"Free to immediately be returned home?" demanded Arsen.

"Well . . . no, not immediately," answered the knight. "He must be further instructed and straitly questioned to establish that his profession be genuine and not just a prevaricant ploy, that he truly understands his new faith and has unquestionably received a Calling to go back and strive to bring his people from out of the darkness of paganism into the truth and light of Christianity."

"And, of course, the poor fucker is kept in servitude to you cocksuckers meantime, right?" Arsen's tone was scathing.

The Spanish knight shrugged. "Life is hard, my lord. In order that all stay fed, all must perform chores of some sort, from the highest to the lowliest. Such is God's Will."

"Well," Arsen said bluntly, "I'm not an excommunicant because I never was one of your fucking communicants to start out with, see. I'm a Monophysite, not a fucking Roman Catholic, and as far as I'm concerned, buster, your fucking Pope and your motherfucking king and his bunghole buddy in Granada can all go take a flying fuck for all I care about them and how they feel like they own this country lock, stock, and fucking barrel. You just tell your own fucking top dog that I said unless he wants to see a whole fucking lot of dead Spanish and Moors laying around here and feeding the buzzards and the possums, he better had just keep them to hell out of this part of the country. I don't like killing, you understand, but a man's gotta do what the fuck he's gotta do, too."

Mike returned then, and catching Arsen's eye, shook his head significantly. No hostiles out in the woods, then.

"I ain't gonna take all your guns away from you like I done the first time," said Arsen. "Just the swivels is in your boats and all the gunpowder you can't carry with you. You and your men go down now and take enough powder to fill up all of your flasks and all the food and supplies you think you can carry, then you can just start hiking back to the coast, because your fucking boats won't be no good to no fucking body once I'm done with them today. I catch any fucking one of you fuckers around here again, you're dead meat. Get me? You unnerstand, Don Felipe? Well, okay, get going, *now*!"

Leaving Mike Sikeena to oversee the carrying out of his orders by the Spanish, Arsen revisited the island long enough to sink every boat he could see, then sailed back upriver. He had said "walk" and that had been exactly what he had meant. It would be a long, time-consuming walk for the Spaniards, much longer and infinitely harder than had been their trip upriver. "Tough titty for them," he thought. "But if I was their CO, I wouldn't do diddly-squat until my p'trol had got back and been debriefed, so the longer it takes Don Felipe and his sad sacks to drag-ass in, the longer we'll have here to get ready for when they come back up here to try and retake this stretch of river away from us. At least, I got me four new swivel guns out of this deal today."

Ser Timoteo, *il Duce* di Bolgia, had talked with the man that Lieutenant Pasquale di Forio and his mounted axemen had escorted back to Corcaigh from the countryside, he and *Le Chevalier* Marc had chatted, walked, eaten, and ridden with the man. Marc had found him distressingly provincial, very peasantlike, and speaking atrocious Norman French; had it been entirely up to the judgment of the French knight, the yokel would have been thanked for coming, gifted a small purse, and sent back to tend his small herd of scrawny kine.

But Captain-of-foot Timoteo liked the man, Flann Mac Corc Ui Fingen, cowherd, farmer, and hereditary Irish king of Munster. Years spent at interviewing prospective recruits for his condottas had given the condottiere a usually reliable sixth sense about men, common or gentle or noble, and he thought to see definite potential in the blunt, honest, open man of thirty-odd years.

True, he did not speak the archaic Norman French that had been the courtly language here in Munster, while still the Fitz Geralds and their ilk had ruled, but certain remaining palace functionaries had averred to Timoteo and Marc that Flann's command of the Irish tongue was so good as to make him sound almost like a scholar, and he could both read and write that language, as well.

Also true, the man was more than just a little rough around the edges, this Timoteo was perfectly willing to admit to anyone. On the occasion of his first meal at the palace in Corcaigh, Marc had sat in utter silence, appalled at the Irishman's eating habits—which he later, privately, had compared very unfavorably to those of a starvling boar-hog scavenging the high carcass of a stag. On reflection, Timoteo thought the statement at least contained one apt simile, for the man was little more than skin, bones, and sinew, and the presence of so much free food at once might have unhinged him a bit.

After the French knight had gone back to his ship to sleep that night, the condottiere had had the table laid once more and then had given the claimant to the Munster crown a crash course in proper manners at high table. He demonstrated the accepted usages of knife, two-tined skewer, spoon, and panoplino-cloth, lectured him on the necessity of using only two fingers and the thumb of only one hand when not using utensils and of the utter gaucheness of plunging one's hand wrist-deep into a bowl to lift out stewed meat. Bones, he said, must be removed from one's mouth and placed upon the appropriate receptacle, not simply spat out upon the carpet beside one's chair. Before drinking from a common cup— those having two handles—one should always make use of the panoplino to thoroughly clean one's lips and beard of grease and food particles. Should one feel the need to rinse one's mouth, one should call for a page or servant to bring a spittoon, not just swish a mouthful of wine about in one's mouth and spit it out onto the carpet. Small pasties should be knifed into pieces suitable to handling with skewer or spoon, not just picked up and bitten into, leaving grease and juices to run out and down into beard and onto clothing. Also, large chunks or thick slices of meat should be cut into smaller pieces upon the platter or trencher, not stuffed into one's mouth until it would hold no more and then bitten off or sliced off at the teeth.

He had spoken and demonstrated these points while he had eaten, then had had Flann served and had prompted him while he ate. He had found the basically sharp commoner-come(distantly)-of-kings to be a quick study, and when next Marc had shared Timoteo's board with the man, he had remarked to the condottiere that the bumpkin was just possibly able to learn the easier things, now if he could only learn a decent French . . .

The man had arrived at the palace clad just as he had been when the axeman had found him—a torn and faded shirt, old, frayed kilt, and rough hide brogans, with only his hairy shanks between them and the ragged lower hem of the kilt. His long-unshorn hair was matted and as dirty and flea-bitten as the rest of him. The first thing that Timoteo had done was to turn him over to servants along with orders to wash him, shear him, shave him, delouse him, and try to find suitable clothing for a gentleman for him, then burn his rags and the fleas and seam-squirrels to which foul vermin they most assuredly gave lodgments.

The late King Tamhas Fitz Gerald had been a much taller, far beefier man than this Flann Mac Corc Ui Fingen, and only his boots had been a fit, but the clothing of King Sean Fitz Robert—who had been both shorter and a bit slighter in build—could be made to cover the flesh of Flann, though it hung a bit here and there, so emaciated was he, but outside the palace itself, most of the ill-fitting clothing could be and in practice was covered by a wide cloak.

Seeing how quickly the man had begun to learn the complicated customs of the high table, the Italian condottiere set him to a couple of hours each day with the brother of the officer who had sought him out and brought him in. Lieutenant Pandolfo di Forio was a renowned master of the sword, and his function in the condotta had for long been that of giving all of the soldiers at least a close familiarity with the weapon, while honing the skills of the officers to as keen as possible a skill. If nothing else, thought Timoteo, learning the light sword would at least add a bit of grace and balance to the Irishman's posture and movements.

After the first such session, Pandolfo had come back to his captain with a broad smile, despite a swelling bump on the side of his pate, a trace of blood-trickle still in his beard, and a certain stiffness of movement that denoted sore limbs.

"I can see promise in the Irishman, Your Grace. I usually, as Your Grace is aware, try a man first with a weapon of which he has a scintilla of knowledge, and he said that he knew somewhat of the pike and the poleax, but was best with the quarterstave, so that is how I took him on.

"Your Grace, the man's fighting style is completely unorthodox; I've never before seen anyone handle the staff like that. But also he is as fast and elusive as a greased shoat. I've the lumps and the bruises to warrant that, and I can only thank God that I didn't try him with the pike or long-axe, else Your Grace might just now be seeking a new swordmaster for the condotta. I mean to start him on the blunted smallsword on the morrow. Once he's mastered the fundamentals and if Your Grace so desire it, I'll go on with him to the Florentine drill—rapier and left-hand dagger—before essaying to teach him broadsword and buckler."

Timoteo shrugged. "Familiarize the man at least with the broadsword, but I can see no need to go farther. I'm trying to make a presentable gentleman out of him, not a blood-hungry paladin like the late

King Tàmhas and the rest of the inbred, lunatic Fitz Whatevers in this pocket kingdom."

After a month of regular feeding and days that started early and ended late and during almost every hour of which he was being tutored or drilled by someone in something, Flann Mac Corc Ui Fingen had gained weight and was developing muscles in places that a cowherd and farmer usually did not need them. He had not yet reached graduation from the blunted smallsword, but Pandolfo expressed pleasure with his latest pupil's progress nonetheless. The king-to-be ("Possibly," thought Timoteo, sometimes) had at least learned to take a certain amount of pride in his appearance and now washed at least once and, sometimes, twice each week without prompting.

Another month saw him beginning to fill out King Sean Fitz Robert's clothes, spending his few free moments practicing alone or seeking out Pandolfo in order to learn more of the intricate art of the sword-and-dagger fencing. One of the palace functionaries who was tutoring the man in the old dialect of Norman French used at the courts of many of the other Irish kinglets told di Bolgia that the man was at least trying to learn and that, therefore, he had hope that he might, someday, accomplish his task. He still fell off any horse that moved faster than a walk with discouraging frequency, but Timoteo noted with approval that the man did not lack for guts, and each time he fell off, he limped far enough to catch the horse and mount again . . . usually to fall off shortly again, then stubbornly repeat the punishing process. Encouragingly, the condottiere remarked to the Irishman that though all of the gentlemen and nobility learned it at a far younger age, everyone learned to stay on a horse in exactly the selfsame embarrassing, painful way.

The third month saw Flann swinging a thick, wide-bladed broadsword and a round, stout, foot-wide buckler with far more speed and synchronization of movements than Pandolfo often had seen in so new and inexperienced a pupil. The swordmaster could easily penetrate the Irishman's guard four times out of five tries, but his brother, Pasquale, whose expertise with the sword was about average for a professional soldier, proved lucky to do it more than twice out of the same number of attempts.

When he reported this to the captain and Timoteo had been out to watch the pupil and the two brothers at it, di Bolgia asked, "Well, what do you teach him now, swordmaster? Greatsword or shortsword?"

Pandolfo had shaken his head. "Neither, Your Grace, they're not used all that much by gentlemen anymore. No, I think, Your Grace approving, I'll turn him over to Antonio to learn the use of axe, mace, and hammer. That is, unless Your Grace would prefer that he first learn the lance or mounted swordwork."

"No, my good Pandolfo," di Bolgia had said, "he's not yet that accomplished a horseman; he'd like as not fall off his charger halfway down the lists. No, send him to Antonio, or let Pietro show him the finer, nastier points of using dirk or dagger, or do both. You might also get a man of about his size and build to teach him scientific wrestling—never can tell when that might be a useful thing to know, eh?"

"If he keeps up his present level of progress," Timoteo told Marc with unconcealed glee, "we may well have ourselves all three rolled into one—paladin, gentleman, *and* kinglet."

"Perhaps," commented the French knight dryly, then mused, "But who will teach him wisdom and find a cure for his provincial naiveté, my fine, Italian friend?"

The condottiere just shrugged. "Oh, he'll work out well enough, I trow, well enough, that is, for Irland.

The only Irlandesi I have met so far who chanced to not be less than just somewhat provincial and naive has been the High King. As for wisdom, my old friend, that is what royal councils and royal advisers are for, you know."

"Another council, eh?" asked Marc. "And who on this one, besides you? I must serve fair warning to not include me; the papal lease on my ship, *L'Impressionant*, will soon expire, and, strictly in confidence, I must tell you that I already have been in receipt of orders from my sovereign king and lord to sail her elsewhere on another mission for the crown. How you and your men get back to Italy is going to be a matter that you and His Grace the Cardinal D'Este will have to work out between you."

"I'm not including me, either," declared the condottiere, but adding, "Well, at least not for long, just long enough perhaps to see this reign off to an auspicious start."

"Then who?" Marc relentlessly probed. "I doubt if you could rake up any experienced Normans willing to serve a non-Norman-descended king, even if said Norman would be acceptable to you and this Flann. So who will you choose? An aggregation, perhaps, of his fellow country bumpkins?"

"Well, the old monk who started all of this, who first brought Flann Mac Corc Ui Fingen to my attention and told me of his claim to the blood-soaked throne of Munster, Brother Eògan. I've spoken with the old man several times recently and he has agreed to sit on the council; he also has made some suggestions of men to fill other places on that council, when formed. One of these is a man called Mouch Mac Collough who lives up near Cashel and is a *brehav* or expert on the Old Irish laws, which like their genealogies were apparently all memorized since the beginning rather than more logically written out for posterity."

Marc sighed and shook his head, saying, "To expect logic out of the dense head of any Irishman, one would have to expect pigs to sing in Church Latin."

"Brother Eògan says that the Old Irish kings were not expected to know the letter of the law, only to give judgments on the bases of the precedents recited by their *brehav*, you see," said Timoteo. "Then the venerable and learned monk has made some other suggestions for the royal council-to-be, as well. He also has asked that I sit on it for as long as I remain in Munster."

"Naturally, he did," remarked Marc, in a sardonic tone. "Old or not, he knows in just whose hands the real, corporeal power lies in this so-called Kingdom of Munster, so long as you and your condotta are about. And believe me, my friend, they will do all within their power to keep you and your soldiers here to protect them for just as long as possible, so I would not advise making any plans for any imminent voyage back to Italy."

"Ah, well," shrugged Timoteo, "both you and I know well that the royal treasury is well stocked, still, from the days of the late King Tàmhas. If the new king and council want to pay my price for the continued protection of me and my condotta, who am I to say them nay? After all, that's the business we're in, you know. And for the most part, discounting only the revolt of the revolting Fitz Gerald ilk, it has been good, easy, bloodless duty for us all."

Marc smiled mockingly. "And this from the man who a few short months back was crying piteously of how he simply had to find a way in which to take his condotta back to help to flush the Spaniards, the Moors, and their barbaric hirelings from the sacred soil of his own, his native land. Has gold then become in so short a time more precious to you than your duchy, my lord *Duçe* di Bolgia?"

"Not entirely," replied Timoteo. "Not that pure, hard, honest gold has not always been very dear to my heart, as it is to most any man's . . . or woman's, for that matter, especially, to any woman's. But news recently received from oversea leads me to the belief that Emperor Egon is doing a far better job than could I and my small condotta have wreaked to bring peace and order to Italy."

Marc grimaced and clenched his fists until the knuckles shone as white as new-fallen snow. "And at what horrendous cost? Did you also hear that that foul fiend of an emperor has also opened his easternmost marches and allowed hordes of barbarians—blood-mad Kalmyks and their infernal ilk—to pass freely through his lands that they might fall upon eastern France like wolves upon a sheepfold? That was not in any way, shape, or form the action of a God-loving Christian ruler. Why, he is as barbaric as the very pagans themselves."

The condottiere sighed, tiredly. "Marc, my friend, I am very sorry to have to say this truth, but what is just now happening in those afflicted parts of France is your own king's fault, to begin. Something had to be done to rein in the overweening Spanish and Moorish factions, lest all Italy be laid waste by them and their imported barbarians. Yet when Emperor Egon made known his intent to march down there with enough force to end it all, your king let it be known that, immediately the Emperor was gone, he meant to set his army to ravaging parts of the Empire and appropriating a few chunks of it here and there.

"At that point, the Emperor had a hard choice to make: He could either stay in the north with all his forces already assembled and let Italy go to hell, or he could march southwards on his mission of mercy toward Italy and the Church, knowing that without him there to protect them, his vassals were going to be suffering invasion and hard pressed to hold their own from out French hands.

"And it's not as if he didn't give warning of just what he meant to do, would assuredly do, were he pressed hard enough by any other power. If you will but recall, Marc, he used these same Kalmyks to bring old Abdul to heel when His late and unlamented Holiness of Rome was making mumblings about preaching a crusade against the Empire and its then-new Emperor, who he felt showed entirely too much sympathy for England and Wales and their excommunicant king, Arthur.

"Therefore, one cannot but assume that your own monarch must have certainly known that he was playing with fire to offer his threats to Emperor Egon. Experience tells us that those reckless or feckless enough to play with fire frequently precipitate some costly conflagrations and often themselves get burnt, and this is precisely what has occurred in the case of your king, Marc.

"So when you wince at the cost of the pipers, Marc, blame not them so much as you blame the man who called the tune—your own, foolish king."

"If you are so very wise," sneered *Le Chevalier*, coldly, "then why are you not a king, rather than just an expatriate nobleman who fights other men's wars for hire like any commoner tradesman?"

"I did not enjoy hurting you, my friend," said Timoteo, with clear sincerity. "But a man, if he is a man, must face the truth squarely, and that which I have just said to you is nothing less than truth.

"As regards being a king, well, I could easily have

made myself such some two or three times over in my checkered military career, even before I got to this pocket kingdom of Munster. Mine is just now the only strong force of any sort or description in all of the former Fitz Gerald holdings—I could declare myself king and hold these lands until hell froze over, did I so desire."

"Then why don't you, instead of playing at king-maker?" snapped *Le Chevalier*, in the same, cold, hostile tone. "The longer you stay in this land, the more like unto these disgusting Irish you are becoming, anyway. You are even so further debasing yourself as to learn to mouth the pig-grunts they choose to call their language, so it cannot be long until you begin to ape their barbaric culture as well, I fear me.

"You deplore the blood-soaked throne of the kings of Munster, yet I always have believed that, despite your solemnly sworn oaths to the contrary, you, your precious brother, and Ser Ugo D'Orsini somehow contrived to murder King Tàmhas Fitz Gerald to serve your own devious, Italian purposes and to further the schemings of the High King, Brian VIII Ui Neill of Mide. And I cannot but wonder just how long King Sean Fitz Robert would have continued to reign and live had not his own relatives done your killing for you a bit prematurely.

"When first I sailed here with you, your condotta, and the Ifriqan condotta of cavalry, I had been given the impression by His Grace Cardinal D'Este, you, and Ser Ugo that you were being retained and sent here to further first the interests of the Church and second, those of the then king of Munster *against* those of the High King, yet—save for the Ifriqans who chose to remain in faith to their oaths to support the legitimate king of Munster, even to the death—I cannot see where you have served any interests than your own in all the time that you have been here. Before the murder of King Tàmhas, you met clandestinely on at least three occasions with his sworn enemy, the High King, and since that regicide, you have taken to meeting with Brian openly.

"From the moment I landed you here on the docks of Corcaigh, you exerted no slightest effort to abide by the wishes of or even to get along with your erstwhile employers' local representative, Archbishop Gissué di Rezzi; rather, you boldly mocked and cruelly baited the poor, pious, earnest old man repeatedly; and was it not common knowledge that he died in Rome by the hands of members of the Spanish-Moorish Faction lest he be elevated to cardinal. I would deeply suspect that you had a hand in his death, too. Were I not under royal orders to immediately proceed elsewhere once the papal lease on His Majesty's warship be legally expired, I would sail her from Corcaigh directly to Palermo and say to His Grace D'Este precisely what I just have said to you, Your Grace di Bolgia."

Timoteo half-smiled. "Then perhaps I should thank the king of France for making it impossible for you to fill the ears of His Grace D'Este with your ill-conceived conglomeration of baseless assumptions, misunderstood actions, gossip, and out-and-out slander, perhaps, eh?"

"Ser Mac, like far too many Northern Europeans, you and the French nobility live too much in the past, or in what you imagine that past to have been. Most of us Southern Europeans, on the other hand, have become realistic adults who live in the present and plan for the future, recognizing fully that the dead past is truly dead along with all its usages, both the good and the bad, the true and the false, the actual and the fabled. His Grace D'Este is, like me, of the south, and were I you, when once your mission for your king be accomplished, I would sail directly for France and there stay, with your own, antique kind; for are you so unwise as to actually go to Palermo, to His Grace D'Este, with your slanders of me, I can tell you here and now almost exactly what will occur: His Grace will receive you graciously, hear you out to the last syllable, thank you profusely, and probably gift you handsomely . . . then see that you are quietly killed somewhere outside his palace and its immediate environs, lest the poison of your accusations possibly taint some of his own Irish schemes. I tell you this as the friend I thought I was to the friend I had thought you were, Ser Marc, as one, last gesture to friendship past.

"Now, if you please, good day. I have important things yet to do here."

CHAPTER THE NINTH

Sprung of sturdy, Northumbrian Borderer stock, Sir Geoffrey Musgrave, of a cadet branch of that powerful family, had served the House of Whyffler for the most of his sixty-odd years, though in present days he served in the same capacity—that of seneschal and *intendens* of both seat and lands—the Baron of Strathtyne, who also was Earl of Rutland, *Markgraf von* Velegrad, and Duke of Norfolk, Sir Bass Foster, Lord Commander of the Horse for His Royal Majesty, Arthur III Tudor, King of England and Wales.

Because it had always been Sir Geoffrey who had stayed behind to mind the everyday affairs of the lands that had originally been the knight's fee of Sir Francis Whyffler (that personage now being styled Sir Francis Whyffler, Duke of Northumberland and King Arthur's royal ambassador to the court of Egon, Emperor of the Holy Roman Empire, whose Empress was Sir Francis's daughter, Arabella) while Sir Frances and Bass Foster went to war in support of the king, he had come to know quite well her whom he first had known simply as Mistress Krystal Kent, then as the *Markgrafin*

Krystal, and, finally, as Her Grace Lady Krystal, the Duchess of Norfolk.

From the very earliest days, Sir Geoffrey—not yet knighted, then—had moved a little in awe of this woman who, though looking nowhere near to her age that was about half his own, seemed so talented at the arts of healing, was so consummate an organizer, always so gay and lighthearted in even the most trying of circumstances and seldom lacking for a jocular word to help dispel the gloom of hard times or unexpected reverses. As a younger son, come of a long line of younger sons, the stark, grey-haired warrior—who was little-traveled and most unsophisticated—had always most highly valued the friendship so freely proffered by the warm and outgoing Krystal Kent, but, cognizant as he always was of his lowly status, if the aging widower lusted after the striking woman, he did so only in his heart, unconsciously, for he never would do or even allow himself to think aught dishonorable.

Geoffrey had had great respect for Bass Foster, of course, even before that man had become his legal lord, overlord, and employer. If he had secretly envied the younger man's wedded possession of Krystal, he had valiantly thrust such impure and honorless thoughts—likely sent by some Imp of Hell to test his faith—away from him and had truly rejoiced at the birth of young Joseph Foster, as much as he had sincerely rejoiced in the knighting and progressive advancements of Sir Bass and Lady Krystal over the years.

But it all seemed to have come so fast. He had but barely gotten accustomed to the Marchioness of Velegrad title when a knight-herald of Arabian antecedents had come riding into Whyffler Hall leading a troop of fearsome Hebridean gallowglasses to announce that Sir Bass now was become Duke of Norfolk, Earl of Rutland, and Baron of Strathtyne (with the seat of said barony at Whyffler Hall) in addition to still holding his foreign, Empire title. Not only that, but the Arab had, on the express orders of his master, bade plain, humble Geoffrey Musgrave to his knees before him and laid upon him the buffet of knighthood—which accolade had been a something that poor Geoffrey had never expected and still was sometimes uncertain he really deserved or even wanted, though to his credit he considered it to be the wish of his liege lord, so bore the trappings of knighthood stoically and conducted himself in the honorable manner he always had, thus actually practicing a code of chivalry to which most other knights only gave lip service.

The old knight knew well that she who now was his liege lady keenly missed the companionship of Sir Bass. She had spoken of it all right often, and he always had tried in his humble way to dwell upon the necessary services that were required by His Majesty of his nobility in all times, but most especially in times of internal war and general turmoil such as these years of late. However, nothing that he ever had said to her seemed to have helped her at all to bear her separation from her husband and lord resignedly as did most women in her position.

That had been the beginning, he knew, that inability for her to simply bear what must be borne, to come to realize that her suffering was just another facet of the awesome, crushing load of responsibility that always attended the possession of high civil or military rank. She had dwelt too long, too hard, too unceasingly upon her loneliness for Sir Bass, had seemed to come to truly believe that he stayed in the south by choice, not bothering apparently to reason that, as the south was where the Royal Horse of which he was Lord

Commander was posted by king's order, her husband had no choice but to bide there near to his troops.

He had sighed as his liege lady kept post-riders virtually glued into their saddles as she penned and sent off letter after letter, each of them more carping and vituperative than its predecessors, to Archbishop Harold, Peter Fairley, Captain Buddy Webster, *Reichsherzog* Wolfgang, His Majesty, Sir Ali ibn Hussein, Carey Carr, and Sir Bass in patiently foredoomed attempts to force her husband to return to and stay permanently at Whyffler Hall. Her initial complaint was that she "had no one about to talk to," and that had been when Sir Geoffrey first had begun to suspect that her reason was becoming unbalanced, for in addition to the two Northumbrian knights' widows in attendance upon her, there were her flock of humbler maidservants, himself, chamberlain Henny Turnbull, the officers of the much-reduced royal artillery garrison still then lodged at Whyffler Hall, Father Edelbert Percy, the officers of the Strathtyne Lances, Sir Feach Mac Murrogh (who commanded her personal guard of gallowglasses), and scores of other servants and humble folk who would have been pleased and deeply honored to converse with the wife of their new baron.

Then, for some reason he never had been able to fathom, she had moved her entire household to the castle that was the accustomed seat of the Earls of Rutland. Not long after, she had sent back her two widow-lady attendants and all of her maids, women who had been with and served her almost since she first had come to Whyffler Hall with him who would become her husband. She herself, however, had not remained as much as six months at Rutland. She had come back in the very dead of winter, draft beasts and a few men had died in getting her and her household back to Strathtyne with her son and her new flock of servants and lady attendants.

The new servants had all been folk of the south or the east or the west; all had felt themselves far superior to the Northumbrians and Borderers and had made no bones about it, putting on airs and constantly criticizing North Country ways, mocking Borderer speech and poking malicious fun at the habits and traditions of the folk of Whyffler Hall and the rest of the barony. Sir Geoffrey had had to be quite harsh in order to prevent physical punishment being wrought upon the flesh and bone of many of these newcome servants by persons who had been given great instigation. He had hated having to do this, for he had not cared at all for the newcomers himself, but they had been hers, the Lady Krystal's, and he had felt that he must protect them as he protected her to the very best of his ability.

The chatelaine's new ladies had been, if anything, even worse, in Sir Geoffrey's keen estimation. All save two were landless widows—in the wake of so many years of fighting in England, the kingdom lay virtually awash with widows, it seemed—and these two, older gentlewomen, were dowerless spinsters, their respective families' fluid wealth having been all dissipated during the war years and the lands having been rendered by resultant circumstances too poor to provide dots and, thereby, husbands for them.

Quite willing and able to do or say anything, no matter how dishonest or dishonorable, in order to retain the sponsorship and security which their current positions assured them, Sir Geoffrey believed, the coterie of gentleborn harpies had done no real slightest service to their mistress, but rather had done no less than actively abet her descent into madness. They never had disagreed with her, not even obliquely.

Instead of performing their true function of gently guiding her in her proper dealings with all strata of society, lending her full support when she was right and gently or jocularly chiding her when she was wrong, they had instead not only publicly approved her every action, no matter how outrageous, how beyond the bounds of courtesy, honor, or decency, but had gone so far as to encourage her to think thoughts and do things that went far past the mere contumelious.

He had himself heard the terrible sextet instigate the duchess to pen letters to Archbishop Harold of York, divers court functionaries, senior officers of the royal army, and even to His Majesty himself that would have caused her husband great difficulties at the very least, had the faithful knight allowed them to ever get out of the barony. As the duchess had gone farther and ever farther into her clear madness, Sir Geoffrey had silently mourned the sweet, kind, friendly woman who had been, but known that there was nothing that he could do to bring her back.

He had, for this reason, been greatly relieved when she had gone down to lodge with her household on the estate of the archbishop of York. Those of her alien servants who had not gone there with her had, without her presence and status to protect them, quickly found Whyffler Hall, the Barony of Strathtyne, indeed, the whole of the borderlands, so unsalubrious to their health and well-being that they could not but quit their service and return to where they had come from, right speedily too, most of them.

After the word had come up to Strathtyne about the regrettable necessity of placing the mad duchess in the care of a nursing order, the two spinsters had made an appearance, apparently expecting to be lodged, fed, and otherwise maintained in perpetuity. After thinking hard on the matter for the month it took his letter to reach His Grace, and the Archbishop of York's reply to come back, Sir Geoffrey had gone to the spinsters and offered them some choices. One was a promise to quickly find them both husbands among the yeomanry or, possibly, among the lesser gentry of Strathtyne or one of the neighboring baronies, perhaps English, perhaps Scots. One was to provide them work under the supervision of the chamberlain of the hall, Henny Turnbull, that they might have the opportunity to earn their keep. One was to convey them to any of several North Country convents, that there they might either take the veil or make other arrangements with the superior. The last was that he see them suitably transported back to York and the disposition of the Archbishop.

When he turned a deaf ear to their protestations that, as Her Grace of Norfolk had repeatedly assured them that they owned a lifetime sinecure of her and her service, it was his bounden duty to keep them at the hall in the style to which they were accustomed so long as they lived and with no common toil or labor expected of them, they had at last and grudgingly agreed to meet with some of the prospective bridegrooms.

Sir Geoffrey had then sent off a galloper with a letter to his friend Sir Michael Scott, laird of that ilk, and presently that worthy had appeared at Whyffler Hall with his servants, mounted gillies, and four widowers, all of the clan's petty gentry. The Scotts had not been long at Whyffler Hall when both spinsters had sought out the seneschal, importuning him to afford them both speedy transport back to York. However, before he would agree, he wrung from them formal, written, well-witnessed documents of voluntary and willing withdrawal from the service of Her Grace of Norfolk. On the eve of their departures, he had their effects searched, and upon finding a multitude of items stolen from the hall among them, he had the two women—gentleborn or no—stripped and striped for the thieves they had proved themselves to be, before sending them on their way.

When first the Archbishop Harold's knight, Sir Rupen Ademian, had come up to Strathtyne to see what had once been the master suite for the old tower cleaned, renovated, and partially rebuilt in order to house the mad duchess and the nursing sisters who would bide with and care for her, Sir Geoffrey had not known whether to rejoice or worry at the possible return of all of the old problems which had attended her last tenure at the hall. Therefore, he had done both.

The letter borne up to Sir Geoffrey by Sir Rupen from the Archbishop had specified that although he was to remain seneschal and *intendens* of His Grace of Norfolk in all mundane matters, just as he always had been, Sir Geoffrey was to recognize that it was to be upon Sir Rupen that the full and unfettered responsibility for the care and welfare of Her Grace was to fall. He was to render Sir Rupen his fullest cooperation, see that his needs and desires were accommodated, and not question any of his decisions in regard to his charges—the duchess and her nurses. The letter had gone on to point out that as she was incontrovertibly mad, orders or requests that came directly from her rather than through her nurses or Sir Rupen were to be invariably disregarded or ignored, especially as regarded demands that she be allowed elsewhere in the tower, the main hall, or upon the grounds unaccompanied by at least one of the sisters.

Still picturing her to himself as she for so long had been, Sir Geoffrey had found it difficult to believe that the frail, sickly, terribly emaciated woman lifted from out the coach and set upon her feet to shufflingly hobble into the hall possibly could be Her Grace, the Lady Krystal Foster, Duchess of Norfolk. Her cheeks were sunken, her eyes dark-ringed and fever-bright, and the hands that he recalled as slim and graceful now resembled nothing so much as the bony claws of some old hag of a beggarwoman, grimy on palms and backs, the nails all cracked and encrusted with filth. Once, when her wimple slipped almost completely off, he could see that much of her ravens-wing-black hair had fallen out, while what remained growing amid the sores and oozing scabs was dull, lifeless, and greying.

She had not acknowledged the greetings of Sir Geoffrey, Henny Turnbull, and other senior members of the hall staff, not even those of the only two of her former maids that the seneschal had been able to hire back. She had just shuffled along where she was guided through chambers and corridors of the main building toward the west wing which had been built onto the ancient tower. Slowly moving, she had said no single word, her expression never had changed . . . until, entering still another chamber, she had confronted a tall, framed mirror, when she had stopped stock-still, staring at the horrible apparition that gazed back at her.

After a moment, she had raised both clenched fists and her ravaged face toward heaven and shrieked, "*OH, God damn you, Bass Foster! You motherfucker, just look what you've done to me!*" Then, screaming unintelligible noises, she had whirled, lifted from its place a solid, heavy chain, and hurled it smashingly into the mirror. That done, still screaming, she had attacked the two sisters like some savage beast and had not slackened until Sir Rupen had stepped in and struck her senseless with his fist. Then he and the somewhat battered nursing nuns had borne her hurriedly through the rest of the hall, up the tower stairs, and into the suite above.

Shaken to his very core by the horrible episode, Sir Geoffrey had somehow managed to get through his various duties for the rest of the day and early evening. That night, in his spartan chamber, he had prayed long and earnestly on his knees before his prie-dieu. Not until he was lying in his bed had he allowed the hot tears to come, to be absorbed by the same pillow which muffled his wrenching sobs.

More than merely familiar with the incredibly labyrinthine manner in which the courts of high churchmen were always operated, Ser Ugo D'Orsini easily weathered the endless delays, readily applied just the proper amounts of golden grease to the succession of greedy palms, and weathered the probing interrogations of the secretaries, armed guards, self-appointed watchdogs, and confidants of Harold, Archbishop of York, with a serene good grace surprising to many of those same interrogators. When asked about this by some of them, he replied simply that he had been them, he would not have trusted a papal knight either, not any farther than he could throw a large destrier. However, despite all that was said to him, from sweetly phrased importunings to near-threats, he had refused stoutly to surrender the impressively sealed letters to any save the man to whom they were addressed, the man he had come to England to see, the Archbishop of York, Harold Kenmore.

At length, however, after much expense and many trials, his dogged persistence triumphed and he was granted audience by the Archbishop. Knowing full well that he was being closely watched, Ser Ugo spent his time between the announcement and the date of the actual meeting innocently enough. He hired on a local who spoke decent French and specialized in such as showing significant points and areas of Yorkminster and the secular city of York to those interested; that took most of a week, moving at a slow, unhurried pace. Then he sought out the knight who ran the Royal Cannon Foundry, Sir Peter Fairley, introduced himself as an Italian knight, and indicated his desire to obtain a brace of the lightweight pocket pistols newly developed by the justly famous gentleman-inventor.

Sir Peter lifted a box from a shelf and bore it over to his incredibly cluttered work table. Reseating himself, the Englishman opened the box and took from it a handgun with graceful, pleasing lines; its grips were of a dark, polished wood, but they were the only wood upon the weapon. The ignition system was a reduced-size flintlock. The trigger folded up into a groove and only fell to the usual position of triggers when the flint-holder was brought to a position of full cock. The barrel—of about twenty bore, Ser Ugo estimated—was of gunmetal and looked exactly like a model of a cannon's tube—complete with the expected reinforces and muzzle swell and even including a carved wooden tompion to seal the bore.

Moving his work-stained fingers with no wasted motion, Sir Peter competently disassembled the compact weapon to show its features to Ser Ugo, hampered in his demonstration, however, by Ser Ugo's less than perfect command of English and his own quite atrocious mastery of French. Finally, he had called in one of the craftsmen recently hired, a wandering Genoan, to translate.

Later, in the inn room where he resided, Ugo had taken his new weapons from out their fitted, fruitwood case to disassemble and reassemble them himself, before finally loading and priming them, then replacing them in their case and locking the case in one of his chests. He was impressed with the quality of the workmanship, of course, but even more so by the new-type lock, one which would never need the time-consuming process of spanning in a tight spot. Even more impressive were the bronze barrels that could be preloaded, attached to the frame with three short twists of the wrist, leaving one with only the momentary task of priming, cocking, and firing; moreover, no less than four barrels were provided for the two pistols, and a special hollow in the wooden butts held a fresh flint in case the ones in the cocks' jaws should shatter unexpectedly. Sir Peter had assured him that parts of one pistol would fit the other and then proved that statement. Ser Ugo, some ounces of gold poorer, felt the money very well spent and now was distinctly admiring of the English Royal Cannon Foundry and the multitalented gentleman who commanded it.

With still more days remaining before his audience and the men set to spy upon his movement having, by now, become familiar if often shadowy figures, Ser Ugo repaired once more to Yorkminster, where he asked directions and, for a mere bit of silver, soon arrived at the library placed hard by the scriptorium. He tried his French on the monk tending the library, but the reply was in such abominable French that he switched to Latin. After he had identified himself and, upon inquiry, modestly admitted his relationship—that of great-great-grandnephew—to the noted religious and philosophical writer Fra Placido Pietro D'Orsini, then spent a full hour listening to fulsome praise of his long-deceased, distant relative, the keeper of the tomes became much more friendly and gladly fetched him the references he sought.

Three days of reading the yellowed, handwritten pages gave him pause to wonder if perhaps the man he was so shortly to see was not really as old as some persons seemed to think and Cardinals D'Este and Sicola firmly disbelieved, modern realists that they were. Of course, his own basically realistic mind insisted, who was to say that—what with all of the vicissitudes of the intervening times, the plagues, the wars, the copyings and recopyings that had taken place over the past time—some records had not been lost, others mistranscribed or deliberately altered for divers reasons that no one now living would ever know or understand. Nonetheless . . . ?

According to the oldest of the records, dating from the reign of the very first of the kings of the Tudor dynasty in England, one Harold Kenmore, Gentleman, had taken some part in the defeat of the Balderites, first relieving the siege of some castle up on the northern border, then taking part in the combined English and Scottish effort that drove the heretical fanatics back and back until they had the poor choice of dying by steel, drowning in the cold sea, or surrendering to face mutilation and the stake. Following the end of the Balderites, the name of Harold Kenmore, Gentleman, had disappeared from the records for around fifteen years, then a Harold Kenmore—the various records here conflicted; one said that this man was a member of the Goldsmiths' Guild, but others named him a churchman, though they could not seem to agree whether he was a priest, a monk, or a monsignor—was brought to the court of King Henry VII Tudor by a relative—again, the records differed, some saying that this man had been a roving Irish warlock and suspected druid, another identifying him as the then High King's father-in-law and the developer of the world-famous Tara Steel, still another averring him to be an English or possibly Scottish adventurer, son-in-law of the High King and an ambassador from Tara to London—of the present *Ard-Righ*'s father, Brian of the Bloody Blades. There, this Harold Kenmore—priest, goldsmith, or whatever—had miraculously cured the lad who became King Arthur II Tudor, the present king's grandfather, of some wasting disease that had all but killed him and utterly baffled every other leech brought to treat him.

The next mention of a Harold Kenmore had been two notes of a Court Alchemist, one Monsignor Harold Kenmore. At some time after that, a Monsignor Harold Kenmore was installed Archbishop of York, this last during the last years of the reign of Henry VII Tudor, to fill one of the numerous vacancies wrought by the arrival in England of the Priests' Plague. But after that, though some gaps existed here and there, the record seemed to be unbroken; no one else seemed to have been installed in the Archbishopric of York for well over a whole century to the present. This was where the mind boggled, for if the records were accurate, if the missing ones followed the course of those available, no other conclusion could be drawn save that the man Ser Ugo would so very soon see in audience was at least more than two centuries old!

Ser Ugo D'Orsini burned to pen and dispatch a long letter which would detail his findings to Cardinal D'Este immediately, but at the same time he knew that to do such with any relative certainty that the missive would reach the prelate at his seat in Palermo, it would have to be sent from Ireland, not England. His head whirling madly with thoughts of all he had read and the suppositions that reading of the records had aroused within his quick mind, he slept precious little on the night preceding his audience with Harold, Archbishop of York.

After being most thoroughly, though most courteously, searched for weapons or anything resembling such, the Roman was ushered through an anteroom in which sat and stood more than a score of armed and armored guards, their polearms leaning against the walls within easy reach, their relaxed awareness stamping them as the veterans or professionals they most surely were.

After passing through doors guarded on both sides by halberdiers, he was escorted into a smaller anteroom in which sat a cassocked priest and two armored men who looked like officers and were each armed with sword, dirk, and a brace of two-foot-long dags of between ten and eight bore. Flanking the doors opposite those by which he had entered were another four halberdiers and two calivermen, the flaring muzzles of their weapons looking quite big enough to easily accommodate Ser Ugo's fist.

After another searching of his person and the *cour bouilli* letter case he bore with him, his escort dropped behind and the cassocked priest strode before him to the doors and nodded to the guards, who flung wide the portals.

"Your Grace, now comes Ser Ugo D'Orsini bearing certain letters from the Italian Faction of the Roman Papacy," the priest announced loudly, then stepped aside that Ser Ugo might enter the chamber beyond.

As he entered, Ser Ugo was quite relieved that, despite the probing searches, no one had discovered the cunningly concealed compartment of the letter case which contained his patron's letter of last resort, the one which was never to have ever been, hopefully. It reposed unsuspected still tightly rolled within a *cour bouilli* tube that had, as the ostensible handle of the case, passed all scrutiny.

The prelate who sat in a cathedra against the far wall of the audience room did not give Ser Ugo the appearance of impossible age. Although his hair and beard were white and his face and finely kept hands both wrinkled and age-spotted, there looked to still be muscle on the tall, slender frame, and when he knelt to kiss the extended ring, he could feel strength in the fingers. The blue eyes were penetrating, and when he spoke, the voice was strong, rich-toned.

"So, Ser Ugo," said the Archbishop in rusty but easily understood Roman dialect, "you come from the Italian Faction, eh? Which one of the cardinals sent you, Prospero Sicola or Bartolomeo D'Este?"

"Both of them, actually, Your Grace," replied Ser Ugo, "but my official patron is Cardinal D'Este, Archbishop of Palermo. He prepared the letter I bear for Your Grace, but both he and Cardinal Sicola, Your Grace will note, signed and sealed it."

So saying, he took from the case the wax-sealed letter and diffidently proffered it, but a wave of the Archbishop's hand directed it to the burly, cassocked man who stood close beside his side. With a sharp knife, the functionary broke the wax and opened the vellum wrappings, then unfolded the ornate, beribboned letter and, careful to not look at the contents, handed it to his master.

When he had read most of the first page, the prelate turned to the equally burly cassocked man who stood at his other side and said, "Brother Cuthbert, please bring over a chair for Ser Ugo and have wine fetched for us all."

Reading, sipping wine, and occasionally throwing a look at Ser Ugo that could have meant much or nothing at all, the prelate finished the letter, carefully scrutinized the seals with a lens, then turned the sheet over and used the lens again, seeking to determine if another seal might once have been in their places. Satisfied, apparently, he then reread the entire lengthy missive from start to finish. Carefully folding the sheets, he handed them to the man who had opened the letter. Then he bespoke Ser Ugo.

"Close on a year has passed since the date on this letter, Ser Ugo. How is one to know that the press of affairs has not wrought changes in the sentiments herein expressed?"

Ugo nodded and set down his goblet. "Your Grace's understandable doubts and qualms were anticipated by my patron. I have here in my case a second letter prepared by him only two months past." He handed the second vellum package to the man with the letter-knife.

When he had read through the second and given the same more than thorough examination to its seals, this time comparing them and their signatures to the first letter's, he spoke again.

"Ser Ugo, these are weighty matters and they will require very much thought, ere I can even start to frame answers to the quite unexpected things offered by your patron and the others. Where are you lodged in York?"

"In a hostelry called the Sign of the Black Horse, in High Street, Your Grace," answered the knight.

"Well, I'll be wanting you much closer to Yorkminster than that, Ser Ugo, much closer indeed, that I may question you at length and at odd hours." He turned to the cleric called Cuthbert and ordered, "Brother, please see to it that accommodations appropriate to a noble envoy are prepared for Ser Ugo and his following, immediately. Send porters and guards to move his effects from his hostelry to his new suite and pay the demands of the hostler."

"Please, Your Grace," protested Ser Ugo, "my patron supplied me with quite adequate funds, and my squires and servants can easily shift my possessions . . ."

The prelate shushed him with a wave of a hand. "I

am certain that you were well provided for by Bartolomeo D'Este, Ser Ugo—it is averred that he is rich as Croesus. Also, however, knowing the unfortunate proclivities of that pack of unhung thieves who arrange my audiences, I am more than sure that you had to lay out more than just a few full ounces of gold, ere you at last entered this chamber, so allow me to reimburse at least a fraction of that expense."

"What can I do save humbly thank Your Grace?" asked Ugo.

The Archbishop grinned. "Tell me how you liked your tour of our Royal Cannon Foundry and the new small arms that Sir Peter Fairley showed you."

He held up his hand as Ser Ugo opened his mouth to speak in reply and said, "But not now—after all, I do have other suppliants waiting, all of whom most likely paid almost as much as did you for their audiences. No, you'll dine with me this day and tell me your impressions of the foundry and the weapons then."

CHAPTER THE TENTH

Tight-drawn were the siege lines around the landward sides of the walled city of Gaillminh, seat of the kings of Connachta, while on the waters that lay just beyond, the interdicting ships prowled like hungry sea-beasts. But the besiegers were themselves being besieged after a fashion, and strong defenses of mounding, ditching, and palisades had had to be erected all around their position to protect them from the Connachta forces not bottled up within the city.

Just below the crest of a rocky hill that lay just out of easy cannon shot of the impressive city defenses stood two of the *Ard-Righ*'s officers, pointing out to Sir Bass Foster the directions from which most of the raids and attacks from out the surrounding countryside seemed to come.

Sir Máel Mac Gréachain, one of Brian the Burly's barons and overall commander of his army in Connachta, handed his brass-cased long-glass to the English condottiere, saying, "If Your Grace will peer off there to the northeast, he will note a hill on which are the grown-over remains of a ring-fort of elder ages. At its north foot, not to be seen from here, lies a gap between it and the long ridge of which Your Grace can see only the steep, westernmost descent. Right many an attack of recent nights has come from out that gap.

"The buggers sneak out of there, quiet as a fox stalking a hen, drop visible sentries with crossbows, and no one knows that they're about until they've scaled the palisade and begun to fire stores or spike guns or murder men in their sleep. Then they flee before any organized force can be set upon them. Cowardly pigs!"

"And on yet other occasions," put in the other officer, another of the *Ard-Righ*'s fighting barons, Sir Cellach Ui Domnaill, "they'll come boiling out of that gap in bright moonlight, roaring slogans and warcries, and while a force is being gathered to repel them, they will only shower down some arrows, loose off a few quarrels and handguns, then retreat as fast as they charged while another band that had moved in from another quarter in full silence strikes devastatingly against an unprotected part of our lines. Spineless assassin cowards, all of them."

Privately, though he of course did not voice the opinion, Bass thought that whoever was organizing and coordinating the hit-and-run night attacks was showing admirable qualities for this backward land and its intemperate inhabitants. For an outnumbered, ill-armed, and most likely ill-supplied force of men, such tactics were the only intelligent way to strike at the entrenched enemy and hope to live to strike again on another night.

What he actually asked was, "Surely, as large as is your force here available, you might have searched out the bases of these irregulars. Light cavalry or even infantry mounted on mules should have been adequate to the job, gentlemen."

Sir Cellach snarled wordlessly, while Sir Máel sighed and said, "Your Grace, we *had*"—he emphasized the use of the past tense—"two squadrons of light cavalry, one of lancers—raised by Sir Cellach, here, out of his own lands and ilk—and one of *galloglaiches*, and between them they razed every village and homesteading for eight leagues and more in an arc outward from our lines without ever finding so much as a bare trace of the cravens we seek; the places none of them contained any men at all of a fighting age or condition, all of the inhabitants being women, children, old men, and a few cripples. Some few of them were brought back here, and I can state that not even under the severest of tortures would they admit to their menfolk being members of these cowardly raiders, insisting even in the extremes of their agonies that all of their men and boys were pent up in Gaillminh with the royal army."

"You stressed your onetime possession of cavalry, Sir Máel," inquired Bass. "Has it been detached, seconded to another area, perhaps?"

Sir Cellach began, then, to curse and blaspheme sulphurously, while Sir Máel just sighed more deeply and shook his head, his scarred face under the rim of his old-fashioned conical helmet mirroring his dejection and frustration.

"Your Grace, when the *galloglaiches* squadron heard the rumor of the *Ard-Righ* readying his forces to mount an invasion of Islay, of the lands of Regulus, they deserted, en masse, and I have reason to believe that they are fighting with the Connachta forces. The forsworn Scottish pig-turds!

"As regards poor Sir Cellach's lancers, alas, with the mounted *galloglaiches* decamped and so much territory to cover, we decided to break the squadron into troops and reinforce them with some mule-mounted light infantry. This was clearly a mistake, for at various times and places, every one of those units has been set upon from ambush and either wiped out entirely or so decimated in strength as to be useless for aught serve camp-perimeter guards.

"So now we own no cavalry save the heavy, which we must save, hold back, in case the craven Connachtas yonder retrieve their misplaced manhood and elect to march out and fight us breast to breast as real men always do."

Bass reflected then that the High King might be progressive and of a modern military bent, but his senior officers assuredly were not. In Sir Máel's most recently spoken words he had branded himself the typical fire-eating, blood-hungry and stupid mediaeval warrior. He was be-deedouble-damned if he would place himself and his men under the command of this man or any others of his archaic breed.

"Sir Máel," he said finally, "I must tell you that, in the event of my report to *Ard-Righ* Brian does result in my condotta being posted here, to Connachta, it will be as an independent command, a completely independent command, no part of your army in any way, saving only perhaps that of supply and remount. That must be understood and accepted at the outset. Is this agreeable to you, sir?"

The overall commander sighed yet again and replied glumly, "Hell, what choice have I, Your Grace? Given a few more weeks of the infernal night-raiding of these cowardly Connachtas and all of my army will consist of men who sit wakeful all night, every night, then stagger about all day, every day, near useless for any purpose.

"Therefore, all right, I agree to Your Grace's terms, although I must most vociferously object on the grounds that, as supreme captain of His High Majesty's Connachta force, I should of rights be in direct charge of each and every one of the units involved therein. *Ard-Righ* Brian is still my monarch, however, and as ever I will follow the orders of my most puissant lord."

There were few words exchanged between Bass and the two barons on the tramp back to where they had left their horses and escorts, nor after that on the ride back to Sir Máel's headquarters area.

Not until they were ridden out well beyond any possible pickets did Bass say aught to his own officers, then he turned in his saddle and waved up *Reichsherzog* Wolfgang, *Barón* Melchoro, Sir Ali, Don Diego, Sir Colum, and Sir Liam to crowd as close to him as his Kalmyk bodyguards, Nugei and Yueh, would permit.

The hulking Wolfgang, uncle of the Holy Roman Emperor, onetime in-law of King Arthur III Tudor, and Bass's overlord for the Mark of Velegrad, was first to speak—for, although he had chosen to serve in a subordinate capacity in Ireland, his civil rank was actually a bit higher than Bass's dukedom. "*Ach*, Bass, the High King ill-served iss by those nobleborn *Lumpen*. Until *Hölle* solid ice becomes, sit there they can without that city to fall they make it. Far too rocky for sapping is the ground about the walls, more sweet *Wasser* than efer they will, haf they, and the High Kink's fleet so very inefficient iss that food und arms und reinforcements almost efery day to reach them do. *Und* the *grösser* guns so far from the walls are emplaced that the balls little force have left when to reach the target they finally do, and often to fall short they do to utter vaste of powder. Pfagh, were such incompetents mine to command, not long their thick heads would they keep on their shoulders. *Ja*!"

Grimacing, Bass nodded. "For his time, that is, the time in which he seems to think he is living—roughly, the thirteenth century—Sir Máel, Baron Ardee, is a progressive officer. His chief complaints seem to be two of the most stupid I ever have heard. He is most upset it seems because the outnumbered garrison of the city back there will not sally out and commit suicide by fighting his force 'breast to breast, as real men should.' The pompous, posturing ass! And that other remnant of the Dark Ages, Sir Cellach, Baron Delvin, is no better and possibly worse. After having razed villages for at least twenty miles out from their siege lines—looting, burning, raping, torturing, killing, the whole nine yards of atrocities—they began sending out impossibly small mixed units of lancers and mounted light infantry and seem to be deeply offended that all of said units met with bad ends out there.

"That's why the dumb bugtits want us, to prevent the irregulars from the countryside attacking the siege lines of nights, killing men, stealing weapons and supplies and disturbing the sleep of dunder-headed noble officers. My principal bit of advice to Brian is going to be that he get his original supreme commander, Count Ardgal, back here before the archaic codes of these two barons lead them to do something disastrous, like staging a full-scale assault on that city's walls and losing, thereby, half or better of the army."

Barón Melchoro—who, before inheriting his father's barony in Portugal, had experienced some years as a roving gentleman-mercenary sword on three continents—spoke up informally, as befitted his status of old friend, ofttimes battle companion, and sometime mentor of a man not born a noble. "Friend Bass, no matter what this High King avows his motives in besieging this city of Gaillminh—the high-royal personage avers only to receive from the King of Connachta his Symbol of Sovereignty, then to join his forces with those of the High King in peace and love and brotherhood—every officer and man with whom I spoke in all that siege camp is expecting and eagerly anticipating, when once the city does fall or capitulate, a full and completely untrammeled intaking, a sack of the fullest nature. The officers all aver that this very thing has ofttimes been promised them, solemnly assured as reward to them, by this one who affects that antique, open-faced helmet, Sir Máel. One therefore is given pause to wonder if his monarch knows of these bloody-minded promises."

"Gentlemen," commented Bass slowly, his face set in a worried frown, "I wonder much of late about the verity of anything this High King says or has said, to me or to others; so very devious is he that it may well be he is deceiving his cousin, my king, as well, as to his true motives for prosecuting this warfare against every ruler on this island who refuses to bend the knee and render up his treasures on command.

"He swears to Arthur that he only seeks to be the kind of king of Ireland as Arthur is of all England and Wales, yet he must know that the best he ever can accomplish here, do what he will, is to become the kind of king that James of Scotland is. England, at least, owns a long history of unity under one strong monarch, while neither Ireland nor Scotland does.

"Within the last hundred years, there were eleven kingdoms vying with each other on this one smallish island, those, plus the little domain of the High King; now there are eight, including the much-expanded domain of Brian, but I am reliably informed that there almost never have been less than five kings here, and seldom has the High King been the greatest of those. So even if Brian temporarily succeeds in his grandiose schemings, just how long will it be before some client king, impatient at the strictures Brian lays down, goes about expelling or killing the High King's men and takes back his lands for him and his people? And who is to say that, even if all the client-kings stay in line, some count or baron or clan chief will not take it into his head to start carving out a new kingdom off pieces of older ones, as not a few of his forebears have done for time immemorial?

"A part of the reason that King Arthur sent us here, as you all know, was to help his dear cousin in holding Ireland against some possible assault by agents of Rome, yet since the demise of Pope Abdul I've seen precious few indications that Brian is making any slightest preparations to do battle of any kind with forces of Rome. Indeed, he has, since his private conversations with a certain papal knight said to be a courier for one of the Roman papal factions, been most reticent to allow any of the higher-ranking Irish clergy to return to take part in the negotiations proceeding at Yorkminster. This leads me to believe that His High Majesty has been in some manner bought back by Rome, so that here we are, in effect, serving the enemy rather than a friendly relative of King Arthur."

"Yes, Your Grace," agreed Sir Colum, Senior Captain of Bass's squadron of *galloglaiches*, "the *Ard-Righ* has changed mightily in late years. I recall that ere the squadron was sent to England, our then chief, Sir Turlogh de Burgh, Baron Lune, and I waited upon the *Ard-Righ*. His High Majesty then was frothing with blood-thirsting rage at Rome and everyone connected therewith. These days, however, right many of those he then had had clapped into fetters and cells are restored to their places and their offices as if never those letters that threatened excommunication of the *Ard-Righ*, full interdiction of every soul loyal to him and a crusade to be preached against Ireland, had ever been writ. When last I visited Sir Turlogh on his barony, I remarked upon it all, and he, too, finds it passing strange."

"And how bides the valiant Sir Turlogh?" inquired Sir Ali.

Sir Colum sighed and shook his head sadly. "*Och*, when that domned Spanisher's mace crumpled the baron's knee-cop and crushed the knee beneath, 'twere a fell stroke. That leg has healed up as stiff as a plank; poor Sir Turlogh no longer can sit a horse at any speed in safety, and so he is running much to fat. He is not at all happy, of course, being almost bound to his seat as he is, but otherwise he is well and healthy. He still talks of that last of his many battles, though, tells any who will listen that they should not think that the last of the English paladins died with the old Norman line, for he has seen a modern-day English paladin fight. Then he always tells of the Battle of Bloody Rye."

Bass had but just opened his mouth to speak again when the first shot rang out up ahead, followed by another, then a ragged fusillade, before a blacksmith chorus of steel ringing and clashing upon steel began to sound. A single rider appeared at the crest of the hill ahead, then descended the steep grade toward the head of the column. As he neared, it could be seen that he was one of the *Reichsherzog*'s Kalmyks, crouched low over the neck of his big-headed steppe pony, his heels drumming at the dull dun barrel, his whip lashing at the straining flanks.

Then the well-oiled machine that was the Duke of Norfolk's condotta sprang abruptly to full life and began to function as smoothly as ever. The pack train came forward at the gallop and squires unloaded the wherewithal to quickly begin to arm their respective lords and themselves. Once fully accoutered, knights mounted their high horses—battle-trained destriers big and strong enough to bear fully armed men at a fair speed for the time it might take to make contact with the enemy ahead—while grooms led their amblers back to the remuda.

Bass turned to the *Reichsherzog*. "Wolfie, take your Kalmyks up to the top of that hill and send back word of what we're up against, what we'll be riding into. When the mules get up there with the guns, you tell them where to set up, too."

"Jawohl, mein Herr Herzog von Norfolk," replied the big man in the fluted armor from atop his tall black horse. Reining about, he cantered back to his Mongol troopers. Unsheathing his sword, he held it high above his head and shouted, *"Voran*! *Alles voran*! *Schnell*!"

Beckoning his own two Kalmyks over to where his squires were affixing the last pieces of his own armor, Bass said, "Nugei, Yueh, you two speak better English than any of his, so go with him and tell him to give you the messages to send back." Seeing the everfaithful Nugei frown and drag his feet slightly, Bass prodded, "Dammit, Nugei, you won't be leaving me unprotected. There are a good three hundred *galloglaiches* here, plus my squires and all my gentlemen, to boot. *Go*!"

Receiving his order, the pack-mules bearing two of his light howitzers, their carriages, ammunition boxes, and accessories set out from the trains at a brisk pace, following the Kalmyks. Bass watched them with pride. Especially wrought for him by Sir Peter Fairley at the Royal Cannon Foundry in York, they and the four others still back at his camp near Lagore were the only weapons of their kind in all of this world. Though only three feet long, the little tubes were quite strong-walled enough to throw iron shot of demiculverin size (about nine pounds), explosive shell, grape, and canister, though themselves weighing but sixteen stone and so easily transported on mule- or horseback, as too was the light but sturdy wheeled carriage; and mounted on that carriage, the little pieces could be fired accurately at any elevation from point-blank level to forty-two degrees—being both rifled and breechloading, utilizing the immensely strong interrupted-screw principle.

After Bass had mounted his leopard-horse stallion, Bruiser, and checked the primings of his saddle-pistols, automatically, he looked back up just in time to see some twenty-odd of Wolfgang's Kalmyks go over the crest of the hill. "Now, goddammit," he thought in exasperation, "what the hell is he doing? I told him to just look over the situation down there, not take part in it."

Halfway to the *Reichsherzog*'s position, the galloping artillery unit was passed by Nugei and Yueh, coming back at a hard gallop. The two reined up before Bass.

"Your Grace," said Nugei, "*Reichsherzog* say that on opposite hill iss Irischers' force of maybe *fier hundert*, about half mounted. Some of the van down iss, fighting hard are the rest, *und Reichsherzog* say that to safe them he must, but to not commit all his Kalmyks he vill not until Your Grace to see the situation hass."

The half-squadron of *galloglaiches* had long been ready to advance by the time their "chief" moved out to lead them on, flanked by his two Kalmyk personal guards, his squires, his bodyguards, and his gentlemen, with his bannerman and his trumpeter close behind him. As he led his troops at a fast walk, Bass noted that Wolfgang had committed another score or so of his Kalmyks, or at least there were many more missing from the hillcrest. Through his battered, otherworld pair of binoculars, he could spy the big German nobleman, now dismounted, at work supervising the unpacking and positioning of the little howitzers on either side of the road and just below the top of the hill, in a position that could not be seen from the other side.

"Your Grace to see can." The *Reichsherzog* waved an armored arm at the opposite hillside, whereon knots of men mounted on horses and ponies or afoot were gathered, watching the small-scale battle boiling back and forth in the narrow vale between the two hills. "No sooner to put in more men do I, than they reciprocate so that to be outnumbered my *Jungen* ever are. A few shells would be a very good sight bursting amongst them, I think. *Ja*!"

Gazing back and forth across that steeper, higher, forested hillside, Bass thought to note a movement in an area more heavily overgrown than most, on the far right flank of the enemy's main force. Again uncasing his precious, unreplaceable binoculars, he fixed them on that area, and what he saw brought his breath hissing between his suddenly clenched teeth.

"Wolfgang," he said, "uncase your glass and look far over to our left there, just a bit down from that big dead tree. See it? Damned right those bastards keep feeding men in a few at a time to just outnumber ours. They hope to sucker us all down there, whereupon—unless I miss my guess—those they've themselves committed will precipitately withdraw and those damned sakers or demiculverins or whatever they have hidden there will fill our troops full of langrage and grape. Nor would I be surprised at all but what there're another brace of the things hidden somewhere over on the right.

"I thought back at Sir Máel's siege lines that a very atypical Irishman must be commanding these Connachta irregulars, and this is but another proof of it, damned if it's not. I'd like to meet that man other than at swordpoints. Have the two gunners called up here, please."

Rearranged so as to sit almost hub to hub on the reverse slope, loaded with solid ball for sighting purposes and each of them laid to precise angles commensurate with their gunners' experience of the prior performances of the individual pieces, the little pack-howitzers were fired, first one, then the other. Immediately the guns had boomed, each gun crew jumped to swab, load, prick the cartridge open, prime, and wheel the piece back up into battery.

Watching with binoculars and long-glass, Bass and the *Reichsherzog* saw the first ball come to earth downhill and a bit to the left of the hidden battery, while the second gun's shot plunged into the thick growth just behind the target.

Being so informed, the two gunners put their heads together for a brief moment, altered somewhat the elevations and traverse of their minuscule pieces, then touched them off, almost together, the blast of hot gases from the hurling-charge igniting the fuzes of the spherical shells with which the tubes had been loaded this time. The flights of the shells through their high trajectory were easily followed by the naked eye, due to the smoking fuzes. Again, one came down a bit to the rear of the concealed battery, but the other did not come to earth at all, rather did it explode in the air about six or eight feet directly above the battery, its blast followed within a split second by another, much louder and more fiery explosion at ground level.

Apparently having been prewarned that the sounds of cannonfire would be their signal to withdraw, the Irish horsemen fighting the Kalmyks down in the narrow vale had begun trying to do just that from the first shot of Bass's howitzers, but the surviving Kalmyks had pursued the Irish so fiercely and doggedly that the irregulars had had no option but to turn and resume fighting for their lives.

The brush and trees around and about the bombarded gun position had, in the wake of the explosions, begun to burn quite merrily, and men on foot, some of them being helped by others, were moving as fast as possible away from the ranged position. A good reason for their haste was revealed to all when, with a terrific roar, another explosion occurred and, almost immediately, both of the hidden guns fired their loads into the vale, fortunately hitting little save earth and grass.

"That'll teach the bastards," thought Bass with relief that it all had gone so well for him and his. "Teach them to not bring kegs of loose powder, next time. A wooden chest of premeasured and wrapped charges is one hell of a lot easier to get away in a hurry in thick brush like that than a heavy, unwieldy barrel of gunpowder."

At this dual discharge there were two more from the far left of the enemy's line. Most of those two loads of murderous langrage, however, took the retreating Irish rather than the Kalmyks they were fighting. The other concealed battery having thus revealed its position, Bass saw his howitzers moved quickly and ranging shots of ball fired at this new target, but before the gunners could assess the degrees off the target of the initial rounds, reload, and relay their pieces, a small column of horsemen was to be seen winding their way down into the vale, the leading rider wearing the unmarked, almost-white surplice of a herald over his armor.

In a trice, Sir Ali's squire had unpacked the knight's own herald-garb from a saddlebag and helped his master to don it.

"Take Sir Colum with you to interpret, Ali," said

Bass. "If the ambushing bastards want to surrender to me, fine. I might even agree to a brief, secured truce, but nothing else. Yes, they do seem to outnumber us a bit, but then all of my forces are mounted *and* professional, not just armed farmers and drovers."

Sir Daveog Mac Diugnan Ui Brehenny, Count Ros Commáin, looked to be in his mid-forties, his dark-red hair and lighter-red beard streaked now here and there with yellowish-white. There was no need of an interpreter with him, for he was capable of conversing in a number of languages—Gaelic, English, German, French, Latin, Italian, and smatterings of Spanish, Catalonian, Moorish, and Portuguese. Not only that, but he was known of old to no less than three of Bass's gentlemen, all of whom had known the man during his days as a highly successful and widely respected mercenary officer on the continent.

Bass's first question as they sat their horses in converse while men of both commands cooperated in fighting the fires set by the artillery shells was, "Why did you attack us on the march back rather than on our advance, may I ask, Sir Daveog?"

The onetime professional soldier smiled and shrugged. "It was your banner, Your Grace. None of us recognized it, and for all we knew, you might've been riding to attack that pile of pigs' filth squatting around and about Gaillminh; we were all of us tracking your column all the way, and had you done so, why we would've all been giving you of our full support.

"However, when we were seeing of how you rode in and were well received and all by the *Ard-Righ*'s noble bumboys there, we knew you for just another pack of invaders, so we planned out and laid this ambuscade. *Och*, and it's all being me own fault, it is. Had I, me ownself, been observing your column but only the once more close than I did, I'd of been recognizing at least the *Reichsherzog* and good old Melchoro, if not Sir Ali—who was but barely a lad when last I was a-seeing of the *bouchal* and had not yet gained all those fine, honorable scars—and I would've been knowing by that that all Your Grace's column were true professionals and best let be by such a makeshift, make-do little force as I own, here."

"Makeshift it may be," remarked Bass admiringly, "but it and your modern methods of fighting have stung the commanders of the *Ard-Righ*'s besieging troops so sorely that they cried to Brian for help. That's why we were ordered up here, this trip, to assess the situation and report back to Brian how I felt it should be done—that is, the flushing out of your bands by my *galloglaiches* and Kalmyks. I have agreed to bring up my full condotta, but only if it be understood in advance that they are mine to fully command and in no way under the jurisdiction of Sir Máel and his officers."

"Astute," said the red-bearded man, "most astute. That man is the best foeman I could be hoping to face under the circumstances, he is that. Give me the time and him not being replaced and it's we'll be a-breaking that bloody siege yet. I own horses and even dogs that are having more sense in their heads than that poor wight. It's thanking Our Sweet Savior I am that Count Ardgal is not being the man I'm having to face and fight with the precious little I own; we soldiered together, Sir Tadg Mac Conall and me, we did, both together and opposing, from time to time. With whatall these besiegers be owning over there, I'd not be lasting long if such a man as Sir Tadg was commanding, rather than that lovely, lovely, old-fashioned pighead Sir Máel."

Bass grinned. "Too bad for your king that he hasn't

a few more like you, Sir Daveog. If he had, like as not he'd be besieging Brian, not the other way around. He owns a good, loyal vassal in you."

"*Hisself*?" yelped the man addressed, as if stung by firecoals, then relaxed a bit, saying, "*Och*, that's right, being a stranger as is Your Grace, you wouldn't be understanding all the internal ways and affairs and relations of *Eireann*, you wouldn't.

"Then, Your Grace, know you that, were it only old *Righ* and *Ri* Flaithri and his fleabitten byblows—all of the lot of them got on diseased camp whores, more likely than not—in that city, I'd be feeling more than a mite inclined to join with Satan hisself, if need be, to bring the walls down around his hairy shanks," declared Sir Daveog, heatedly. "It's stallions and stud-bulls I'm owning of with longer and more honorable pedigrees than that well-damned, hell-spawned, land-stealing, murdering coward of a *Ri* of Ui Laidhigh. It's I'd not be a-pissing down the whoreson's poxy throat were his cesspool stomach all ablaze!"

Perplexedly, Bass just shook his head slowly. "But I had just assumed that you were one of *Righ* Flaithri's most loyal supporters. You are one of his nobles, aren't you, one of his vassals?"

"Christ and all the Holy Saints forbid such!" prayed Sir Daveog fervently. "When it was leaving me home I was to go a-warring, as a lad, I was a third-born son of the *Righ* of Ros Commáin, Your Grace, *Righ* Diugnan Mac Kielthi Ui Flanaghan and *Ri* of that ilk as well. Four of us sons by the first wife, there were, Your Grace, the eldest and second eldest were, of course, kept close by my sire to be assuring the clansmen a choice in the electing of a new chief when ever God would be a-taking the *Ri*, and when I—the third—chose the life of a soldier, the fourth was sent off to be educated for the priesthood.

"It was many's the long year I'd been a-learning of me soldier's profession, when the fell word was brought me that me royal sire had fallen in battle against a plaguey *ri* what had seized the throne of Connachta and was striking out at all his neighbors for to increase the size of his holdings. But as it's in Hungary I was then, a-serving of good King Bela Czintos; the sad word was of course old when I was a-getting of it. Fortunately, the time was good for me leaving. King Bela's armies—hisself's own, plus those of his two most powerful vassals, Duke Friederich and Archcount Vlad—along of my condottas and those of the justly famous condottiere Sir Wenceslaus, Count Horeszko, had but just thoroughly defeated the southeastern *ordus* of the Khan of the Tatars and what with the unbelievably rich loot of their baggage trains and base camp, it was every high-ranking professional officer was just then owning enough of a fortune for to buy the most of my carefully assembled condottas off of me. Indeed, good King Bela hisself it was, when he heard of how I must so speedily be a-taking of me leave of his lands and triumphant armies, bought of me *Landesknechten* and right many of me guns, then Archcount Vlad took some and old Sir Wenceslaus the most of the rest."

"And one imagines that they were overjoyed to gain them at any price, old comrade," remarked *Barón* Melchoro, "for your mastery at forming up and training first-rate units was ever one of your finest and most famous qualities."

The old condottiere continued, "So I rode down to Venetzia along of me household and some dozens Rus Goth axemen as were then me personal guards, traded off the most of me great treasure of loot for a letter of credit from the bankers of the Church, then hired us a ship with much of what were left and set sail for

Eireann. We were twice over set upon by sea-robbers, that sailing, but with so many fighting men shipped aboard, we overcame the both of them and took not a small amount of loot besides, and not to even be a-mentioning the welcome bits of diversion these little episodes were a-giving me and me trusty Rus Goths, God be a-keeping all the brave *bouchals*.

"When we landed in Dublin, Your Grace, and the *Ard-Righ* was after getting the word that it was to *Eireann* I was returning, he bade me stop at Tara, and I did, hoping that he might be giving me support against the Connachta curs, seeing as how his sire and mine had always been on good terms; also, Mide had been at war or close to always with Connachta time out of mind.

"But devil a word did the bastard speak of friendship or aid, no, he was just wanting to hire on my Rus Goths to join his own numbers of them. Seeing how badly he was wanting them, I worked him around to trading me *galloglaiches* three for one, then paid the hire of some *bonnaghts* he was not using just then and went on me way to the Kingdom of Ros Commáin. And oh, alas, the terrible horror I was a-finding in the lands that had been me home, Your Grace."

CHAPTER THE ELEVENTH

With the fires all beaten out, smothered out, or quenched with water from the brook that ran down the center of the narrow and grassy vale, chuckling over and around stones, Bass had had the train and the remuda brought up and camp pitched on the recent battleground. Some of Sir Daveog's riders had gone off somewhere and returned with a brace of sleek beeves and a wainload of ale, army bread, and oddments.

Upon Bass's courteous refusal to partake of the thin supplies of the Irish count's irregulars, Sir Daveog had laughed quite merrily. "*Och*, Your Grace, Your Grace, this provender be but a gift of the *Ard-Righ*. Intended it were for Sir Máel, but it was a-thinking I was that the man needs not so much as Brian sends him, so lest he o'ereat and be afflicted with the plagued gout, I have me *bouchals* take modest toll of every supply train as comes acrost of me lands, I do. It's keeping us well supplied with food, His High Majesty does, not even to mention all the fine horses, waggons and wains, mules, oxen, and oddments of armor, small arms, and suchlike. *Och*, 'tis a rarely generous man the burly bastard is to me and mine. It's often I'm a-thinking that it's his guilty conscience a-plaguing him for helping one of Mide's oldest enemies break up the lands of one of his dynasty's oldest and best friends, I am."

And so the beeves were butchered and flayed and dressed for the thick greenwood spits and the recent enemies joined to drink High King Brian's ale, eat his beef and his bread, then sleep well under the stars riding high above the little vale and the hills rising up around it.

In his oral report, Bass laid it on the line to the High King. Conversing with his gentlemen and at some length with the charming and voluble Count Ros Commáin had all gone to confirm his own beliefs that Brian was, to use an expression of his own world and times, playing both ends against the middle and truly out to benefit no one but Brian, in the end. He was become certain that the man had lied to him repeatedly, lied to King Arthur, and was very likely lying to his pet papal knight, as well.

"Your Majesty, the siege is not advancing toward any conclusion for a number of very good reasons, most of them the faults of Sir Máel and the commanders of your blockading fleet. This so-called blockade is proving completely ineffective, for the city is being almost nightly resupplied, rearmed, and reinforced by sea, by way of small craft that lie up during daylight hours, then dash in at night through shallows and shoal-waters of depths known to them, safe for them, but suicidal for most of your fleet to attempt.

"The *Reichsherzog* Wolfgang, of my staff, who has conducted more sieges than any other man I've met, states that Sir Máel has positioned his siege guns much too far back from the walls and so would risk bursting those guns did he have enough powder rammed into them to do an adequate job from where they sit. He has commenced not one set of approaching entrenchments from any point of his lines. Indeed, the only works he has thrown up at all are around his outer perimeter, intended to protect his camps from the incursions of irregulars.

"In conversation with Sir Máel and Sir Cellach, I determined that there were no great, crashing battles that lost them all their cavalry, as Your Majesty's parting words had led me to believe, rather did the squadron of *galloglaiches* desert en masse, while a serious tactical error on Sir Máel's part cost him all of the lancers and an equal number of mounted light infantry, as well."

Brian shrugged, frowning. "I only told you that which letters had told me, Your Grace of Norfolk. Why would the *galloglaiches* have deserted? They always are paid on time and in full in unclipped coin. Or did those two foolish barons mistreat them, perhaps, do you think?"

Then Bass shrugged. "I have no way of knowing that last, of course, Your Majesty, but your barons tell that the desertion was a result of the *galloglaiches* hearing that the army was to be brought back to Dublin, enshipped, and thrown against the Regulus of the Isles."

Brian cracked a big, prominent knuckle, his face clouding. "The noble fools, Máel and Cellach, damn them both, didn't they tell the army that no such thing was actually my intent?"

"If they did, Your Majesty," replied Bass, "it is obvious that their words were not believed, it would seem."

"Where in the hell could that squadron have gotten to, then?" mused the *Ard-Righ*, "Had they sailed back for Lewis out of any port on this island, my agents would have heard of it and I would know. Nor have I had word of any unattached *galloglaiches* seeking employment anywhere or living off the countryside, even."

"No, Your Majesty," Bass informed him, "the mounted axemen found good employment almost at once with Count Ros Commáin, who now is using them against Sir Máel and company to some great effect, I am given to understand. Granting that they all must possess some firm and rather detailed knowledge of that arc of encampments, I'd imagine that their new employers have found them to be quite a worthwhile investment."

"Daveog?" the High King almost shouted. "Daveog Mac Diugnan Ui Brehenny? You mean to say that that shoat is responsible for all these outrages against my army and supply trains? But his sire was my ally, and my sire's before me. He hates *Righ* Flaithri with a bottomless and unholy passion, too, so why would he fight to protect him and Gaillminh from my army? It boggles the mind, Your Grace, being beyond all comprehension of rational men. Huh! Wait, mayhap that's it, then. With all he's suffered over the years, mayhap the poor *bouchal*'s wits have slipped away from him."

Bass shook his head. "I think otherwise, Your Majesty. I talked with Sir Daveog at some length, over parts of two days. He avers that, having seen more than enough of war in his lifetime, he would have gladly kept out of this one, had your troops not razed some of the homesteadings and a village of his vassals in the western parts of the Barony of Clonmacnowen. Sir Cellach's lancers also descended upon the hall of the baron of those lands, received his honorable surrender, then looted, raped, and, finally, burned the place down with the too-trusting baron nailed by hands and feet to a door.

"When told of this atrocity, Sir Daveog says that it was then he sent the flaming cross to rouse all his county. He says that not a few came to join his hosts from the baronies that had been his father's and now are held by Your Majesty or by *Righ* Flaithri, and then when the *galloglaiches* came riding by and were amenable to the taking of his pay, he found himself in command of a rather sizable force."

"But, dammit," expostulated the *Ard-Righ*, "surely that Sir Daveog has seen enough, experienced enough, over his years of soldiering to know that things like that just have a bad habit of happening in war. Surely he cannot believe that I or any of my noble officers attacked his lands deliberately? Clonmacnowen is, after all, a border barony; both *Righ* Flaithri and Daveog claim it, and both have held it at one time or another, too. I would imagine that the captain of Sir Cellach's lances, whoever that may be, thought himself quite legitimately despoiling Connachta lands. He could've come to me at Lagore or Tara, made supplication, and I'd've seen things made right again for him; he did not need to start making undeclared war upon my troops. In fact, had he—with all his vast and valuable experience—simply presented his lands all to me and taken them back in feoff, become one of my vassals, I'd've put *him* in charge of my army in Connachta."

"Your Majesty," said Bass slowly, wording this carefully, "he gave me the impression that he considered coming to you for redress, but then decided against it. He says that he does not trust Your Majesty and that any other Irishman who does is a deluded fool."

Bass tensed himself, knowing the *Ard-Righ*'s often fiery temper. But he waited in vain for any outburst. Brian just shook his head and sighed.

"*Och*, the *bouchal* still holds against me my seizing of six of the baronies that were once part of the short-lived Kingdom of Ros Commáin. He cannot seem to realize even yet that had I—an old friend and ally of his late sire—not taken them for Mide, Flaithri certainly would've taken them for his own as he took the most of the others, and then I'd've had that forsworn, land-hungry usurper of Connachta far closer to Tara than could've been easily borne.

"But that's neither here nor there, just now. I would imagine that he bade you offer terms of some sort, something that he wants me to grant him before he'll cease to harass my siege forces and seize my supply trains?"

"Yes, Your Majesty, he did," Bass said, grave-faced. "Sir Daveog, Count Ros Commáin, demands immediate return of his baronies of Clonlogan, Shrule, Ardagh, West Kilkenny, Rathcline, and Moydow. He bids you withdraw all your troops from off the lands of Ros Commáin and Connachta and all ships from the coastal waters off the city of Gaillminh he . . ."

"He's protecting his bitter enemy, the man who murdered and debased his own blood kindred, seized much of his lands, and then depoiled the rest? He's protecting *Righ* Flaithri and Gaillminh?" burst out Brian, in astonishment. "If so, then I was right to begin, he's gone stark, staring mad!"

"Your Majesty," said Bass, in a lowered voice, "*Righ* Flaithri is no longer in Gaillminh; it is being held by his sons in his name. *Righ* Flaithri tried to sail west, to *Magna Eireann*, but his ship was flung back ashore somewhat north of its point of departure. He and a few other survivors sought shelter in a certain monastery, the abbot of which happened to be another son of the late *Righ* Diugnan, who had them all disarmed and conveyed to Sir Daveog. And he bade me tell Your Majesty that, as he now holds something he called 'an odd lump of amber with a dragon in it,' he is the rightful, God-chosen *Righ* of Connachta and he expects that all good and God-loving monarchs such as Your Majesty will see him soon in his lawful place.

"However, he adds, he is certain that he can bring about the peaceful capitulation of Gaillminh and, therefore, will not need your troops or ships to effect it; it is for this reason that he demands you withdraw them. However, he insists that the siege guns be left in place, their value to serve as at least partial reparations for the despoliation of the surrounding countryside."

"And if I don't do all these . . . these . . . these *things*?" Brian grated from between clenched teeth, while knots of jaw muscle worked under almost livid skin. He squeezed the arms of his cathedra so tightly in his powerful hands that three pieces of inlay popped out of the tormented wood to clatter down upon the floor, completely unnoticed. "Just what are the threats of this arrogant, presumptuous bastard, then?"

Bass steeled himself to not allow a single smile or, far worse, a chuckle, to show or escape him, for in Brian's present rage, such could very easily be fatal. "Then, Your Majesty, Sir Daveog says that he will simply continue his current strategy and tactics until the siege forces either are taken off by the fleet or surrender to him. Should it be the latter, he says that he will take everything of value of them, hold the noblemen and gentlemen to ransom, hire all the good troops to his service, and sell the rest for slaves to certain Europeans of his old acquaintance. Then, after his coronation, he will march his army eastward and take back the six named baronies, plus any others he fancies at the time. He sounds to be most sincere, Your Majesty. No threats, no bluster, no vituperation, only soberly worded notification of intent."

"May the Lord God smite him with every loathsome pest in all this world!" snarled the *Ard-Righ*, his features all twisted and jerking in his towering rage. Suddenly, he clenched a fist, raised it, and brought the side of it crashing down on the arm of the cathedra with such force as to tear it away from both the back and the seat and send it, shattered, tumbling across the floor with a great clatter that brought both the outer guards half through the door with ready pole-axes and looks of concern.

"Get to hell out of here and close those doors, you Gothic pigs!" roared the *Ard-Righ*. "If ever I want you, I'll send a swineherd after you!"

As the doors closed behind the Rus Goth guardsmen, Brian sat up very erectly and took quite a few very deep breaths, before saying, "Your Grace, I take it Sir Daveog is gathering his host around and about the walled city of Ros Commáin, then? And he is holding *Righ* Flaithri there, as well?"

"No, Your Majesty." Bass shook his head. "Count Ros Commáin has dispersed his court. He and most of his barons and gentlemen live and move with his hosts about the countryside, biding nowhere for long. All that he would say of *Righ* Flaithri was that the fairies had shown him where to hide him away."

The *Ard-Righ* dismissed Bass without so much as one word of thanks for the long ride and his report. Then he just sat, brooding darkly, until he heard the portcullis at the outer gate creak up and the bridge slam down. At that, he came to his feet, opened the door, jerked a poleaxe from one of the guards, broke the thick haft, just below the iron bardings, over his knee, then slammed the door behind him and proceeded to use the weapon to demolish each and every stick of expensive furniture in the chamber, roaring curses and foul obscenities and horrible blasphemies in every language he knew, all the while.

* * *

Later, seated in his secret room, Brian the Burly handled his treasured symbols of Irish sovereignty, talking to them as to another human.

"Dammit, nothing at all has worked exactly right, exactly as I'd planned it, since that plaguey English duke came over here to *Eireann*. The only burdens I can't blame on him are the damned Italian mercenaries, the cursed di Bolgias—they were here before him.

"But back to him. When first he and his condotta arrived here, I sent him up to Ulaid to fetch back their Magical Jewel, by hook or by crook. Well, he brought it back, right enough, though by then the damned thing was nothing but an old yellow diamond with no iota of power or significance. The king it had come from was by then dead, murdered by one of his own, but there was a new king, one of the damned Italians, no less. One of the ancient, original Jewels, missing and unseen by any man for hundreds of years, turns up stuck into the bare foot of this foul Italian knight, so the idiotic northerner pigs crowned him their king.

"And as if that were not enough to pile upon me, he proceeds to give his kingdom to and take it back in feoff from, not me, the *Ard-Righ* of *Eireann*, as he should've done, but the Regulus of the goddam Hebrides, the Scottish Western Isles, by all that's holy.

"Then there is the still-unsolved murder of the *Righ* of Airgialla, my faithful liegeman and client, Ronan. The English duke had, in passing through Airgialla on my orders, been given the loan of a slavegirl bedwarmer by poor Ronan. He took a fancy to her, and on his march back through Airgialla from Ulaid, he and his condotta proceeded to tramp into Ard Macha, take away the slavegirl by force of arms, loot more than a hundred ounces of gold from the treasury, then all but sack the palace and city before they finally left. The duke stopped and robbed and terrorized no less than two of Ronan's messengers so that the Englishman had sent the slavegirl out of the realm long before I'd heard about it and could move to make him return her to her royal owner.

"Not only was *Righ* Ronan murdered that fell night up there, but his *Ban-Righ* and several of his noblemen as well, and his infant son disappeared along with the wet nurse. For a while, some senile lunatic who had been on the royal council, I think, was proclaiming himself Priest-King of Airgialla, coronated and crowned by God Almighty, according to him. But then none other than our sly, devious Italian, *Righ* Roberto of Ulaid, proceeds to take over Airgialla and announce that he intends to rule it as regent for Ronan's infant son, whom he is fostering in Ulaid, knowing that if I attack him, I'll shortly have the thrice-damned Regulus—that bloodthirsty old bastard Aonghas Mac Dhomhnuill—after me and *Eireann* if not the King of Scotland—who is another of that terrible old man's vassals—and my own blood-kin cousin, Arthur of England and Wales, too.

"It's clear as crystal to anyone that either *Righ Roberto* or his overlord, the Lord of the Isles, is guilty of having Ronan and all those others of his court cruelly murdered, but I have not yet reasoned out just why they did it, for Airgialla has never been all that rich a kingdom. They always made most of their income from slave-raiding, looting isolated island steadings, as had all their Norse ancestors from time immemorial, fishing and trading. So the realm is simply not much of a prize.

"It looked for a while as if the other Italian mercenary—*Righ Roberto*'s elder brother, Ser Timoteo, *Dux* di Bolgia, was going to work out and help to advance my plans. When he and his managed to kill that mad *Righ* Tàmhas Fitz Gerald so adroitly that it was widely mourned as a tragic accident—trust the poxy Italians for being fine and notably infamous assassins—then got the Magical Jewel, the Star of Munster, up here to me so that I could replace it with the copy I had had made, things looked extremely promising for Brian, yes they did.

"But hardly had our choice, *Righ* Sean Fitz Robert, been crowned, than the damned Fitz Geralds got him away from the most of his guards on the pretext of electing him *Ri* of Fitz Gerald, then murdered him. They put *Righ* Sean's head on a spear, raised up a mob in Corcaigh, and somehow persuaded a light squadron of Ifriqan mercenary horse to come over to them, then tried to kill off di Bolgia and all of his men. One of the Italians got away, out of Corcaigh, though, a young papal knight, Ser Ugo D'Orsini, and rode here to me more dead than alive. But by the time I, my gentlemen and guards, along with Duke Bass and most of his condotta got down to Corcaigh, that damned iron-hard, nine-lived Italian, di Bolgia, and his condotta had killed every Fitz Gerald in Corcaigh—which meant damned nearly every one of the males of that overly inbred ilk in all of Munster, God be praised—so there was nothing for it but to turn all of my force around and ride back to Lagore.

"I had just about decided to send agents down to Munster to seek out a man of the old line of kings of Munster, those who had reigned before the Fitz Geralds. I was going to see him crowned, give him to know that he reigned only by my forbearance, and then all of southeastern *Eireann* would be mine in one way or another and Munster would be at peace within its own borders for the first time in near seven hundred years, with the common people and the new-old nobility elevated by this new-old-line king recognizing me as the man who had delivered them finally from the oppression of the Normans and, therefore, never dreaming of rising up against me.

"But now, but now, goddam him, that cursed Italian has stolen my thunder, may worms eat his lights! Some ancient monk came to him, it is said, babbling of some damned cowherder who was the rightful *Righ* of Munster, and di Bolgia not only had the clod brought to Corcaigh, he has had him crowned *Righ* Flann of Munster. Worse luck, my own damned *filids* avow that the pig most assuredly *is* the true, hereditary Irish *righ*.

"So now I have no more power and influence in Munster than I had when the insane Fitz Geralds ruled there, while that foreign bastard out of Italy is hailed as the savior of the kingdom, sits on the goddam royal council, and commands all of the warriors, too.

"Meanwhile, I had sent the Duke of Norfolk and *his* condotta north to try to reason with my usually very *un*reasonable cousins, the Northern Ui Neills. When did fate have him arrive? Just on the very eve of a battle between the *Righ* of Ui Neill and the *Righ* of Breiffne over some strip of marches along their shared border. Had it been me, I'd've sat back and let them beat each other into the ground, then taken my forces in and conquered them both, but not our Duke of Norfolk, oh, no, not him, goddam it.

"This Englishman proceeds to make peace between them, so impresses them both that they and their *filids* dig up some hoary, ancient bit of prophecy about the man who will come from beyond this world to finally unite all of *Eireann*, bring a long-lasting peace between all the *righs*, though he will never himself be a *righ*.

"Now this infernal mess of dog's-vomit in the west! I send him—because, after all, he is a famous and revered leader of warriors and owns too a well-qualified staff of noble officers—to look over the situation as regards this stalemated and hideously costly siege of Connachta's capital city, Gaillminh. So he goes, he sees, and he decides who and what is wrong there, right enough, confirming some of my own suspicions, too.

"But then, on his return journey, he runs across that damned Daveog of Ros Commáin, with his ultimatums and threats. If the shoat out of that old boar Diugnan *does* have the Magical Jewel of Connachta . . . hell, he does, I'm certain of that, and that damned Flaithri, too; I hope he does to him what Flaithri had done to his brother, then keeps him around to further torment for a while, the old cur deserves no better. The usurper has no real friends in all of his stolen kingdom; only his possession of the Magical Jewel, the Dragon of Connachta, has kept him on his ill-gotten throne this long. So if that damned Daveog can get word to the nobles of Connachta that he has the Dragon, the bastards will have him crowned within the bare blinking of an eye, depend on it, and I'll be far deeper in the shit than I was to start.

"I don't know, maybe I should've backed Daveog when he came back from Europe after his sire was killed. Between us, we could surely have crushed Flaithri then, and now Daveog would be not only back on the throne of his ancestors, but he'd be in some measure beholden to me for the fact. But, at the time, it just seemed to me the better move to let Flaithri defeat Daveog and take enough of his lands that the Kingdom of Ros Commáin would be reduced to a county at best and therefore there would be one less *righ* for me to move against when I was ready to move."

The *Ard-Righ* sighed gustily and fingered the plush-lined hole in the tray, the opening that was meant to hold the Dragon of Connachta. Sighing again, he then began to speak once more to the cold baubles of gold and precious stones.

"Well, the winter is approaching, anyway. I'll just summon the army and fleet back from Connachta. I'll have to cede those six baronies, too, I suppose, else I'd have to keep them constantly garrisoned, knowing Daveog. I'll even leave the bastard the siege guns . . . but they'll all be well spiked, too, damn him. I've won and lost battles, and I long ago learned that when you're faced with an impossible situation, the only sane thing to do is to withdraw in the best possible order, regroup, form new battlelines, and be ready to regain the offensive immediately an opening of any sort is presented you. That's the strategy called for by this situation, and that's what I have to do. But I don't have to like doing it, God dam it all to the deepest, hottest, foulest pit that Satan owns!"

After he had calmed himself to rationality once more by deep breathing and fondling of his tray of jewels, he again began to speak to the stone walls and the treasure chests.

"But this Duke of Norfolk, now, what am I to do with him? When I consider all that he, with the very best of motives, has nonetheless cost me and my plans for *Eireann*, I often think that the best thing would be the arrangement of his quick, quiet demise, his and his principal officers'. But there's the problem: *Eireann* is a small, insular land wherein secrets are exceeding difficult to keep secret for long, no matter how elaborate the precautions taken, so all too soon, there would be speculation if nothing more that I had managed the deaths of at least three foreign noblemen, one the uncle of the Emperor and another very, very dear to Cousin Arthur, whose good favor I cannot yet afford to jeopardize. So what to do with this sometimes useful but always dangerous English nobleman? Send him back to England and Arthur? No, it goes against my grain to so easily, so willingly give up so much available force. Send him and his condotta back to Ulaid? No, Ulaid *and* Airgialla are lost to me and to *Eireann* for so long as *Righ* Roberto di Bolgia lives on and reigns on, for his newfound overlord is reputed to be quick to come to the aid of any threatened vassal and that terrible old man owns at least as powerful a host as do I; moreover, should I fight him, the goddam *galloglaiches* would desert my hosts, all of them, and should I have the luck to seem to be getting the best of old Aonghas, why he'd surely call in his plaguey vassals and their damned hosts, not to mention his allies and his vassals' allies. And against such numbers as those, well, that would be the very end of Brian and of *Eireann*, too, most likely.

"All right, then, send this *Sassenach* duke to Munster, perhaps, see if he can improve matters there? Maybe get the *Dux* di Bolgia to take his condotta back to Italy and cease plaguing me? Hah! Damned unlikely. Much more probably, this peace-loving warlord of Cousin Arthur's would make di Bolgia a fast friend, join the two condottas into one, and then I'd have a real threat, a mobile threat, ready to leap out of Munster at my very throat at any time.

"And not to Connachta, either. Not again, not for any purpose. Were I to so do, no doubt he'd bring that damned Daveog back here to replace me as *Ard-Righ*, and the way he's managed to cozen all the other *righs* of the north, they'd likely as not back him up, too. Already they and the *filids* are hailing this damned foreigner as a 'God-sent king-maker for *Eireann*, the long-awaited one, he-who-moves-between-worlds,' whatever the hell that last means.

"So where is there to send this troublemaking man? Hmm. Why not . . . ? Yes, why not?"

* * *

Don Guillermo disliked having to sit and watch men flogged so early in the day, for what with the formal, military proceedings, the affairs invariably consumed at least an hour of the cooler mornings in which, without such a discipline formation, he usually got a good percentage of his necessary office work done before the interior areas of most of the near-windowless fort became so stifling. But in cases like this, ones wherein he had personally passed sentence, he felt it his duty to attend. And this matter was, indeed, of a serious nature, for humbler soldiers could be a childishly superstitious breed, and if talk of this fine fort being haunted by the ghost of the French officer who had blown its predecessor and himself up rather than surrender it to its present *comandante*, Don Guillermo himself, was allowed to continue in the barracks untrammeled, then soldiers would soon be deserting right and left; such had happened elsewhere, over the years.

Don Guillermo was a deeply religious man, and as such, he knew that ghosts and malignant revenants and specters did not, could not be. Men or women died, their bodies quickly became corruption, and their souls went on to purgatory or hell or, in very rare instances, directly to God in His Heaven; they did not ever linger about in the world of the living. A very wise old priest and imam had told him so when he was a young man, in Spain.

Of course, it could not be expected that a common, crude, profane soldier of mixed blood—some of them being as little as one-eighth Spanish or Moorish descent—and therefore cursed with all of the superstition, ghost-ridden, stubborn stupidity, and basic childishness of their principal and most inferior racial lines—a mere *criollo* could ever comprehend the civilized reasoning of a pious Spaniard or Moor; no, the only way to stop such dangerous speculation was to make malefactors to suffer and bleed and scream in the sight and sound of their base sorts. Let them think such thoughts as their simple minds would easily hold, but let them keep their big, flapping tongues under tight rein, was the opinion of the *comandante*.

At last the thing was done, the sentence fully carried out by the best efforts of a Spanish braided *fustigar alacrán*—a real one, fabricated in the ancient city of Saragasso, wherein they had been made in exactly the same way since the time of the Old Roman Empire, done up of finished leather, not the rawhide of cheaper imitations, with leaden pellets and bronzen barbs permanently integrated in the tails.

As the knight stood up, he noted a tiny gobbet of bloody flesh adhering to the leg of his left boot and impatiently flicked the thing off with the tip of his stick. There was nothing he could do about the fine droplets of blood, however. He sighed. More time to be wasted going back to his quarters and changing boots, but far better that than to be plagued by following flies for the rest of the day. Next flogging, he must have his chair positioned differently. While his squire, Bruno, pulled off the boots and turned them over to a waiting slave to be cleaned and repolished, then fetched the other pair of everyday boots from the clothespress, Don Guillermo was thinking.

"Who in the hell is stealing all this cannon powder? And apropos the thefts, what in the names of twenty saints are they doing with it? Casks of gunpower are, at best, heavy, bulky, unwieldy things; manpower alone cannot bear them easily or far under most conditions, they must be rolled, and rolling makes noise and the rollers have to be damned careful in the rolling, too, since the hoops are soft copper rather than tough iron. The town and the lands about it have been turned upside down and inside out repeatedly and devil a trace of that stolen powder to be found, over a ton of the precious stuff now missing. And doubling the locks and tripling the night guards on the magazine apparently does no good at all; the thieves still manage somehow to dance in and out with as much powder as they want, unseen, unheard, through solid walls and bolted doors with locks that look always to have been untouched.

"It's said in hoary legend that the white-robed white-skinned pagans that dwell somewhere north and west of here are capable of such impossibilities, but I've never put any stock in such tales . . up until now, that is. But if it's true, if some of those witches have drifted down here, what would they want with my cannon powder, pray tell? They are said to not war or hunt or own even small arms, much less cannon; they live on only grain and plants, and indios are said either to virtually worship them or to avoid them like the plague.

"The Irish, directly north of here, seem to ignore these pagans, but the French, to the north of the Irish, have been actively if sporadically hunting them for at least a century now, trying to track them down and either convert or kill them off. If they've had any success on any of their expeditions into the interior, I've heard no word of it . . . and you know damned well that, being French, they'd be crowing their silly heads off if they'd succeeded in even the tiniest of ways.

"Don Felipe . . . where in the hell is that young man, I wonder? He is most conscientious, shows exceeding promise, so it is most unlike him to take so long at so commonplace a task as scouting out those damned, indio-arming, excommunicant interlopers upriver in the Shawnee lands. The lad should at least have sent a message down here to me if circumstances were going to delay his return. He would have, I am certain, knowing him well as I do, unless . . . ?

"No, he is too astute and experienced a fighter, his party is too large and too well armed that at least a few would not have survived any attack or ambush that those indios and those whoever-they-ares could mount."

After standing and stamping down firmly into his boots, the *comandante* left his quarters for the second time that morning and strode briskly down the stone-walled corridor toward the business section of the fort. There was always much for him and his small staff to do and little enough time in which to do it. Days simply had too few hours, it seemed.

CHAPTER THE TWELFTH

Dwarfing almost all other shipping of any type, a towering warship and its companion vessels proceeded slowly up the River Liffey. At the naval quay, she was carefully warped in, and a party that a German might have described as "*herrischer*, *herrlischer Herren*" alit and waited a bit impatiently until horses were found for them. Once mounted, the newcomers divided into two parties, one riding toward the *Herrenhaus* of the Empire's ambassador to the court of the High King and the other exiting the city and making directly for the camp of the English *Herzog* and his condotta.

"*Ach*, *mein alte Freund*, *mein guter Kamerad*, *mein prächtiger Vassall*, Bass, it truly painful iss to leave you after so many goot years, but needed I am in *und* by the Empire. For me *und mein Jungen*, a great varship vaits in Dublin, *und* so return I must, this very day."

Bass was stunned. "It's not . . . ? Nothing's happened to Egon, has it, Wolfie? Pray God not!"

"*Nein*, *nein*." The *Reichsherzog* shook his head. "At last writing, *mein Neffe* und sovereign in Italy was *und* butchering *Spanishchen*, *Moorischen*, *und* their kind in great numbers. *Nein*, the Electors to call me back haf because of difficulties mit the Kalmyks. Because a blood brother I am to the Great Khan, better is thought that to deal with him be to me left. Also, two of the Kalmyks still mit me hiss grandsons are.

"But not all of *mein Jungen* to go back vish. Nugei *und* Yueh to stay mit you vould, of course. Nugei's nephew, Batu, vould stay mit Sir Ali, *und* his half brother in the service of *Barón* Melchoro vould remain. Some *dreizehn* more vould not for reasons various go back mit the rest; to order them I could *und* obey they vould assuredly, but to do such I vould prefer not to do. *Ja*, *und* so left am I mit a problem, for not efen goot *Deutsch* do the most of them to speak, far less *Engelisch und Irisch* so into your service vould you take these fine fighters, *mein alte Freund*? Much more vould my mind rest could I know that safe mit you they were, *und* happy in the service of a great lord that respect *und* admire they all do."

Bass and his entourage of course rode with Wolfgang and his Kalmyks to Dublin, through it, and so down to the naval basin on the south bank of the River Liffey. One by one, the smaller ships of the Empire's convoy were warped in close enough for each to receive its lading of Kalmyks, their gear, and their ponies.

Bass felt miserable. He knew already just how much he was going to miss this old and very dear friend, this man whom he had known longer than most of the other people in all this world. On the ride down to Dublin, he had tried to persuade the *Reichsherzog* to take back the Mark of Velegrad that he might bestow it and its lands and city upon a knight who could and would live there and see it prosper.

"*Ach*, *nein*, *nein*, Bass Foster, *mein Vassall* you are *und mein Vassall* you vill remain. The *Mark* in goot hands is in your absence, nefer to fear, *Kamerad*, *und* a strong garrison the *Schloss* holds, as alvays. Besides, as uncertain as is our vorld, *Kamerad*, *gut* it often iss to know that to haf a bolt-hole vun does, lands *und* assured safety in another realm; to villingly gif up such a possible salvation vun should not, nor vill I to let you do so. So say no vord more on this subject, *Kamerad*. So short is our remaining time, so let us to talk it avay mit other, more pleasant things. *Ja*? *Ach*, *ja*!"

When the last ship was loaded and the multidecked warship was preparing to cast off the mooring lines, the tall, powerful *Reichsherzog*, his scarred face tear-drenched, sobbingly embraced and bussed each of them in turn—Don Diego, Sir Colum, Sir Liam, Sir Calum, Sir Conn, Sir Ali, Nugei, Yueh, Batu and his half brother, Ordei, Melchoro, and then Bass, once more. Wolfgang projected irresistible amounts of emotion—he cried and sobbed, wrenchingly, Bass cried, Melchoro cried, Sir Ali cried, Don Diego cried, Sir Colum cried, Sir Liam cried, Sir Calum cried, and Sir Conn cried. Nugei, Yueh, Batu, and Ordei did not cry, but began a soft, sad-sounding chant that was picked up by the Kalmyks aboard the smaller ships now waiting out offshore. Presently, all of the Empire noblemen and ship's officers, Wolfgang's squires, his page, and not a few of the common sailors were weeping, at which point the always very sensitive and emotional Irish on the quay began to cry, as well.

Obviously, Bass thought to himself on the slow ride back to his camp, no one had ever gotten around to telling the fierce, usually brave, and often violent warriors of this world that tears or any display of emotion was unmanly, that "real men" did not cry. It had taken him years to learn to overcome that stupid and unnatural admonition and he was very glad that his own son, little Joseph Foster, would never be burdened with so ridiculous a piece of emotional garbage.

"I wonder how little Joe is making out in fosterage?" he half-whispered to himself. "And his . . . and Krystal, Krys, I wonder if she's any better. Damn, what a terrible thing, her cracking up like she did. The Krys I married and the one of the last few years were just not the same person at all. I wonder if it was my fault. Hal swears it wasn't, that she was never strung together too tight, in this world or the other one, and would've whacked out eventually anyway. But . . . I can't help but wonder . . . ?"

When he had returned to York after seeing Her Grace of Norfolk established in her tower suite at Whyffler Hall, with the two nuns of the nursing order and some ladies and commoner maids to care for her, Rupen had, at Sir Geoffrey's firm insistence, taken a couple of the Strathtyne Lancers with him. Therefore, on his next visit to the border, these lancers had guided him and his contingent of the Horse Guards of the Archbishop through the shorter but much more rugged and dangerous course of the cross-country route, that which he once before had ridden in company with Bass Foster and his wild Irish rogues.

A few months of warmth, care, access to bathing facilities, and frequent changes of clothing, as well as copious amounts of varied and well-prepared foods, had rendered the mad duchess into much more the image of the woman Rupen had first met at the Archbishop's country manor than the haglike creature he had brought up here. She was clearly healthier, physically, but as he quickly discovered, she still was mad as a March hare, still precipitately violent, still very dangerous.

"Sir Knight," Sister Fatima, who looked a bit more

battered about the face than Rupen recalled her and who now walked with a slight but perceptible limp, told him soon after his arrival from York, "we can not allow you to be alone with her, you or anyone else, male or female, not ever. Her fits of rage are become much more frequent here, and her devil-spawned cunning has increased, as well. She slew one of her ladies—a knight's widow—outright, and just last week she half-blinded and permanently crippled a poor girl of a maidservant. We have had to ask the seneschal, Sir Geoffrey Musgrave, to absent himself from these premises, since she is become wont to attack him on sight, apparently under the mad impression that it is her husband, His Grace of Norfolk, that she is trying to slay. You know well her strength, the strength of her madness, Sir Knight, so you know just how deadly she could be. Therefore, I pray you, as you love God, exercise the utmost caution when anywhere near to her, for you are a very good man and it would much pain me to see her injure or slay you, too."

"Damn, it's good to have you back here," said Krystal in the twentieth-century English to which she and Rupen had both been born, reared, and educated. "It's so good to have somebody I can talk to, somebody who knows the other world, not just this goddam primitive, stinking, uncomfortable excuse for a place to live.

"You know, these yokels all are firmly convinced that this hole we're in is a fucking palace, for Christ's sake, even those damned nuns. No central heating, no air conditioning, no electricity, not even any running water, much less a shower . . . oh, God, God, what I'd give for a nice, hot shower with sweet, mild soap and shampoo and some bath gel and an electric razor to shave my legs and my underarms. You know, one of my ladies used to do it, and do it well, too, before I was taken away and locked up; now under this sack of a dress, I'm just as hairy as a fucking ape. I've asked them to prepare rooms for me elsewhere in the hall, but so far, no dice. These rooms all are small and cramped and drafty, you know. I wouldn't want my son, Joe, to try to live up here. I wrote to Hal, you know, and ordered him to send my son up here from wherever my son-of-a-bitch husband had him sent. Joe is six now, and it's high time I started teaching him his Hebrew. Did Hal send him up with you?"

"No, Mrs. Foster," replied Rupen carefully, "I rode up here with only some guardsmen. We took the cross-country route from York, across the mountains."

"Yes, of course," she said, "and that's no trip for a child, even a strong and active child like Joe. Hal will be sending him up here by the road then, I presume. How soon, do you know?"

Rupen knew—he had been with the Archbishop when he received and read the madwoman's letter.

"I can't say that I do, Mrs. Foster. The Archbishop is such a busy man, and you must know how slowly messages and travelers can move in this world. Also, winter is almost upon us, and I doubt that the Archbishop or you, his mother, would want the boy essaying the so-called roads in a coach. Would you, ma'am?" He was sorry to have to mislead her, but he thought his prevarications better for all concerned than to tell her the truth, that Archbishop Harold thought her son should remain as far from her as possible, that her patent insanity not adversely affect his own developing, immature mind.

Wrinkling up her brows, she said, "No, I suppose it won't hurt to wait a few more months, until the road is passable or at least as passable as that road ever is. But Joe must come up here in the spring, no later, you hear? Hal, of all people, must know just how important is early religious education. Joe was baptized, you know, I let his goddam asshole father talk me into it. But baptized or not, he's still my son and I'm still his mother and that means that he is Jewish, not a goddam *goy*. I wish to God I could find a rabbi, but none of these fuckers here seem to even know what the frigging word means, and when I tried to explain, they ran in some fucking priest and—would you believe? —not even that pious-mouthed peckerhead knew what a rabbi is."

"Yes, Mrs. Foster," replied Rupen, "I can easily believe that. You see, ma'am, there are no Jews in all of England or Wales, in this world. I am given to understand that there is a small colony of Jews in Edinburgh, and other colonies are scattered about in or near to European cities, with larger numbers in North Africa and the Middle East. But not in England, Mrs. Foster."

"Well," she grated from between clenched teeth, "there are at least two Jews in this world's England, anyway, come hell or high water: me and my son. Poor Joe doesn't look at all like my father, though, he looks just like his goddam wasp father, the *schmuck* . . . . Do you know what the Yiddish word '*schmuck*' means?"

"Yes, Mrs. Foster. I don't speak Yiddish, though I do speak a bit of High German, but I know what that word means, nonetheless."

"You're a German?" she demanded to know. "You don't look at all like a German. You actually look more Jewish than I do."

"No," he replied, "I'm not a German, I'm an American, though I was born in Syria. I was five or so when my folks emigrated to the States."

"Oh, shit!" she said disgustedly. "A fucking Arab, huh?"

He shook his head. "No, ma'am, I'm pure Armenian. My folks were driven out of Armenia in 1915 by the Turks and the Kurds and ended up in Damascus. It took them ten years of damned hard work, but they finally scraped together enough money to make it to the U.S."

"What did you do in that other world, our old world?" she asked. "Peddle oriental rugs and Middle Eastern brassware?"

He grinned. "Not quite, Mrs. Foster . . ."

"Hold it!" she snapped, but then softened the demand with a smile. "If I hear 'Mrs. Foster' one more time, I'm going to throw something solid at you or puke up my guts or both. My name is Krystal."

"All right, Krystal, my name is Rupen, Rupen Ademian," said Rupen.

"Now that we've got that matter straight," she went on, "you were telling me that you didn't peddle rugs and hookahs, right? So what was your line of work, then, Rupen?"

He grinned again. "Varied, Krystal, quite varied. Most recently, for the ten years or so before coming here, I'd been a partner in the Confederate States Armaments Company, Incorporated, of Richmond, Virginia."

She wrinkled up her nose and said dubiously, "Antiques? Funny, you don't look the type, Rupen."

He shook his head. "No, not antiques, not originals. Reproductions of nineteenth-century rifles and pistols, cap-locks, accessories, bayonets, swords, that sort of thing, eventually even some small cannon."

"You mean that people can actually make a living selling copies of old guns and swords and things? It seems to me that any really knowledgeable person, especially one with laboratory facilities, could tell almost immediately that they were modern-made fakes, Rupen." She frowned.

"Oh, they were clearly marked, labeled as repros, Mrs . . . Krystal. No deception was ever intended or practiced. You see, there was and is a large segment of the shooters who wanted to shoot with, even hunt with, the older types of firearms, but all of the originals were, in addition to being too valuable to risk damaging, too old to be at all safe to load and shoot, so the people would buy originals—if they could find them and afford them—to hang on the wall and admire and repros to shoot," he informed her. "Ours were made by firms that faithfully copied originals, but fabricated the repros in our modern, stronger metals and test-fired them with overcharges just to be sure they were safe. We handled quality products, you see, Krystal, and we had earned a damned good reputation in the field of repros."

Her face registered amazement. "You mean that you actually had competition, that other people made and were able to sell these high-class fake guns? God, I didn't know just how many well-heeled nuts there were in that world, I guess. But you said that that was your most recent line of work, Rupen. What did you do before that? Sell fake works of art, maybe? Or ersatz Persian rugs?"

"No," he responded. "I was a buyer for Rappahanock Arms Company, a branch of Ademian Enterprises U.S.A., the firm founded by my late father, Vasil Ademian, and presently chaired by my younger brother, Kogh Ademian."

The mad duchess raised one eyebrow. "Rappahannock Arms I've never heard of, but I recall hearing about Ademian Enterprises, and none of what I heard was good, as I remember it; one of my boyfriends, Dan Dershkowitz, and his group used to demonstrate against Ademian and all of the other nearby death-merchants, while the war in Vietnam was going full-blast. Wasn't it napalm you made?"

"Not napalm, Krystal, shell cases, just as we did with not a bit of complaint or protest from anybody in the U.S. all during World War Two and the Korean War and so on. But I was serving in the army during both World War Two and Korea, and after Korea, that part of Ademian, the manufacturing and research end, was not the one that employed me.

"I started out just buying up stocks of surplus military rifles and pistols and shipping them back to the States for Rappahannock to sell to smaller dealers or direct to the customers."

She sighed and said, "Rupen, you're going to think me incredibly naive or stupid or both, but I just don't understand any of this. Why would anyone pay good money for old army guns?"

Holding up his spread hand, he ticked off the fingers. "Collectors, first, people who maybe want one of every rifle or pistol used in a particular war or during a particular period of history, or who want one each of all the variants made by a particular factory. Second, the types who, rather than buy a comparatively expensive new hunting rifle, would prefer to buy an old but sound military action and use it as the basis for a virtually handmade hunting piece, a one-of-a-kind item. Third, men who fought in certain wars and, having learned there to love or hate or respect a certain weapon, want one of their own. Fourth, the shoot-'em-trade-'ems—people who will buy a weapon, pistols in particular, shoot a hundred rounds or so with it, then sell it or trade it for a different one they've never shot or handled before. Fifth, those who want an inexpensive weapon for personal or home protection. I estimate that ninety percent or more of our mail-order sales were to the last-three-named types of customer, though."

She shook her head. "In your way, though, you were just as bad as the other part of your company, Rupen. Didn't you ever stop to think how many of the rifles and all you shipped into the country would be bought by criminals, to hurt and kill innocent people with?"

"No. To begin with, I don't think that manufacturing war material for your government or for friendly foreign governments is bad. And as for providing criminals with firearms, you really are naive if you think any career criminal is going to try to saw off a forty-odd-inch bolt-action military rifle to use to hold up a bank when any hardware store can provide him with a cheap revolver or a good shotgun, which last is one hell of a lot more intimidating a thing to point at victims than a .30 caliber rifle, anyway. Now, I do admit that it is barely possible that some few nuts here and there used those old, heavy, slow-firing pieces in the commission of a few felonies, sniping attacks, that sort of thing; but a professional hit man—and believe it or not, I knew at least one such—prides himself on a smooth, clean job and therefore tries to utilize only the best, most modern tools for the job. The one that I knew, for instance, preferred Weatherby hunting rifles, a quite expensive domestically manufactured piece, or a silenced .32 caliber pistol; since he used custom-loaded, explosive bullets and invariably shot for the head, a .32 was all he needed.

"But anyway, back to my career in the surplus arms business. I traveled all over the free world tracking down caches of old weapons, and frequently I'd find myself being offered other kinds of military hardware and equipment, mostly, though, things I couldn't legally sell or for which there was no domestic market, but I kept noting these offers down and filing them away. Then one day I ran into a country that was very anxious to buy the identical items that another government had offered to sell me only a couple of weeks earlier. So I hotfooted it back to government A's country, bought up the lot, and arranged for it to be shipped to government B's country at a markup just sufficient to cover shipping charges and my own expenses. Barely a month later, I fell into the identical kind of situation and did it over again.

"I wasn't really aware just what I was getting into, of course, or I'd've just put A in touch with B and gone on my way. Things just snowballed, and before long I was so busy brokering transfers of military material from one point to another that it was damned seldom I could make the time to perform what was my primary job for my firm. At length, I just tossed this new and unbelievably lucrative business into the lap of Ademian Enterprises, worked with them for long enough to be sure they were on the right track, then went into partnership with another of my brothers, Bagrat, in the Confederate Arms deal."

"How about the rest of your group that were projected into this world, Rupen?" the woman asked. "Were they all into the same dirty, inhuman business of making war and killing, too?"

Rupen bit his tongue. After all, the woman was a certifiable lunatic. "Some were connected to one branch or another of Ademian Enterprises, some weren't. We were just an ethnic band, not in any way professional musicians, just doing it as a hobby, sort of. We played almost every weekend at a Greek restaurant for next to zip, moneywise, but it was fun.

"We weren't all Armenians in the band, either, and only one of the belly dancers was. Our bassist was a Greek dentist, our guitarist and second oud was a

Lebanese, and Greg Sinclair, our second dumbeg—that's a kind of Middle Eastern drum, Krystal—was only a quarter Armenian. Our lead belly dancer was a third-generation Norwegian-German and was also—believe it or not, but it's true—a resident emergency-room specialist at the one of the hospitals run by the Medical College of Virginia."

"How did she find the time?" queried Krystal, disbelievingly. "I was a psychiatric and neurological resident at Johns Hopkins and I often had to make an appointment to sleep a few hours or use the toilet."

Rupen just shrugged. "Don't ask me, but she did. No, she couldn't hardly ever make practice sessions and she missed a whole lot of the weekly Greek-restaurant appearances, too. But she was such a great damn dancer, so expressive, so good at building up a real rapport with an audience, that we were overjoyed to forgive her absences and gratefully accept her at any gig she could make."

"Rupen," Krystal asked wistfully, "why doesn't Hal ever come to see me? I recall, shortly after we first went to York, how much I enjoyed talking to him, playing chess with him."

"You cannot believe just how busy that poor man is, what with all the endless conferences about setting up a new papacy and a seat for it somewhere to the north of Rome. He does have great regard for you, for your welfare, and I'm certain he'd come up here had he the opportunity," he assured her blandly.

"You lying Armenian cocksucker!" she suddenly snarled, her voice gone hard and icy.

At hearing these words, Sister Fatima, who had been sitting in silence, reading by the firelight, looked up and set aside the slender volume. She could not understand the language, but she was quick to recognize the threat in the mad duchess's voice and tone.

"That goddam old faggot won't come near me because he knows goddam good and well I mean to kill him for what he and that damn no-good *goy* husband of mine did to me, taking my son and having me hauled off and locked up in a fucking filthy little cell and damned near starved to death and not allowed to bathe and being eaten alive by bugs and roaches and fleas and lice and bitten by fucking rats in my sleep and having to eat what garbage they did give me off the goddam floor like a goddam dog, knowing that I'd had to piss and shit on that same goddam floor because they wouldn't leave me a fucking bucket. And Hal and Bass Foster did all that to me, so you're fucking-A right I mean to kill the both of the two bastards the first goddam chance I get. They tried to have me killed.

"Isn't that really what that mealy-mouthed so-called Archbishop sent *you* up here for? To kill me? *Isn't it*? *ISN'T IT*?" she shrieked, coming suddenly to her feet, grasping a heavy bronze candleholder from off the table, and hurling herself at the still-seated man with mad rage in her eyes and froth partially hiding her bared teeth, the muscles of her face all jerking.

Rupen barely made it onto his feet in time to catch the shaft of the candleholder on the palm of his hand and wrench the deadly weapon away from her, but then he had to drop it and use both of his hands to try to protect his face and eyes from her clawing nails.

Resignedly, her lips moving in silent prayer, Sister Fatima took from beneath her apron a leather cudgel over a foot long and, limping to a point just behind the raging duchess, raised it and struck, in just the right spot and just hard enough.

Rupen only saw Krystal suddenly stiffen, then her eyes rolled up and she crumpled bonelessly to the floor.

* * *

Mike Sikeena left his carrier to hang a few inches above the ground outside the stone crypt and, after banging on the door and being told to enter, descended the steps quickly, looking very worried. "Arsen, big doings at the fucking Spanish fort and town, downriver there."

Arsen, who was just then helping Ilsa to remove a long, jagged wood splinter from the foot of an Indian child, looked up. "What kinda big doings, Mike? The fucking place burn down? I hope, I hope, I hope."

"Aw, naw, Arsen." Mike shook his head. "What it is, it's three ships down there, must of sailed in late yesterday or real early this morning, is what I figger. And it's a whole hell of a lot more men around there now, too, dressed a little diff'rent from the Spanish and the Moors. And, get this, buddy, they're most of them talking *French*; it's a fucking peculiar-sounding kind of French, lots of words I don't understand, but it's still fucking French."

"How big are the ships, Mike? Are they carrying cannon, or did you see them that close?" asked Arsen.

Mike nodded. "Yeah, Arsen, they all three got guns, both the swivel kinds and the bigger ones on what you call trucks. The two littler ships are both sixty or seventy feet long and they're up on either side of the jetty, you know. But the biggest one must need too much water to get that close, 'cause it's anchored out in the river, and, man, that one's got a whole pisspot full of guns of both kinds, some of those fuckers damn big ones, bores big enough to stick your fucking head into."

The *comandante* of the fortress and town at Boca Osa was not in the least pleased to be forced to afford lodging to armed troops of the excommunicant French trespassers, still less to courteously entertain their snobbish officers, some of whom he recognized anyway as men he and his expeditionary force had driven out of this very town after their suicidal commander had blown up the French fort with him in it. But the Cuban *guarda costa* caravel that had come up the river with the two French warship-troopships had borne along a letter from His Excellency in Habana ordering cooperation and straitly forbidding any violence against the French unless they first should unmistakably demonstrate hostile intent or treachery, so Don Guillermo and his officers were left no option save to swallow their true feelings, ethnic prejudice, and basic distrust and behave as if the French interlopers were really friendly allies.

At the obligatory formal meal on the second evening after the arrival of these infamously cunning confreres, Don Guillermo sat as host, trying to be politely jovial to these men he hated while at the same time riding tight, glowering herd on his own hotblooded officers lest one of them say or do that which their instincts and his own all called insistently to be done, in all of its violence and bloodshed.

While *Capitaine Sieur* Maurice Maria de Mont Souris picked with a look of clear disdain at a fowl—reeking of garlic and spices and yellow-orange with saffron—Don Guillermo, to whom had quickly been reported the Frenchman's prying about every nook and cranny of the fort, while an accompanying aide had rendered sketches and noted armaments, asked, "And what does my lord think of our Castillo de San Diego, in the wake of his thorough inspection-tour?"

Sieur Maurice Maria sniffed, shrugged Gallically, and said in a coolish tone, "When it was called the Fort of Saint Denis, I recall it being much cleaner." After a long, insulting pause, he smiled icily and added,

"Architecturally speaking, of course. The walls are thick enough and adequately inclined, but is it to be held for long, it needs heavier ordnance; why, my good ship out yonder mounts cannon throwing half again as much poundage as your heaviest and long culverins throwing four or five pounds more than your largest. You never could last long here under a serious bombardment from a fleet of modern ships such as my *Indomptable*. Thick as are your walls here, it is to be expected that they would not remain long of solid fabric battered with seventy-pound iron shot."

Don Felipe, but just days before returned from a scouting mission upriver, had opened his mouth to make a heated reply, but a hard look from Don Guillermos silenced him, his rejoinder to ever remain unspoken.

But each and every one of them was, all too soon, to recall the words that *had* been spoken.

Arsen and Mike skimmed down the river in their carriers, well up above the thick fog until just before the last turn, when they sank down into the damp and chilly embrace of the soup-thick mists and proceeded more slowly toward the faint yellow glow of the lantern hung at the masthead of the largest ship, where she lay at anchor in the channel of the Río Oso.

Unknown to them, a sentry on the river wall of the fort—one of the reinforcements for the garrison sent up aboard the Cuban ship and standing his first tour of guard duty at his new posting—saw and called the attention of his passing superior to the greenish glows moving through the bank of fog.

"*Sarjento*? *Sarjento*, look, see, out yonder! What could they be, river monsters of some kind?"

The sergeant, also just up from his own former posting at the Castillo de San Marcos, many leagues south of Boca Osa, snorted and said, "Hardly, you ignorant creole scum! I've seen almost the same as that fog over water at San Agostino, and an officer down there—a most learned Moor—told me that in many swamps, the peat ferments and that from that fermenting peat, a thick gas rises up and the winds carry clouds of it over water and out to sea. For some reason we do not understand, God causes this gas to often glow, just like those two blobs out there. The officer said that the substance is called 'swamp gas.'

"Now stop seeing monsters in the river and keep your eyes set on that damned French ship. Remember what you were told earlier—at the first sight of anything suspicious aboard her, you're to fire your arquebus to alarm the fort."

When Mike Sikeena had adroitly and silently clubbed down the two sentries on the foredeck and the quarterdeck, both he and Arsen guided their opened carriers along the rank of iron guns positioned in the waist of the ship, unplugging touchholes, filling these holes with fine priming powder from flasks they carried, then going on to the next gun, not stopping until all of the larboard deck guns had been primed to fire. Next they glided far enough to the starboard side to be out of any danger in case a gun burst and began using the carrier heat-rods to touch off the guns. Because they had not remembered to remove the tompions from the muzzles or even to open the gunports, the iron balls and belching fire from the discharging guns wrought a goodly amount of damage to the ship's larboard rails, and because the tubes had not been aimed at all, only three of the balls struck any part of the fort, one plowed into the Cuban *guarda costa* where she lay moored at the dockside, and the other two landed in the town.

While the fort resounded with the peal of bugles,

the rattle of drums, and the occasional windborne shout in Spanish, Moorish, or some other tongue, Arsen and Mike used their heat-rods to burn through every bit of rigging they passed for the length of the ship, then parted the anchor chains before heading back into the fog, into the night, and back upriver. For miles of their trip, as they moved slowly in the still-opened carriers, they could hear the distant thunder of cannon from the area they just had left.

Naturally, they could not know just how much chaos they really had wrought. One of the lines they had severed had been that by which the big lantern had been hoist to and held at the masthead, and when it came plunging down on deck, it had smashed and the oil spreading out from it had been fired by the still-lit wick to confront the crewmen and officers who came spilling out from the passages with an immediate concern that, for the moment, occupied them so thoroughly that they did not at once notice the fact that the ship was no longer secured by its anchor and was drifting with the river current, stern-foremost, down toward the treacherous bars and mudbanks just above the mouth of the Río Oso.

Don Guillermo came to the top of the ramparts huffing with the exertion of racing so fast up so many steps. He was wearing only his small clothes, boots, a purple-plumed morion, and a baldric. His hair, beard and mustachios were tousled and disordered, but his wheellock dag was spanned and primed and his swordblade was bared.

"What the hell is afoot?" he yelled at the nearest officer, one of the new ones sent up from Cuba. "Did the French pigs fire on us?"

The young officer waved out at the mist-shrouded river and said excitedly, "They did, *Comandante*, they loosed off every deck gun that would bear, and now they've cut loose their anchor and are headed downriver . . . although there appears to be a fire aboard, no sails have been set, and they are going stern-foremost, it would appear. It is most peculiar."

"The French are always most peculiar, man," snapped the fort commander. "Not to mention their inborn treachery and total lack of honor." At sight of one of his original officers, he roared, "Don Anselmo, my compliments to *Maestro* Pablo, and tell him to hull that French scow before she gets beyond range. I'll teach that foppish bastard to fire on the fort of a sleeping ally! And have the whole garrison formed up, fully armed. So anxious was that French turd to strike at us that he forgot a half-hundred of his soldiers were either ashore or aboard that coaster of his moored at the dock. Not one of them is to escape alive. Hear me, man?"

Aboard the caravel *Indomptable*, the *Sieur* de Mont Souris, less fully dressed than Don Guillermo, demanded of the sailing master, "How the hell did this fire start? And who was the one responsible for firing off those guns?"

"*Monsieur*, I do not know how the guns were fired. Whoever did it first struck down the deck guards. But the fire apparently was started by the masthead lantern falling into the waist. Also, the anchor chains somehow parted and the ship is drifting with the current," replied that harried seaman.

"Then, you numbskull, get the sails unfurled, ere my beautiful ship be driven onto a mudbank!" the *Sieur* shrieked in rage.

"*Monsieur*, it would appear that the fire or something has parted too much of the standing rigging. I would be fearful of sending men up to add their weights to those masts or to put the strain of drawing sails on them until the rigging be repaired."

"Well, then, damn your worm-ridden guts, you Gascon cur-dog, man a boat and send a messenger ashore to the fort before those Spanish clods and the braying jackass who commands them decide they've been deliberately attacked and return fire. Have you no brain of your own? Must your betters always think for you?"

But it was too late. The stricken Cuban *guarda costa*, her rudder smashed and her hull holed by the third cannon's twelve-pound ball, carefully aimed her stern-chaser—the only gun that now would bear on the slowly moving French caravel, a long demiculverin—and spat out a nine-pound iron sphere that crashed its way through the brightly painted rail of the quarterdeck, throwing deadly splinters of wood in every direction, then took off the leg of one of the men trying to force the rudder about, before caroming off the base of the mizzenmast and splashing into the river.

But the worst was yet to come. The first scream of the crippled seaman still was ringing in the damp air when the entire river wall of the Castillo de San Diego belched forth long, thick spears of flame from first the lower, then the upper batteries. *Sieur* Maurice Maria de Mont Souris, however, was never aware of what the balls hurled by the "mere forty-pounder" cannon he had derided earlier wrought upon his beautiful ship, for one of the splinters hurled from the rail had pierced through his eye and deep into his head, forever ending his abilities to think for his inferiors.

ABOUT THE AUTHOR

Robert Adams lives in Seminole County, Florida. Like the characters in his books, he is partial to fencing and fancy swordplay, hunting and riding, good food and drink. At one time Robert could be found slaving over a hot forge, making a new sword or busily reconstructing a historically accurate military costume, but, unfortunately, he no longer has time for this as he's far too busy writing.

For more information about Robert Adams and his books, contact the National Horseclans Society, P.O. Box 1770, Apopka, FL 32704-1770.